VIP Lounge

Also by Ed Decter

The One

VIP Lounge

a Chloe Gamble novel

By Ed Decter
and Laura J. Burns

Simon Pulse
New York London Toronto Sydney

SIMON PULSE

An imprint of Simon & Schuster Children's Publishing Division

1230 Avenue of the Americas, New York, NY 10020

First Simon Pulse paperback edition December 2009

Copyright © 2009 by Frontier Pictures, Inc. and Ed Decter

All rights reserved, including the right of reproduction in whole or in part in any form.

SIMON PULSE and colophon are registered trademarks of Simon & Schuster, Inc.

For information about special discounts for bulk purchases, please contact Simon & Schuster Special Sales at 1-866-506-1949 or business@simonandschuster.com.

The Simon & Schuster Speakers Bureau can bring authors to your live event. For more information or to book an event contact the Simon & Schuster Speakers Bureau at 1-866-248-3049 or visit our website at www.simonspeakers.com.

Designed by Mike Rosamilia

The text of this book was set in Adobe Caslon Pro.

Manufactured in the United States of America

2 4 6 8 10 9 7 5 3 1

Library of Congress Control Number 2009930941

ISBN 978-1-4169-5436-1

ISBN 978-1-4169-9836-5 (eBook)

*To Jon Messeri, Bob Ellis, Lisa Legow, Barbara Shulman,
Peter Guarino, and Bob Mumby, best friends who somehow
made New Jersey a fun place to grow up*
—Ed Decter

Acknowledgments

Thanks to Frank Beddor, author, producer, impresario, and great friend who put me down this path. And, of course, Cheryl and Abigail, who make the path worthwhile.

—Ed Decter

Thanks to P.G.S., who will help me figure out any plot point at any time, and never even gets the credit for it!

—Laura J. Burns

Snap Network Takes a Gamble on COVER BAND

Brand-new teen network Snap is unveiling its flagship series "Cover Band." The one-hour premiere of the undercover detective show will launch the net's aggressive slate of programming targeting the edgier market left behind by the Disney Channel.

Internet sensation Chloe Gamble will headline the series about a teenage rock band that rocks by night, solves crimes by day. The network snatched up Texas native Gamble after her YouTube music video became an overnight hit. Details on the show are being kept under wraps, but the viral vixen is expected to sing in each episode. The entire "Cover" band will tour to pro-mote the show, with musical stage performances to play in twenty cities. The Snap Network already has a bustling online social networking site and expects gains in various new media markets including an online crime-solving game component to the show. Gamble is represented by Nika Mays of the Hal Turman Agency.

Chapter one

Nika Mays's Manuscript Notes: Overnight Success

Hurricane Chloe. That's what I called Chloe Gamble in the weeks after she landed her first starring role. The girl wasn't even on the airwaves yet, but Hollywood knew her. And Hollywood wanted her. That's a heady thing for a sixteen-year-old girl. Hell, it was a heady thing for me, and I'd been out of Stanford for three years already.

Here's the thing about Hollywood: It can change your life in a single second. One day an actress is a waitress who owes two months on her rent. The next day she's a star, with four magazine covers scheduled and a shiny new BMW. One day a writer is an office drone answering phones in some cubicle at a nameless corporation and the next day he's got a studio deal and a blurb on the front of *Variety*. One day a director is renting out pornos at a video store and the next day he's Quentin Tarantino.

It doesn't happen all the time. It doesn't even happen very often. But it happens. Maybe an actress has had four hundred awful meetings—meetings where she's told that she's too fat, too old, too green, too talentless, too washed-up, or just "not right." Four hundred meetings that led nowhere. And then, for no reason other than luck, the four-hundred-and-first meeting goes well. The actress meets the right casting director with the right project at the right time, and that's it. Before the actress gets to her car, her agents have been contacted. Negotiations begin. Other projects come pouring in, just because the formerly available actress is now completely unavailable. The gossip columns and the paparazzi hear about it and start making up stories. *Boom!* The actress is famous. Life changed.

All of my classmates from Palo Alto thought I was crazy for putting up with the sexist, low-paying, and old-school atmosphere at the Hal Turman Agency. But every time one of them asked me why I didn't leave Hollywood and get a normal job, I would tell them: Normal is the last thing I want. I want to wake up wondering if *this could be the day.* That's what keeps us all in show business.

It happened for me the day Chloe Gamble got cast on *Cover Band.* That morning, I was still a nobody, an assistant at a Ventura Boulevard child talent agency with one sixteen-year-old unproven client on my roster. Then I closed the deal: Chloe to star in the flagship show for the new Snap Network. One deal—a few phone calls back and forth, a little hardball negotiation, and done. Life changed.

By the time I arrived at the office the next day, my world was transformed. The assistants at the agency had started answering my phone for me, even though I'd been one of them just a day before. Hal's top agent, Donnie Uslan (who hated me), asked me to lunch. And I had twenty-three calls on *my* call sheet—not Hal Turman's call sheet, *mine.* Some of the calls were talent managers, wanting me to agent their clients. They'd heard I made a deal for Chloe Gamble. I'd somehow managed to resurrect her career after she made the apocalyptically bad decision to crash a network test at NBC. Now these talent managers who I had never met before wanted me to work my magic for their stable of young actors and actresses.

Chloe was the newest thing, and that meant everybody wanted a piece of her. A few were music managers, wanting to handle the recording side of Chloe's career, and there were one or two songwriters trying to send me demos that were "perfect" for Chloe. I spent the whole morning working the phone, feeling my way through the first flush of Hurricane Chloe.

"Nika! Do I have you to thank for this?" Hal Turman bellowed from his office. I figured that was his way of calling me in for a chat, so I grabbed my sweater from my cubicle and went into his office. I'd learned long ago that Hal had a very specific reason for keeping his inner sanctum as cold as a meat locker. So I made sure to cover up so Hal could look me in the eye.

"I just got a call from some rag about my hipness quotient," Hal said. He stared at me, his bushy eyebrows drawn together in confusion. "Now what in the hell is a hipness quotient?"

"Who called?" I asked.

"Something called H Meter." Hal waved the pink

message paper around. "Must be one of those new magazines."

"Hal, H Meter is a Hollywood blog," I told him, snatching the paper so I could read the message for myself. "They're saying that the agency's hipness rating just went up because of Chloe's new show."

"Honey, you can call it a quotient or a rating and I still don't know what it's supposed to mean," Hal said. "Don't try to tell me that there are Nielsen ratings on what's hip."

"Well, no." I smiled. "It's just a blog that tracks the Business and decides who has good buzz or bad buzz, who's getting more famous, who's in disgrace, you know . . ."

"What is this *blog* garbage?" Hal asked. "I hear them talking about it on CNN, for God's sake."

I thought about trying to teach him a little about the digital age and the Internet, but what would be the point? Hal still referred to the computer on his desk as the "word processor."

"Tell you what, I'll handle our New Media department," I said.

"You'll handle it?"

"I'll create it," I said. "For a twenty-five thousand dollar raise."

Hal's eyes narrowed. He'd been in the business a long time. He was a dinosaur, but he was a dinosaur who knew how to negotiate.

I might have overplayed my hand. Hal had given me a raise just the week before. But he looked at me now, his old eyes calculating. The long silence was a technique I had watched him use countless times. It was designed to make the other party feel "greedy" and cause them to lower their price. I knew that I had to stay quiet, no matter how uncomfortable I felt.

"This 'New Media' department, it'll help us keep our *hip quotient*?"

I nodded.

"Fine. You're Head of New Media. You earned your ten-thousand-dollar raise." Hal motioned me toward the door.

I knew I had asked for way too much money. I had expected Hal to lecture me or laugh at me, or *both*, but I had not expected him to give me a ten-thousand-dollar raise. That's when I knew how important Chloe was to the agency. Hal felt he was making a *comeback*. I hadn't overplayed my hand at all—I had underplayed it.

"I'll need an office. And my own assistant," I said.

Hal narrowed his eyes again, but this time I could see angry lines forming on his brow.

"Have them clear out the break room; you can turn that into your office," Hal said. "And you can *share* an assistant with Michael. And for your information, there was nothing wrong with the *old media*. It built this fucking building."

He turned away, and I walked out with a new title, new digs, and some more money. Life changed.

And it wasn't just me.

Travis Gamble had a new life too. About twenty minutes after Chloe landed *Cover Band*, word leaked out that Travis was her twin brother. Video grabs of his guest shot on the sitcom *Shallow People*, shirtless and hot, were up on YouTube almost instantly. Before, he was just a cute male model. Now, he was part of a hot acting family—a *young*, hot acting family. The tabloids love that. Look at Britney and Jamie Lynn, or Lindsay and Ali. Hell, even Paris and Nikki.

Travis wasn't even officially my client when Hurricane Chloe hit. But right away the calls started. I had serious bookers calling me about modeling jobs in New York and these weren't just for underwear catalog shoots. I had casting directors calling about TV and film auditions. Travis had always struck me as a kid with his feet on the ground, but when McG's company wants you to read for a role, even the most sensible teenager in the world is going to jump at the chance. I rushed over agency papers right away. My client list had doubled!

The next thing I had to do was find a reputable modeling agent for Travis, so that I could focus on his acting career. That's Hollywood—one week you're just a high school soccer star. The next week, you've got two agents and a dual career. Like I said, life changed.

Then there was Chloe Gamble herself. From the biggest screw-up the town had ever seen to the star of a shiny new TV show in record time. Chloe's life went from zero to sixty overnight. No more school, no more general meet and greets, no more lurid horror movies—she was past all that in the blink of an eye. As soon as she closed on *Cover Band*, Chloe's life became a whirlwind of photo shoots, magazine interviews, wardrobe and makeup tests, music rehearsals, and must-be-seen-at parties. The struggling girl who'd clawed her way out of Spurlock, Texas, was now Chloe Gamble, the star.

She was enjoying every moment of it. But she still kept a very keen eye on the bottom line.

"How much do I get paid?" Chloe asked me three days after she'd started work on the preproduction of *Cover Band*. "For all the extra stuff, I mean."

"What 'extra stuff'?" I asked.

"The photo shoots and the network promos and all those interviews with websites! I mean, it's a lot of fun, but how much do they pay me for that?"

I had to laugh. In some ways Chloe was the shrewdest person I'd ever met and in many ways she was still a sixteen-year-old kid.

"They don't pay you anything extra," I said. Chloe's eyes went wide with surprise.

"The Snap Network isn't paying you all that money just to *act* in the show. They're also paying you to *sell* the show. Your job—your only job—is to *sell* the product known as *Cover Band*. That means acting, but it also means promoting," I explained. "We have to get your face on every single blog, gossip site, magazine, and TV show that will have you, because that gives the show a chance to be successful. People will want to see more of you, so they'll watch the show, and the show will stay on the air. Good ratings equal survival in TV. Think of it as investing in yourself."

Chloe understood, but her mind was focused on only one thing. "But I need to pay the rent and the bills. And I have to buy a new outfit for every single party and interview. If I wanted to invest, I'd rather do it with somebody else's money."

"Well, I can help with the clothes," I said. "Head over to wardrobe at the studio and get Amanda to lend you an outfit whenever you need one."

"The producers agreed to hire Amanda?" Chloe's eyes brightened.

Chloe had asked me to help her friend Amanda Pierce get a job on the show. It wasn't difficult; Amanda was a fairly well-known costume designer who lived at the Oakwood Apartments where Chloe lived with Travis and their mother, Early. Amanda had taken a risk and hired the hard-drinking Early as a minimum wage seamstress and Chloe wanted to repay the favor by having Amanda be the costumer on *Cover Band*.

"Not only did she get hired, but she's already been out shopping for you. You'll have plenty to wear for all the interviews and promotional stuff."

"My agent rocks!"

"Remember that when the really big agencies come after you," I said as Chloe breezed out of my

office (my own office—with a door and everything!).
I knew I'd avoided a potential storm. When it came
to money, Chloe was fierce. She saw each dollar she
made as an insurance policy against ever having
to go back to Spurlock, Texas, and her rat of a
father. That's why I'd been avoiding telling her
that she didn't even have a real contract yet. And
without a contract, Chloe would have no paycheck. I
was hoping to solve this problem before Hurricane
Chloe had turned into F5 Tornado Chloe.

Chloe's *Cover Band* papers were on my desk,
waiting for signatures. Hal thought I'd taken care
of the whole thing already, but I was holding the
contract back, waiting for my insanely handsome
new lawyer friend to look it over. I had questions,
and Sean Piper would have the answers. I hoped.

He was an associate at Webster and White, a
huge entertainment law firm. He was doing me a
favor by looking over these contracts and I hoped
to return the favor by delivering him a new client
who was the star of her own hit TV show. Maybe
signing a hot new actress would give Sean an edge,
bring him to the attention of the partners of his
firm. Maybe it would change his life.

And maybe that would change mine.

It could all change in an instant. That's what

I knew, and right then I thought it was a good thing. Of course, that was before the police got involved.

Testing

"I love playin' dress-up and all, but how come we have to go through all this?" I asked. For the last three hours I had been in and out of makeup and wardrobe trailers and had tried on about a dozen outfits (lots of short skirts and skinny jeans) and an equal number of hair styles and makeup choices.

"You the star, girl. If you look good, we all look good! Then we can all have us a nice long run and make us some money!" Keesha laughed as she applied coal-black liner to my eyes.

"Amen to that," I said, and laughed along with her.

Keesha, who was listed as the "head of the makeup department" on the call sheet, was from Baton Rouge. Maybe that's why we got along so well; we were two Southern girls who said whatever the hell we were thinking.

It was a real luxury not having to do my own makeup. Back on the pageant circuit in Texas, I always had to do it by myself. I suppose my mama could have helped, but help is not something my mama gives, only receives. But now I had the head of the makeup department to do my face, the head of the hair department to do my hair, and the head of the wardrobe department to do my costumes.

I noticed the rest of the actors who had been cast on the show had *assistants* do their hair, makeup, and wardrobe. I had all the department heads. I also noticed everyone—the producers, the writers, the network executives, and the crew—treated me just a little bit better than they treated everyone else. When I was around they smiled more, laughed harder at my jokes, and ran to find me Fiji water. Sure, it felt great to be treated like royalty, but it felt kind of *odd*, like everyone was acting phony.

Even my friend Amanda had changed. Amanda had been kind enough (or desperate enough) to hire my mama to sew when we really needed the money. So I owed her bigtime. But on her first day of work she arrived with a box of T-shirts that had "Team Chloe" printed on the fronts—pink for women, blue for men. Everyone on the crew put one on. I know I should have enjoyed it more, but I felt sort of *pressured*, like everyone was depending on me to pay their bills or something.

"Do you like them, Clo?" Amanda had said.

"They rock. That was so sweet of you!" I said.

"Thank you for the job!" Amanda said and gave me a big hug.

How did this happen? How did I go from the NBC security "watch list" to someone who helped people get actual jobs? Truth was, I had no idea. But I knew for sure that I never wanted it to change. I had to make myself a success, especially now that so many people were depending on me.

"You seem a million miles away, girl," Keesha said. "Homesick?"

I laughed. "You've never been to Spurlock."

"But I been to Baton Rouge and I'm here to tell you, bigger ain't better."

"That's not what I've been told," a guy's voice said from the doorway of the makeup trailer. I swung the chair around to get a good look. He was thin, but broad-shouldered and ripped. His hair was thick and dark, his eyes were big and blue, and suddenly, I totally knew who he was.

"Junior Junior!" I said. For years, he'd played the oldest boy on *The More the Merrier*, a show about a family with five children and a dad named Junior.

"I'm *praying* this show makes people stop calling me that," he said. "I was Junior Junior from the time I was three. They had to keep telling me my real name was Jonas."

"Huh," I said. "Am I supposed to feel sorry for you now, Mr. TV Star? Because I totally don't."

His eyes widened in surprise, and then he laughed.

"Chloe Gamble," I said.

"How you doing, Ms. YouTube Star? Jonas Beck." He came over to shake hands. Up close, I could see that his skin was perfect. And he had the straightest, whitest teeth I had ever seen. I wondered if he used those Crest whitening strips like they advertised on TV. Hell, the guy had been on TV his whole life, even though he was only a year or two older than me. He could probably afford the kind you get at the dentist's office. I couldn't believe I was sitting around in a makeup trailer shooting the shit with Jonas Beck! He was totally cool and really relaxed, I guess because he had so much experience and everything. All of a sudden a weird thought popped into my head—why was Jonas Beck in the *Cover Band* makeup trailer?

"You visiting someone on the lot?" I asked Jonas.

He looked stunned. "Didn't anyone tell you?"

"Tell me what?"

"I'm joining the cast of the show."

I was floored. "Junior Junior" Jonas Beck was in *my* show? Or maybe it wasn't *my* show anymore; maybe Jonas was now the star of the show.

"Oh! Great!" I said, but I was really confused. The band in the show was supposed to be all girls. "So, you're joining the band?"

"Me? I suck at singing. No, I'm playing your best-friend-who-secretly-has-a-crush-on-you-but-doesn't-want-to-risk-ruining-the-friendship-but-eventually-in-year-three-becomes-your-boyfriend. It's not groundbreaking but it is a *huge* step up from Junior Junior."

I laughed with Jonas, but I was even more confused. In the *Cover Band* script I read there was no best-friend-slash-love-interest!

Jonas could read the expression on my face. "They rewrote the script, Chloe. It happens all the time, sometimes a few times a week."

I'm not proud of this but all I was thinking at that moment was that the best friend character is never the star, which meant that *Cover Band* wasn't Jonas Beck's show, it was still *mine*. How cool was that?

I relaxed back in my chair. "I knew a beauty queen in Texas who carried a *Tiger Beat* poster of you to all of her pageants," I told him.

"Really?" Jonas was laughing. "An actual beauty queen?"

"No, sadly for her. I beat her every time," I said. "I guess she was just a beauty princess. Still, you can bet she'll be watching this show if she hears you're on it!"

"If she tells three or four million of her friends, we'll have a hit."

I decided Jonas Beck was going to be my friend. And he was gorgeous. Girls across the country would gladly slit my throat to take my place here, hanging with Jonas Beck in a Hollywood makeup trailer. I looked into his stunning blue eyes and waited for my heartbeat to speed up, or that tingly feeling to make its way up my spine. But I got nothing.

"This will be fun," Jonas said as he took the chair next to mine.

"If we ever get started," I said. "Do we actually shoot scenes, or just have lots of meetings and wardrobe tests?"

Jonas laughed. "It starts slow, but don't worry, it'll get fast in a hurry. Once we're in production, things speed by."

"When is that?" I asked.

"First table read should be this week," Jonas said. "Have you been to your trailer yet this morning?"

I shook my head.

"There's a script waiting for you," he said. "If you want, we can run lines."

"I have a band practice after this makeup test," I told him. "They finally cast the drummer yesterday, so now we've got the whole band. They're teaching me how to play guitar!"

"We're ready for you, Ms. Gamble," a second assistant director called from the door.

"Now, Duane, I told you to call me Chloe! Ms. Gamble's my grandmamma."

Duane, the second AD, smiled and said, "Then what do they call your mother?"

"A hot mess, that's what," I said.

"I hear you, girl!" Keesha chimed in.

"You going to that Teen Dream kickoff party tonight?" Jonas asked as I stood up.

"Nika—my agent—she says I have to," I told him. "It's a new perfume or something, right?"

"Yeah, but it's sponsored by Forever 21. Lots of paparazzi. It's a must-go." Jonas gave me a mischievous smile. "It'll be more fun together. You could be my date."

"Should I wear this?" I twirled around in the plaid miniskirt I was wearing. It was supposed to be the uniform of the all-girls prep school that my character in the show attended. It looked more like the outfit Britney wore in that old ". . . Baby One More Time" video, only sluttier.

"The paparazzi would love it!"

"Well, then, I am *definitely* going to wear this," I said. "Why not make some noise?"

I figured Jonas would watch me as I headed out the door—most guys do—but when I glanced back, Jonas's eyes were closed and Keesha was powdering his face.

I followed Duane toward the soundstage where they were building the set for *Cover Band*, wishing I had some tea to perk me up (I refuse to drink coffee; it ruins your skin). As soon as the makeup test and the band practice were done, I had to work with my guitar teacher for an hour and then knock off some calculus problems with the on-set tutor.

"Duane, can we make a quick detour to that craft services trailer?"

"What do you need?"

"Oh, nothing, just some tea."

Duane pushed a button on his walkie-talkie. "Craft services, a tea for Number One!"

Just as we made it to the soundstage door, a guy from craft services named Chuy ran over with some tea and honey.

A flash went off, making me jump. My friend Jude Morgan grinned at me from behind the camera.

"How does it feel to be 'Number One'?" she asked.

"Rocks!" I said. "What did they say?"

"I met with this photo editor guy Bob Lavett at the net-work."

"And?"

"And, he hired me, but—"

"But nothing! You got the job!"

I wrapped my arms around Jude. She was pretty much the first person I'd met in Los Angeles and she took pictures of me for free and shot the YouTube video that made everything happen. She was also becoming my best friend and I was so psyched that Nika was able to get her an interview to be the on-set photographer for the show.

"Yeah, I got the job for *two weeks*. I have to show that Bob Lavett guy every image I take, and after two weeks, if he likes what he sees, I get the gig for real."

"Then you have nothing to worry about! You'll be taking pictures of *me*!"

Jude laughed. "Not everyone's as hot as you are, Clo."

"Don't I know it! Ask them pageant panthers about it!"

"Chloe, thanks. This is waaay the biggest gig I've ever had," Jude said quietly.

"Don't you get weird on me. Remember"—I pointed to the soundstage and all the trailers—"all this is thanks to a little someone named you."

Duane looked at me impatiently. "Chloe?"

"Gotta skedaddle," I said to Jude.

"Who else was in makeup?"

"Jonas Beck."

"Ooh. Gotta get him or Bob Lavett will have my ass!"

"Bob Lavett wishes!"

"Later!" Jude took off toward the makeup trailer with a wave.

Duane pushed the button on his walkie. "Number One on set!"

I looked at Duane and said, "Sorry, I never got people jobs before."

"Get used to it, Number One."

When I got back to the Oakwood, my ears were still ringing from band practice and my head was spinning from too many new guitar chords and too much calculus. I desperately needed a nap before going to the Teen Dream party. Plus I had to swing by Amanda's apartment and see if she had any stiletto heels I could borrow to complete the naughty prep-school look I was going for.

As I headed down the hallway toward our apartment, I mentally ran through how much time I had to get some beauty sleep.

"Wow, that is *cold*," a guy called after me.

I turned around, and laughed. "Max. I didn't even see you." Max Tyrell was a musician who lived at the Oakwood, but in my mind he was always linked to Kimber Reeve, the actress who I most despised in this world. She'd ditched him (and her apartment at the Oakwood) the instant she got famous.

"I'm easy to miss," Kimber Reeve's ex-boyfriend said. He was joking. Max had hair practically down to his waist, all of it in dreads, making him extremely hard to miss. I guess he was kind of good-looking (in an alt rock kind of way). Another thing I liked about him was the fact that he hated Kimber. "So where have you been, Ms. Chloe? Haven't seen you around lately."

"I'm working all the time," I said, and I couldn't keep the goofy grin off my face.

"Right, I heard about your show. Good for you," he said. "Don't give up the music, though."

"Never," I said.

"I still have the perfect guitar riff to open your YouTube song," he added, turning back to a bulletin board. He stapled a flyer to it. I leaned in to check it out.

"Wait. Your band is playing at Spaceland?" I said.

He nodded. "Come if you can."

I frowned. Spaceland was a pretty well-known club, and I'd always assumed that Max's band was just some grungy cover band. "You're in The Ruffians? Now how come I didn't know that?"

"You've heard of us?"

"Yeah. Keesha—the makeup lady at my show—she was playing a Ruffians CD the other day."

He nodded, smiling. "Must be a fan. We only sell CDs at our shows. You can download most of our stuff, though."

I studied his face for a minute. "Y'know, rule number nineteen on my Don't Do list is not to date out-of-work musicians."

Max raised one eyebrow. "Most people have a To Do list, not a Don't Do list."

"I ain't most people," I said. "My point is, you're the real deal."

"I am."

"Kimber shouldn't have dumped you," I said.

"She'll regret it someday," he said.

We both laughed. Max turned his stack of flyers over and scribbled a number on the back of one. "Listen, I'm out of the Oakwood at the end of the week. My drummer and I got a place in Silver Lake. But keep in touch."

"I will," I said, taking the flyer.

Max kissed me on both cheeks, then headed off down the hallway. It was weird but I felt a little sad seeing him go. Pilot season was over, and every day somebody else moved out of the Oakwood. When Trav and me and our mama first got here, this place had seemed like the center of the whole Hollywood scene.

I made a mental note to make an effort to check out The Ruffians at Spaceland. Stuffing the band flyer in my bag, I headed for our apartment.

"I am your *mama*, darlin', and that means I don't take orders from my own children," Mama was saying as I walked in. Her voice was slurred, which meant she'd been hitting it pretty hard. Even though I hadn't gotten even one paycheck from *Cover Band* yet, Mama felt that the ten percent of my income I was going to pay her to manage my "expenses" entitled her to leave her seamstress job with Amanda. So that meant that Mama had a lot of free time on her hands, and free time was my mama's enemy.

"What's Mama up to now?" I asked Travis.

"I am not up to anything," my mama said. "All I'm doin' is havin' a little fun."

"With that porn producer who hangs out at the pool," Trav told me. "I found her getting a back rub from Alex the perv today."

"What happened to your country singer?" I asked Mama.

She shrugged, examining her fingernails. She somehow had paid for a manicure.

"Mama, could you please try to keep your eyes on the prize just this once?" I said. "I'm starring in a show for twelve-year-olds. I need to be a role model, and that does not include having a mama in the porn industry."

"Oh, hush up, Clo, I ain't in no *industry*." My mama rolled her eyes. "Alex was just putting the sunscreen on my back."

I shot Travis a look. He was pretty pissed. So was I. Mama's new love life was our least favorite thing about moving to Los

Angeles. Not that we blamed her—our daddy had been tom-catting around just about as long as we could remember. But Mama had no learning curve when it came to men. She'd taken off to Branson, Missouri, with some country music star named Lester Orcutt and been gone for weeks. We had to track her down and carry her drunk ass back home to the Oakwood. God only knew what would happen if she started sleeping with a porn producer.

"I'm serious, Mama," I said. "I agreed to give you a percentage of my TV money so that you'd behave yourself. You mess up that career for me, you can kiss your money good-bye."

My mama glared at Travis. "See what happens when you shoot your mouth off? You got Chloe all upset, poor thing, after she's been workin' so hard on her show."

"Save it, Mama," Travis said. "Chloe knows you don't give a crap how hard she works. You just don't want her to cut you off."

I leaned against the kitchen counter to watch. Usually it's me and my mama hollering at each other, and Travis playing referee. This was something new.

"You be careful, mister, or I might go telling *your* little secrets," Mama said. "Did you know about this, Clo? Your brother is about to get booted from his soccer team."

"What?" I cried.

Mama snatched a paper off the table. By the way Trav lunged to stop her, I could tell it was something important.

"What's this about?" I asked, grabbing the paper. It was

a letter to Mama from Coach Ibanez at St. Paul's Academy, the high school where me and Trav were on scholarship. My brother's soccer talents were what got us the free ride. "Why does he want to meet with Mama?"

"It's nothing." My brother pulled the letter out of my hands. "Mama's just trying to distract you from her porno boyfriend."

"Well, it worked," I said. "Why's the coach want to see Mama?"

"Your brother has been skipping out on soccer matches to go to his little auditions," Mama said in an annoying singsong voice.

"I have not," Trav snapped. "I've missed some practices, is all. Maybe a scrimmage or two. Who cares?"

I have witnessed some truly shocking things in my life, but I don't think a single one of them ever threw me so much as hearing Travis say that. My brother had been playing soccer since before I could remember. He loved it more than anything except for me.

"Trav, what the hell?" I said. "You can't put underwear modeling over soccer."

"It's not just modeling. Nika's getting me auditions for *acting* jobs."

I decided to deal with that little revelation later. After Travis had gotten a gig on a sitcom, I'd told Nika she should represent Travis, but I'd been sort of kidding. Or at least I hadn't expected it to turn so real so fast.

"You got to stay in good with the coach or else we are both shit out of luck when it comes to school," I said to my brother. "We'll end up slumming at Hollywood High with the gangbangers."

"So you get to have the cool acting career while I have to skip auditions and play high school soccer?" Travis said. "How is that fair?"

"What are you talking about? You don't want an acting career," I said. "That's *my* thing, not yours."

"What, are you threatened by me?" my twin asked. "Think I'm gonna steal some precious attention away from you?"

I just stared at him. The thing is, me and Trav don't fight. Never have. We've had each other's backs since we were born— we had to, with loser parents like ours. To have my very own twin stand there sassing me, well, it left me speechless.

Trav too. He didn't say a word, but his face looked as astonished as mine must have.

"Well, aren't you two just peas in a pod!" Mama cracked, totally thrilled to see us at each other.

"Shut up, Mama, I haven't forgotten about your pervert," I said.

"Clo . . ." Travis held his hands out to me. "You know I didn't mean—"

"Yes, you did," I cut him off. "You think I'm so self-centered I'd freak out if you took the spotlight off me."

Travis opened his mouth to answer, but I didn't let him.

"Well, you're right," I said. "I don't care if you say it. I want all the attention, all the time. I need it like . . . like a drug. You don't. You like hanging with your friends, fixing cars, playing soccer and having a normal life."

"Yeah . . ." Trav didn't sound convinced.

"Trav, it's my fault we're in Los Angeles instead of back in Spurlock shooting the shit and getting ready for prom. We're here because of me, not because you wanted to leave Coop and everybody. You would've been totally happy to stay in Texas. You think I don't know that?"

"It's cool. I like it here," Travis said.

"You're just saying that so I don't feel guilty. But I feel guilty all the time that I dragged you here," I said. "I do not like guilt, Travis. I want you to have school and friends and soccer here, too, so I can stop worrying about you and concentrate on selfish ol' me."

"I'm not just being nice. I really do like LA," Travis said. "I liked guest starring on that TV show. They paid me crazy money to just walk around and say two lines. I got to meet famous people. I got to be on TV, for God's sake. There are girls leaving their damn panties in my locker at school, Clo. I want to keep doing it, acting and modeling and whatever I can get. Maybe you thought of it first, but it's working out for me, too."

"Of course it is, 'cause you're gorgeous. And I'm proud of you," I said. "But you're not like me. You're not crazy-focused on yourself all the time, and if you want to get really success-ful in Hollywood, you have to be. Look at me. I don't have friends from school. Everything is about getting to where I want to go. Even this party I have tonight is for work. And the friends that I do have are starting to be my *employees*. It's not normal."

"Screw normal. I had an offer to fly to Brazil last week," Travis said. "You hear me? Brazil!"

"To do what?" I asked.

"A bathing suit spread for some fashion magazine."

"Ooh! I'll go with you," Mama put in. "Like a chaperone."

"Mama! Travis can't go to Brazil, he's got school," I snapped. I frowned at my brother. "That's what you told them, right?"

He shrugged. "I told Nika I didn't have a passport, and she said it would be too much of a pain in the butt to rush it through for just one job. But I drove over to the Federal Build-ing in Westwood and applied for one."

"Well, do you want to be an actor or do you just want to go flying all over the world?" I asked.

"I don't know," Trav said.

"And which is it—acting?" I pressed. "Or do you just want to pose in your boxers all the time?"

"I don't know, Chloe. Jesus." My brother's jaw got tight, which is what happens when he gets angry.

"Trav, it's goin' good *now*. But what if it stops goin' good?

What if for some reason it ends? Then you don't even have a high school diploma and you're just a loser."

"Hey!" Mama squawked, case in point.

"What if it stops goin' good for *you*?" Travis said.

"*I got no choice.* I only want one thing. Always have. You got a choice. Do you want it as bad as I do?"

"I don't know," Travis said again. He ran his hand through his sandy hair, frustrated. "I haven't thought it all through. I'm just getting a lot of meetings and job offers and it's really cool."

"That doesn't sound like a plan," I said.

"*You're* the plan girl," he said. "Maybe I don't need a plan. Just . . . just back off and let me think about all this stuff."

"Fine. But school is what you need for your future. And you need soccer to stay in school," I said. "Just go to practice from now on, will you?"

He didn't answer.

"Just for the rest of this school year. It's only a few more months," I said. "Deal?"

Travis sighed. "Deal. Can we drop it now?"

He still wasn't meeting my eye. I wondered if maybe I'd pushed him too far. I've made a bunch of mistakes in my life, done a few things I regret, but I couldn't live with myself if I screwed up Trav's life. Could not and would not let that happen.

"What should we do about Mama and her porn king?" Travis asked.

I glanced over at my mama, who was now watching a QVC jewelry show on the TV in the living room and pretending not to hear us. "I'm too tired to try talking sense into her right now," I said.

"Okay. You need the Escalade tonight?" Trav asked. "I was thinking of going out with some of the guys from school."

"Don't need it. I'm getting picked up for this Forever 21 event."

"Studio sending a limo or something?"

"Nope. I have a date!"

"No kidding? Anyone I know?"

"Junior Junior from *The More the Merrier*."

"You're shittin' me."

"Am not," I said. "He's got those big blue eyes, and he's got the six-pack, and I'm pretty sure he's also got a boyfriend."

Travis's mouth dropped open. "Junior Junior is gay?"

"He likes to be called Jonas."

"So why are you wasting your time going out with him?"

"Are you kidding? He's just about the most perfect boyfriend I'll ever have!"

"There's a blind item on Perez Hilton about a certain up-and-coming TV star seen with Jonas Beck at a Forever 21 party last night," Nika said the next day as I sat down in her office. "Who could that be?"

"Yup." I grinned. "We held hands and everything. Just

doing my part to get everyone talking about *Cover Band*."

"It's working," Nika said.

"If only Kimber Reeve hadn't shown up, it would've been a perfect night," I said with a sigh. Kimber was my biggest competition in this town, and we both knew it. Still, I'd gotten more attention last night, and we both knew that, too. Kimber hadn't been smart enough to bring along a famous boy of her own. I doubt she'd make that mistake again.

"Put her out of your head. You need to concentrate on your own stuff, not hers," Nika said while she applied some lip gloss.

"Since when do you glam up at nine in the morning?" I asked.

"I've got a meeting." Nika glanced at her watch. "In, like, five minutes."

"I'm not staying long. I just want to know where my money is," I said. "It's been a week since I started work."

"You don't get your first paycheck until episode one is shot," Nika said, then she blotted her lips. "But that's not why you're here. You could've called me to ask that."

"Fine, you're right," I said. "I wanted to talk to you about Trav."

"He's amazing. I've got three meetings set up this week with modeling agencies. He gets so many calls that I just can't handle that side of it anymore, and besides, it's not my industry," she said. "Trav needs a real modeling rep, and then I'll focus on the legit acting gigs. Hey, do you think your acting teacher would take him on?"

"Um . . . here's the thing," I said. "You need to back off on getting jobs for Trav."

"What?" Nika was stunned.

"All the modeling, and now the acting stuff . . . it's not Trav's main focus. Or it shouldn't be. He's got soccer. He can't go to auditions when he should be at practice. And he can't take jobs that are going to conflict with soccer matches."

Nika put away her makeup and narrowed her eyes at me. "How often does he have practice?"

"Four days a week after school. Matches on Saturdays, sometimes Friday nights," I said.

"You're basically telling me I can't book him work."

"Just until soccer season is over," I said.

"I don't like to say no to jobs," she said. "Travis is hot right now, he's got momentum in his career. If we lay low until soccer season is over, he might not have that. The offers may not be there anymore."

"Oh." I felt a brief flicker of guilt, but I ignored it. Travis needed to stay in school so he could get a diploma, go to college, and not end up like our loser parents. That's what was best for him. "Well, if that's what happens, we'll deal with it," I said. "There's no choice. Travis and me are in school on a scholarship, and if he gets kicked off the soccer team, we get kicked out of school."

Nika frowned. "Is this what Travis wants?"

"That's just it. He doesn't know what he wants," I said. "And it doesn't matter. You know I can't afford to pay for that school—I haven't even gotten a paycheck yet and when I do, ten percent of it goes to you and ten percent of it goes to my mama for expenses, and fifteen percent gets sucked out to go to that child actor account—"

"Coogan account," Nika said. "And that money is still yours. It's just being held in trust until you're eighteen."

"Whatever. The point is, I make $11,500 an episode, but I only take home $7,475. That's not enough. There's taxes. Rent is three thousand and then there's food and bills. St. Paul's costs twenty-four thousand a year. Times two, for me and Travis. Will they let me use my Coogan account money for that?"

"No," Nika said. "And it wouldn't be enough anyway."

"See the problem? Travis has got to keep his scholarship."

Before Nika could answer, the girl from the front desk stuck her head in the door. "Nika, your nine o'clock is here," she said. "And *yum*, by the way."

"Okay Let me think about all this, Chloe." Nika adjusted her hair, that, I decided, she recently had straightened.

I laughed. "No wonder you were trying to get rid of me," I said. "You don't have a meeting, you're having office sex."

"Don't be ridiculous," Nika said. "I'm not trying to get rid of you. In fact, this meeting is about you. Sean is the lawyer who looked over your agency papers for me."

"Why do I need a lawyer?" I asked.

"Because people are trying to con you." The voice was deep, and when I turned to see who it belonged to, I understood why Nika wanted to look good. The guy was hot, and his dark suit and short hair only made him hotter.

"Are you going to protect me?" I asked.

"I am." He smiled, looking even better.

"Sean Piper, Chloe Gamble," Nika said from the desk.

"Chloe needs no introduction. I saw the YouTube video." Sean gave me a nice, firm handshake and I held on a little longer than I had to. I figured he was about Nika's age, mid-twenties. The oldest guy I'd ever been with was some Ag major who went to college in Lubbock, and, trust me, that was nothing special. But this Sean the lawyer, well, he looked like everything special.

"So what's the holdup?" Nika was saying.

"Live performances and record deal," Sean told her.

"I knew it," Nika said with a sigh. "It shouldn't be bundled in there."

"It should be if you're the Snap Network and you want to own everything about the show," Sean said. "But if you're Chloe, you want it separate."

"Excuse me, but just what the heck are y'all talking about?" I said.

Nika hesitated before she spoke. "Your contract."

"I thought that was all done and gone," I said.

"There's a few things we want to rework," Sean said.

"Don't I get a say in what I want?"

"Nope." Nika smiled. "You'll say you want whatever gets you paid the fastest."

"That's right," I said. "I have bills to pay."

"Your bills can wait. You can't go into a job like this with a bad contract," Sean said.

"Excuse me, but I can do whatever I want," I told him. "Just how long do you expect my bills—and my mama's, and my brother's—to wait?"

"As long as it takes." Sean dropped into Nika's other guest chair and loosened his tie. "When you're a huge success, you'll thank me for this."

"When I'm kicked out of my apartment, I won't," I said. "You gonna let me sleep at your place?"

He ignored that comment. "Let me explain it to you, Chloe," he said. "There's a lot of music in the show."

"Well, yeah, it's a show about a rock band," I said. "And?"

"The network is planning tie-in albums and tours," Sean said. "The way the contract is written, those things fall under the category of *promotional* duties. You won't get paid for them."

"Nika told me promotional stuff was included in my salary for the show," I said.

"Promotional stuff like interviews," Nika put in. "And publicity photos."

"The music issue . . . well, there could potentially be a lot at stake," Sean said.

"When you say 'a lot at stake,' do you mean *money*?" I said.

"I do. You're a singer, the entire reason the network cast you in the show is because you're a *singer*, and you could, in theory, cut your own album and go on your own tour. But the Snap Network is asking you to do musical tours as a *representative of the show*. So I think we can argue that they should compensate you separately for that."

"Or else they should take out the language about Chloe being required to do the songs and the tours," Nika said.

"Hold on, they can't do the tour without me," I said. "That would be like a Hannah Montana tour without Miley Cyrus."

"Right, which is why they won't agree to that," Sean said. He leaned toward me, and I caught a whiff of his hair. I could smell his shampoo. I don't know why, but that turns me on. I can't stand guys who wear "fragrances." They remind me of my daddy and the Stetson cologne he would put on every time he went out in search of pretty young things. But Sean smelled *clean*.

I must have been staring at him because he suddenly shifted back away from me and said, "I'm going to make them agree to a separate deal for the tours and the songs."

I turned to Nika. "You said negotiations were over. There is no way I'm letting this job fall through."

"Don't worry, Clo, it won't," Nika said.

"I'll battle it out with the legal department at Snap," Sean said. "Nika can play good cop and I'll be bad cop. You just worry about doing a good job so they want to keep you around."

"Which means getting to work on time, and I think your call time is in twenty minutes," Nika said, looking at her watch.

She was trying to take my mind off the contract, but that wasn't about to happen any time soon. "If you mess this up for me, I will hurt you and I am not even playing," I told Sean. "Nika . . ."

My agent stood up and came around the desk. "Chloe, relax. This is my job and Sean's. Go to the set and act as if you don't even know any of this is happening. That's what you have an agent for, to do the dirty work."

"Okay. I'm trusting you both. Don't fuck up." I shot a glance at Sean. He was checking out my legs. "My brother dropped me here on the way to school. Think maybe you could drive me to the studio?" I asked him.

His eyes shot back up to mine and he actually blushed. "Sure."

"But . . . are we finished?" Nika said to Sean.

"Yeah. I'll copy you on all the back and forth. Okay, Good Cop?"

"Got it, Bad Cop." Nika said as she slumped back in her chair.

"You ready, Chloe?"

"Born ready, Mr. Piper."

Sean didn't even look at me again while we headed outside and climbed into his little Audi. But I could tell he wanted to. The air in the car was practically vibrating with tension.

"So you met Nika through her friend Marc, right?"

"Right," Sean said while fiddling with the air-conditioning.

"You two date much?"

"What? No. We're like buddies."

"Fuck buddies?"

"Absolutely not. Behave."

"That's not my strong suit."

I crossed my legs and took my time about it. Sean made a big show of checking his side- and rearview mirrors.

"This guy I know, a sound guy, said I should write songs for an album," I told him as he turned onto the freeway on-ramp. "Do you really think I could do that?"

"Not if I get your contract hammered out. They might agree to separate out the music in terms of payment, but they'll insist on owning everything you do while the show is on the air." He shot me a smile. "That's what I'll have to agree to in the end."

"You make it sound like I'm a slave or something," I said.

"Only until the show hits big. Once you're a huge star, we'll just renegotiate everything."

"That's what Nika says too," I said. I let my hand rest on the gearshift in between us. We drove on in silence for a while, me inches away from him and him pretending not to notice. "So do you work for me now, Sean?" I finally asked.

"No," he said.

"I thought you were my lawyer."

"For me and my firm to formally represent you on this deal, we'd have to take five percent of it. Nika said you would hate that idea."

"Damn straight, I would."

Sean smiled and said, "So, when—not if—I do a good job, you may end up engaging me as your lawyer, but at the moment I'm doing a favor for Nika."

"And for *me*. Don't forget about me, Sean."

"How could anyone?"

"So you're not my lawyer," I said as I let my hand touch his. "Then what am I to you?"

Sean glanced over at me. "You're *trouble*, that's what you are. We're here."

I looked up, surprised to see the gates of the studio in front of us. The ride had been too short. "You want to come see my trailer?" I asked. "It's pretty sweet."

"No, thank you." Sean pulled the car to a stop just inside the gates. "Can you walk from here?"

"Yeah, that's my soundstage." I pointed to the big building with a *Cover Band* billboard over the doors. Jonas was right outside, talking on his cell. "And that's my costar," I added. "Jonas Beck, you know who he is?"

"Junior Junior, right?" Sean said.

"You couldn't have been studying all the time at law school," I said. "You sure you don't want to check out my trailer?"

"Time for you to get going, Chloe," Sean said, as if he was my big brother or something, dropping me off at school. "Good luck with the show."

"See ya," I said curtly. I climbed out, making sure he got an eyeful of my legs and butt. Then I glided over to Jonas and pulled the cell away from his ear.

"Hey, gorgeous," he said.

"Hey, yourself." I grabbed his shoulders, stood on my toes, and kissed him on the lips. I could tell he was surprised, but he kissed me back. Perfect.

Except that when I glanced over my shoulder, Sean's Audi was already gone.

"What was that for?" Jonas asked.

"Um, to say thanks for making that Teen Dream party fun last night," I said, a little shaken. How could that guy just drive away from me? "Sorry I got you on all the gossip sites."

"Are you kidding? It's awesome publicity. Wear insanely short skirts every time we go out!" Jonas looped his arm over my shoulders and pulled me toward the trailers. "News of the day is that they set the first table read for Friday morning. After that, we're in the fast lane."

"After all this preproduction stuff, I could use me some fast lane."

"Have you seen you?" Jonas said.

"What?"

Jonas pointed to the side of the soundstage. There was a *gigantic* billboard advertising *Cover Band*, and right smack-dab in the center was a picture of me. My face must have been ten feet tall.

"Thoughts?" Jonas said.

"We're friends now, right?"

"Of course."

"And friends can keep secrets."

"What's your big secret, Chloe?"

"That there billboard," I pulled Jonas very close to me and I whispered the rest, "gave me a big beautiful orgasm."

E-mail from Travis Gamble

Coop. What up? I gotta vent, man, I'm so pissed off. Remember I told you about that gig I almost got down in Brazil? Nika said the bookers were disappointed when I passed, and she was gonna hit them up for something else in San Diego next week. So I called her about it today, and she was all "we're not booking anything for you until the summer." I'm like, WTF? Turns out my sister told her to back off on finding me work. Nika actually turned down an audition for a guest spot on *CSI* today! Goddamn Chloe, can you believe that shit? I mean, I told her I'd stay away from gigs that conflict with soccer, but the San Diego thing was over a weekend. I figured Nika could ask them to let me show up late, after the match on Saturday morning. You know what, though? Screw it. My sister thinks she can go behind my back like that to try and control me—not happening. I'm telling Nika to book that thing and I'll go down on Friday night. So I'll miss the soccer match, BFD. Later, Coop, I'm calling Nika right now.

chapter two

Rewrite

"Just what is goin' on with this script?" I said on Thursday. I'd
only gotten up to page three, but it was like a whole new script
already. "There's not even a single word left from the one I
read before."

Amanda chuckled from the lounge chair next to me. She
was wrapped in some kind of giant muumuu while Jude and
I—and my mama—were all in bikinis. But she didn't seem to
mind, and hell, it kept Mama from complaining about having
to view Amanda's extra poundage. The pool at the Oakwood
was always crowded with hot bodies, but that never stopped
Amanda from sunbathing. I guess I was supposed to be
impressed with her self-confidence, but I actually thought she

should go on a diet. Unlike Mama, though, I wasn't stupid enough to say that out loud.

"What's funny?" I asked. Amanda might be big, but she was also experienced in Hollywood.

"Honey, from the first draft to the shooting script, there's usually nothing the same. Sometimes it's not even the same plot."

"Why? There was nothing wrong with the first script," I said.

"It didn't have that cute boy in it," Mama put in, shocking me. I'd never seen her read anything longer than the label of a wine bottle. She must've been deeply bored to bother reading the thirty-page *Cover Band* script.

"But Jonas is only in one new scene so far," I said. "The other scenes are the same, kinda, but all the words are different." I flipped through a few more pages. "Wow, you're right about the plot, Mandy. It used to be the band looking for an art thief, but now we're cracking an honest-to-God spy ring."

Mama snorted. "That's ridiculous."

"You sound like Hal Turman," I said. "I guess you old people don't believe that high school kids can be sophisticated secret agents."

"Don't you call me old, Clo, I'm still hotter'n half the girls here." Mama turned away from me, sulking. I knew the "old" crack would get to her.

"They've got us breaking up a scheme to steal secrets from

a military base near the high school," I said. "Why would they change it from art to something so serious? We're singing dumb pop songs one second and sneaking into a fallout shelter the next."

"If I had to guess? Some network focus group indicated that tweens are concerned about national security, as if they even know what that means, so the Snap people told the writers to make the plot reflect that." Amanda yawned and hauled herself over onto her stomach. "Your mama's right. It's ridiculous."

"See?" Mama said in an injured voice.

"It's still cute, though," I said, scanning the script. "The new dialogue is funny. I won't bother memorizing it for the table read—what's the point if it's gonna change so much?"

"What on earth is this table read you're all goin' on about?" Mama said. "Some kind of fancy lunch?"

"It's the first step in producing a TV episode," I told her. "Jonas says it's when all the actors sit around a table and read the script out loud so that the people who wrote it can hear whether or not the dialogue sounds good."

"Why would anyone want to watch you sit around and read?" Mama said. "Bor-ing. Y'all are in a weird business."

"Are you going?" I asked Amanda.

"Sure. Jude too."

I turned to look at Jude, who was half asleep with some photography magazine over her face. "Yup," she mumbled.

"Gotta shoot the table read. Bob Lavett wants the whole process on film."

"Huh," I said. "I didn't know it was such a deal. Guess I better put on some makeup."

"Hey." Travis's shadow fell over us. He threw himself onto the lounge chair next to Mama.

"Where you been, sugar?" she said. "I've been missin' that sweet face."

"I have a little thing called school, Mama," he told her. "You get up early, you go to classes all day—"

"You go to soccer practice after," I put in. I tried to give Trav a wink, but he wasn't looking at me.

"Today's a school day?" Mama looked astonished to hear it. I guess when your only responsibility is making sure your tan lines are even, you tend to lose track of the days. "How come you been home all day, Clo?"

"I had a band rehearsal this morning," I said. "And I met with my set tutor for an hour after that. You were still sleeping it off, Mama."

"Yeah, she just called," Trav said. "That tutor. Said to tell you she's puking her guts out so she can't see you tomorrow."

"She said that?" I had a hard time picturing Deborah, the most boring person on earth, saying that she was puking.

Travis shrugged, his eyes closed while he took in the sun.

"Cool. No chemistry for me." I closed my eyes too. Then I opened them again. "Crap!"

"What?" Amanda asked.

"My set tutor is sick," I said. "But she's my chaperone! I'm not allowed to go to work without a guardian because I'm a minor. Dammit! How'm I supposed to go to the table read?"

"I can be your guardian for the day," Jude said. "I'm twenty-two."

"No, that won't work. Nika had to get the school to approve Deborah as my guardian on-set, and there were all kinds of papers to sign. I can't just drag along any old adult, it's got to be legal." I chewed on my lip, thinking it through. "I better call her back and tell her to chug some Pepto. She can't call in sick."

"She sounded like shit," Travis said. "You want to make her hurl at the table read?"

"Your mama can go. She's legal," Amanda said, making a face like she thought I might smack her.

"Hey, yeah!" Mama sat bolt upright. "I'm still your mama. I'm allowed to chaperone."

"No, Mama, I don't want you making a fool of yourself in front of the whole crew," I said.

"I don't appreciate that kind of talk, young lady," Mama said. "I deserve some respect."

"No, you don't," Trav mumbled.

"You want to tell me what choice you have, Clo?" Mama asked.

I thought about it. Deborah puking from a stomach flu or

Mama puking from a hangover. Was there really a difference?

"Don't worry, honey, I'll keep your mama in line," Amanda said. "Me and Jude both, we'll handle it." Jude nodded.

"I have had just about enough of this attitude," my mama snapped. "Y'all treat me like I'm some kind of *embarrassment.* I'll have you know that I was the homecoming queen at my high school—"

"Until they stripped you of the title 'cause you were knocked up with twins," Trav cut in.

But there was no stopping Mama. "I won twenty-seven beauty pageants back in the day. Not even Chloe won that much." Mama's chin began to tremble. "I am a desirable woman. I will not be hidden away like something shameful."

"Maybe if you stopped boozing and hanging out with porn kings and started acting like a proper mama, we wouldn't need to hide you all the time," Travis said.

For once Mama kept her mouth shut. And I had to admit that Trav was being a little hard on her. Not that a word he said was wrong, but there was something in his tone that felt nasty.

"There's not much time to figure it out, Clo. You just have to make a decision," Jude said, always the voice of reason.

"Okay," I said. "I guess I got no choice. Mama will come."

Mama bounced up and down in her lounge chair, clapping like an excited three-year-old.

"I hope I don't regret this," I said.

Nika Mays's Manuscript Notes:
Table Read

Every episode of every television show you've ever seen started with a table read. Technically, the episode starts before that, with a concept hatched in the writers room and worked into an outline, then a first draft, then a revised script, yada yada yada. Maybe some writers' agent will write a book about that process. But for my purposes—for Chloe's purposes—it starts with the table read.

By the time the table read is scheduled, the script has been read and fought over by all the writers and producers, the studio executives, and the network executives. As far as the words on the page go, everybody is theoretically on board. But you never really know how words on the page are going to sound until actual human beings start saying them. That's why the table read is so important—it's the first time anybody gets to see whether the episode will work.

For a brand-new show, the table read is make-or-break. The actors don't know their characters yet. The writers don't know the actors' strengths and weaknesses. Nobody can tell if the cast members have chemistry, or if they're funny, or if they can pull off the snappy dialogue that's been worked over by so many writers and execs. And let's face it—no matter how brilliant the script is, a bad actor will still ruin it. Which is why it's so dangerous to build an entire TV show around a single actor, especially an unknown actor. Hal says it's like putting all your eggs in one basket—if the main actor sucks, the show sucks.

You'd better believe that Leslie Scott, the chairman of the Snap Network, was thinking exactly those thoughts as she got ready to attend Chloe Gamble's first table read on *Cover Band*. Leslie had handed over a big, important show to a completely unknown quantity. No one knew for sure whether Chloe could act, not even me.

What I did know was that Leslie Scott would be at the table read, her attention fixed on Chloe like a laser beam. If my client wasn't up to the task, she'd be removed. Instantly. Because Leslie wasn't going to be alone. Her bosses would be there too—the people who owned the network. People who made a network chairman seem like middle management. People who cared about one thing and one thing only: money. If they didn't think Chloe would bring in viewers, then they would replace her with someone who would. In television, viewers equal money. The more viewers, the more money the network can charge advertisers for a slot during the show. And all of that money was riding on Chloe Gamble's slender shoulders.

So when I picked up Chloe for her first table read, it was hard to tell who was more horrified—me, to see Early Gamble waiting with her. Or Chloe, to see Hal Turman tagging along with me.

"What the hell is he doing here?" Chloe hissed, nodding toward Hal in the driver's seat of his huge Mercedes. He probably heard her, but he was so busy leering at her mother that he didn't answer.

"He's your agent, he's going to the table read," I said. "What the hell is your mother doing here?"

"My set tutor's sick. I need a chaperone," Chloe said. "And I thought *you* were my agent."

"I am, but every one of the agency's clients is Hal's client," I said.

"Get in the car," Hal boomed. "We've got to be early."

"I already am!" Chloe's mom chirped, running around the big car to shake Hal's hand through the window. "Earlene Gamble, but call me Early. What a beautiful watch." She turned Hal's wrist and admired his twenty-thousand-dollar Rolex.

"Mama, that man is old enough to be your grandfather," Chloe snapped. "Get in the car."

"I'll just ride up here with Mr. Turman," Early said. "Keep him company."

Hal didn't put up a fight, I noticed. I'd met his wife a couple of times at office parties—she was as old as him and he seemed kind of scared of her. He might ogle Chloe's mom, but there was no way he'd do anything else. Hal was old-school that way, and besides, he'd probably seen hundreds of women like Early in his time.

"Let her," I whispered, steering Chloe into the backseat.

"She's like a cat in heat when she smells money." Chloe rolled her eyes.

"We cannot let your mother come to the table read," I said in a low voice as Hal pulled out of the Oakwood parking lot. "We'll have to leave her in your trailer or something."

"She won't let us, she's all excited about the table read." Chloe sounded resigned. "Amanda and Jude said they'll keep an eye on her."

I took a deep breath, trying to calm my racing heart. Today was important, and Earlene Gamble had a way of screwing up important things.

"I don't need Hal Turman," Chloe said, not even

bothering to lower her voice. "I know how to read just fine."

"It isn't just reading and you know it," I said. I thought back over our recent talks, trying to remember if we'd discussed the table read. We hadn't. "Don't you?"

She grinned. "Don't have an aneurysm, I know it's not like reading out loud in English class. It'll be fine."

"Fine!" Hal cried. "Fine will get you bupkes, young lady. Nika, didn't you go over this with her?"

"Well . . ." I grasped for some excuse, some reason that I hadn't talked to Chloe about the table read. Nothing.

"Jesus!" Hal exploded. "This is Agenting 101! Maybe you let your fancy office get in the way of doing your job!"

Chloe stared at me, waiting for me to defend myself. I couldn't. Hal was absolutely right. Why hadn't it even occurred to me to prep Chloe? I'd been so busy worrying about contracts and money and fielding calls with offers for Chloe and her brother, and Chloe always seemed so on top of everything. . . .

"You're right, Hal," I said. "There's no excuse."

I thought Chloe might fall off the seat, she looked so shocked at my spineless answer. But what could I do? I'd forgotten Hal's Golden Rule: Take Care of the Client. Sending Chloe to her first table read with no prep—that was *not* taking care of her.

"What on earth are you all gettin' excited about?" Chloe said. "It's fine. I even got Alan to give me a little coaching last night. I'll be great."

"Who's Alan?" Hal boomed from the front.

"Alan Leiber, Chloe's acting teacher," I told him.

"She don't need no teacher, that girl was born dramatic," Early commented.

Hal didn't answer. He was eyeing Chloe in the rearview. "Did he coach you on how to behave professionally?" he asked. "Did he tell you you've got to be the first one there and the last one to leave?"

"Uh, no." Chloe glanced over at me with a smirk.

"Then he's a crap acting coach," Hal muttered.

"We went over every single scene—," Chloe started.

"Did he tell you the performance starts the

instant you step out of this car?" Hal cut her off. "Did he tell you that the vultures are circling your set already?"

"Tell me, Hal, you got any other clients?" Chloe said. "Or are you planning to tag along for every single scene I shoot?"

"I won't have to. The table read is more important than any piddling little scene." Hal was so busy lecturing that he blew right through a stop sign. I clutched Chloe's hand. But she didn't even seem to notice. She gave a loud sigh and rolled her eyes.

"You better drop that attitude when we get to the studio, missy," Hal said. "These people bought a fun, sassy girl but they won't be as patient as I am if you turn yourself into a diva."

"I sure hope you'll forgive my Chloe, Mr. Turman," Early put in. "I've tried again and again to teach her she ought to respect her elders—"

"People get fired at table reads!" Hal talked right over her. "You remember that next time you feel like rolling your eyes at me. Everyone and his brother will be there just to see if you're going to make a fool of yourself. And even if you don't, they'll still fire you if they think you're not good enough. So you just drop the starlet act and make sure you do a full-out performance in there, Miss Gamble."

"Think of it as acting in a play," I told Chloe.

Hal snorted. "A play where the audience can fire you."

Chloe looked at me, her expression a mix of amusement and worry. "Is he for real?" she said. "Snap wanted me for this show so much that they caved and gave me more money."

"That's the past, Clo," I said. "Now they're looking at the future. They're going to watch this read like hawks. If they don't like an actor's performance, they'll recast and start again. If they think the show doesn't work, they'll pull the plug before they spend any more money."

Now Chloe looked downright scared. "They can do that?"

"Of course they can," I said.

It took less than a second for the fear to vanish from her eyes. Less than a second for the familiar fire to start up. "So I got to be good enough to make sure the whole show works," Chloe said.

I nodded.

"Well, that sucks," Chloe said.

I laughed, but Hal didn't. He just looked at her in the rearview. "Heavy is the head that wears the crown," he said. "You're the big fish today, honey. I hope you're up to it."

"Jesus, when's the fun part start?" Chloe asked.

"It's not show fun, honey," Hal said. "It's show *business*."

Debut

"How come you didn't bring my cute lawyer today?" I asked Nika as we headed across the studio lot toward the conference room where the table read would be.

"She brought me instead," Nika's friend Marc said, rushing down the walkway to meet us. He kissed me on the cheek.

"What's that for?" I asked.

"For making me your own personal public relations hack," he said. "Not that you need one. You're brilliant on your own. Who told you to start dating Junior Junior?"

"I wouldn't exactly call it dating," I said.

"Girl, call it whatever you want, it was a stroke of genius." Marc glanced past us and frowned. "Is that your mama draped all over Hal Turman?"

"Yes. And you can't spin our way out of it," Nika told him.

"Well, maybe I can stuff her in a closet somewhere," Marc said. He put on a smile. "Early Gamble! Come give me a kiss!" He went over and practically dragged Mama away from Hal, acting like they were best friends even though he'd only met Mama once.

"That won't work for long," I said. "Mama was a beauty queen. She's met a million fabulous gays on the pageant circuit—and she doesn't have much patience for them."

"How bad is she going to be?" Nika asked. "She won't have an outburst in the middle of the read, right?"

"She ain't dumb," I said. "But she is an attention whore. If she feels like people are ignoring her, she acts out just like a five-year-old."

"Well, nobody's going to be paying attention to her here. They'll all be focused on you." Nika's perfect eyebrows were drawn together, and she looked worried.

"Why don't we all go hang in my trailer until this thing starts," I said once Marc had pulled my mama over to us. "We're half an hour early."

Nika just nodded toward a group of people near the doors to the building. There were about five of them, all standing together, and all ignoring one another by talking on their cells. "Leslie Scott, already here. Bo Haynes, already here."

I recognized them, of course. Bo headed up development at the Snap Network, which seemed to mean that he was in charge of making new shows, and when it's a new network with all new shows, that was a big deal. And Leslie, well, she ran the whole network. But she lived in New York.

"Leslie didn't fly out to LA just for this table read, did she?" I asked. "I mean, she had meetings here or something too, right?"

"She's here to see you, Clo." Nika looked me straight in the eye. "Hal's obnoxious, but he knows his shit. When he says this read is a big deal, it's a big deal."

I glanced back at the people near the door. The two big fish and a few other network execs. I'd wowed these folks before to land the job. I'd wow them again, no problem.

"Leslie!" Hal boomed, totally ignoring the fact that she was on the phone. He stalked right up to her, hand out. "How was the flight?" Leslie managed to look annoyed and smile at the same time while she muted her phone and shook hands.

"Stressful. I came with Quinn," she said. "He's waiting inside."

Beside me, I felt Nika stiffen up. I guess Mama did too, because she immediately pounced. "Who's Quinn? The big boss?"

"No, Mama, Leslie's the big boss," I said, trying to pull her past the execs without them noticing how low-cut her shirt was or how much her breath smelled like alcohol.

"Actually, Quinn is," Marc said. "Dave Quinn. Leslie reports to him. He's the CEO of EdisonCorp, the company that owns the network."

Mama looked thrilled to be right, but I didn't care. "I didn't know there was a bigger honcho than Leslie," I said.

"Everyone's got a boss." Nika frowned at Hal, who was busy telling some story to Leslie and her flunkies. Judging from their stiff smiles, it was a boring story.

"Let's just go in and get this over with," I said.

"Clo, we can't start until everyone is here," Nika said. She gave an exaggerated glance toward my mama. "And Quinn is in there. I don't think we want alone time with him right now."

I sighed. Alone time with the boss was exactly what I needed, but my agent was right. Mama would make a fool of herself—and me.

"Are there going to be refreshments at this shindig?" my mama asked, right on cue.

"No, Mama, they're not serving alcohol," I said. "It's only ten in the morning."

"There could be mimosas," Mama said. "They're classy."

Hal's loud laugh stopped me in my tracks before I could reply. A quick glance told me that he was the only one laughing, and that Leslie Scott and Bo Haynes had gone from mildly bothered to seriously annoyed. Between Hal and Mama, I was starting to feel stressed. And Nika's nervousness was getting to me too. She was pretending to be all calm and normal, but I can see through people pretty easily.

"Know what? I'm gonna hit the bathroom," I said. I didn't even wait for an answer, I just took off into the building leaving Nika and Marc to deal with my mama. I'd never been in there before—it was an office building, and I was always on the soundstage or in my trailer. But right in the lobby I found what I needed—a little sign that said RESTROOMS and an arrow. I followed it around a corner and down a hallway, and straight to Jonas Beck.

He was sitting on the marble floor with his back against the wall, flipping though the *Cover Band* script.

"Hey," I said, sitting beside him. "You hiding?"

"Damn straight," Jonas said. "How about you?"

"I needed space to clear my head," I told him. "I guess this table read is a big deal. I can't be getting distracted by other people's stress."

Jonas nodded. "My agent and my manager are busy freaking out in my trailer. I don't do freak-outs."

"Do people really get fired at these things?" I said.

"On *The More the Merrier*, table reads were kind of a joke," he said. "But I really only remember the ones from season six and seven. I wasn't even in kindergarten for the first read of the first episode. At the beginning, all the big players are still paying attention."

"So basically you're telling me that it'll be no big deal in five years," I said.

He smiled. "Sorry. I guess that's not very helpful."

I took a deep breath, trying to calm myself. It didn't work. It had never occurred to me that I could get fired, that everything I had done to land this job could end up being for nothing. I pulled out my BlackBerry and texted Jude to get her ass here and babysit Mama. Maybe if I could remove one stress factor, the rest wouldn't seem so bad.

The door to the ladies' room opened, and a little girl came out with her mom. The kid stopped in her tracks and a huge smile spread across her freckled face. "You're Chloe!" she cried. "You're my big sister!"

Her mom laughed. "She's your character's big sister, Maddie."

The little girl rolled her eyes. "I *know*, Mom." She was probably only eight or so, but she shot me a look that said *mothers are lame*, just like she was a miniature teenager. I liked her right away.

"Isn't it funny—the only cast members I haven't met yet are the ones playing my own family," I said. "You're obviously Madison Wills." I held out my hand to shake, but Maddie threw herself into my arms instead, hugging me like I really was her sister.

"I sang 'I Could Care' for my school's talent show last month," she said. "I totally won. I'm gonna start writing my own songs just like you do."

"Good for you," I said.

"No time for chatting, Maddie. We've got to run lines some more before the read," her mother said. "We want to be perfect, right?"

They headed off toward the lobby. I glanced at Jonas.

"Bring back any childhood memories?" I asked him, teasing. "Are you sad to see another child forced into the Hollywood machine by an overbearing stage mom?"

"Nah. Most kids are in the Biz because they want to be and they wouldn't stop nagging their parents about it," Jonas said. "And that mother is not even remotely overbearing. You want to see that, you've got to meet *my* mom."

The little girl had calmed my stress, but talking about mothers brought it right back up. I took another deep breath.

"Calming? Centering?" Jonas asked.

I nodded. "My acting teacher says breathing is very important for me. Usually I'd make fun of crap like that, but it actually does help me focus."

"Alan Leiber," he said.

"Yeah," I said, surprised. "You too?"

"From the time I was ten. He's the best acting coach in town." Jonas smiled. "Tell you what. Let's just channel Alan for this table read. We'll forget about all the suits watching us and we'll pretend we're doing a scene for Alan."

"Okay. I can do that." I thought about my teacher, who was the only teacher I'd ever had that taught me anything worth learning. "I can definitely do that."

"Alan would say we need to listen," Jonas said. "Not act, not force it. Just listen to each other. Deal?"

"Deal," I said.

"Then let's go blow their minds, Chloe Gamble."

"Where the hell did you get off to, Clo?" my mama whined as soon as I stepped into the conference room with Jonas. "You're supposed to stay where I can see you, that's what Nika says."

I opened my mouth to answer her the way I normally would, but one look from Nika made me shut it again. The room was filled with people, and clearly nothing had formally started yet. But everyone was watching, and they were watching me. I had to be *on*. I had to be bright, cheerful, fun-loving Chloe. That's who Snap wanted. Not the girl with the drunken attention whore of a mother.

"Sorry, Mama, I just had to go visit the little girls' room," I said. "Is Jude here yet?"

"Yeah, but she's working." Nika nodded toward Jude, who was busy shooting pics of my bandmates.

I caught Jude's eye, and she winced. "Sorry," she mouthed.

Great, I thought. *So much for her helping me corral Mama.*

"Okay, where's Amanda?" I said.

"Some stick-up-her-butt stage mother has her trapped over by the food table." Mama snickered. "Of course that's the first place Amanda headed."

"Well, shit, what am I gonna do with my mama?" I whispered to Nika, the panic starting to rise in me again.

"I am standing right here," Mama snapped. "I don't know why you gotta be so mean to your own flesh and blood! I do not need to be—"

"Here's our girl!" Hal's loud voice cut her off, but when I turned toward him I got a nasty surprise. He had Leslie with him, and a guy in a suit that had to be Dave Quinn. The big boss. "Say hello to Miss Chloe Gamble. Sorry to interrupt," Hal added with a glance at Mama.

"That's completely okay," I said. I didn't dare look at Mama myself. She'd been interrupted in the middle of a complaint and that usually didn't sit well.

"Mr. Quinn, it's so great to meet y'all," I said, reaching for Dave Quinn's hand. He was thin and tan, maybe fifty or so, and wearing a tie that must've cost as much as my entire *Cover Band* salary.

"Chloe. I hear you're the next big thing," he said.

"I won't stop until I am," I told him.

Quinn smiled, but I wasn't fooled. This guy would be happy if I succeeded, but he didn't give a crap if I failed. Far as he was concerned, I could be replaced. That meant I had to prove to him that I couldn't be. "Thanks so much for coming to my table read," I said, treating him and Leslie to a sunny good ol' girl smile. "It just warms my heart to get this kind of support from the Snap Network."

Leslie's mouth twisted a little, and I wondered if I was pouring it on too thick. I was going for total self-confidence, not total ass-kisser.

"I don't believe we've met," Mama piped up. "I'm Mrs. Earlene Gamble, Chloe's mama." I shot her a panicked look, willing her to shut up. But Mama was busy performing. She had a huge pageant smile on her face as she held out her hand to Dave Quinn.

"Dave," he said. He seemed a little surprised that she had dared to speak to him, but he shook her hand. Mama turned immediately to Leslie.

"And you must be the network head that my Chloe's always talking about. Why, she thinks you are just so impressive. I think it's wonderful that my girl has such a good role model."

"Thank you." Leslie's shoulders relaxed for the first time today.

"I don't mind saying, I'm more'n a little excited to be here," my mama said. "I know y'all must go to these things all the time, but I'm still starstruck. Just being at a real Hollywood studio is a dream come true."

Quinn chuckled. "I forget that sometimes."

"When you work here, it starts to seem mundane," Leslie agreed.

"That's why Chloe has me—to keep her from ever thinkin' her life is *mundane*. She may be the most talented girl in the room, but I promise you she will keep her feet on the ground." Mama gave Quinn a wink.

"I like a girl with her feet on the ground," he said.

Nika was staring at me in shock, but I just felt like laughing. Mama was doing the full-on Girl Next Door, one of the classic beauty pageant roles, a sure crowd-pleaser almost everywhere. It sounds like a no-brainer—everybody likes a down-home good girl—but it's surprisingly hard to pull off. You have to forget all the unkind or sarcastic or just plain smart thoughts in your head and try to warm the world with your smile. If you get caught *acting*, it ruins the whole effect.

My mama taught me the Girl Next Door back when I was still in the junior pageants. I'd been doing it for so long that I'd just about forgotten that Mama did it first.

"We're counting on this show, Chloe," Quinn went on, finally glancing back at me. "Let's see what we've got."

He turned and walked away, Leslie trailing him. As soon as their backs were turned, I grabbed Nika's arm. "Did he like me?" I said.

"He liked *me*," my mama said.

Nika actually laughed. "He sure did, Mrs. Gamble."

"Everybody likes the Girl Next Door," I said.

"You just remember that when your head starts getting big, Clo," Mama said. "I taught you everything you know."

Usually that would annoy me, but right now Mama wasn't on my shit list. She'd put on her act and she was pulling it off fine.

I took a deep breath. Calming. Centering.

"Ready?" my agent asked.

"Born ready." I walked over to where Jonas was waiting at the head of the room, and it was like giving some kind of signal. The second my butt hit the chair, everyone else scurried for their seats too.

"Okay, everyone, let's get started. We're here for the first table read of *Cover Band*," Josh Golden announced.

"First of many!" his wife, Diane, added with forced cheer.

Everyone applauded, and I took the opportunity to look around. The room was big, with six long tables set up in a square. Little Madison Wills, the girls from my band, and all the other actors sat at the tables, with me and Jonas at the top of the room. Josh and Diane Golden, the head writers—showrunners, Jonas and Nika called them—sat right next to me. On their other side was Norman Kendall, the director for the first episode. A bunch of chairs were lined up around the walls too, and every single one of them was filled. I didn't know who all those people were, though I recognized a few faces from all the boring executive meetings Nika had made me go to. And I noticed Gene Whitaker, the casting director, sitting near the door. Leslie Scott and Bo Haynes sat at the table opposite ours, on either side of Dave Quinn. They were the ones who mattered. I didn't even have to think about anyone else in the room.

"Don, will you read stage directions?" Diane asked.

Don, the first assistant director, nodded and cleared his throat. When he started to read, his voice sounded thin in the big room, like it was hard for him to talk through all the tension. I don't know what he had to be nervous about, but he definitely was. Everyone was, even Diane and Josh. They were smiling, but their eyes were terrified.

It's up to me, I thought. *I have to make sure every one of these people has a job tomorrow.*

Under the table, Jonas took my hand. The first scene was just the two of us—Lucie Blayne and her best friend Sam Kelleher—walking down the hallway at school. For some reason, Lucie always hangs out with semi-nerd Sam even though she's the lead singer in a hugely popular rock band. Sam is the only one at school who knows that Lucie is also a spy. Not one page of the plot would ever happen in real life, but whatever. Real-life nerds didn't look like Jonas Beck, either. I didn't have to think about whether the script was realistic or not, I only had to listen.

My eyes went to the script and I started to read:

LUCIE

Sorry I couldn't make it back in time, Sam.

The gig ran long.

SAM

(whispers)

And by "gig" you mean "mission."

LUCIE

No, I mean gig. There was an after-party.

SAM

And by "after-party" you mean "secret
rendezvous."

LUCIE

No, I mean party. How was your birthday?

SAM

Great. And by "great" I mean, just my parents
and me.

By the time we reached the end of Scene One, I'd completely forgotten about the fear in the room. Hell, I'd forgotten about the other people in the room! Jonas and I had never even run lines together, but the dialogue rolled right out of us as if we actually were the dorks having this cute little convo. I wasn't as sweet as my character, and I had a feeling Jonas wasn't, either, but it didn't matter. While we read, we were best friends and there was a nice little streak of flirtation and it was a blast.

It was so much fun that when my bandmates began reading in the next scene, they seemed to be having a good time too. I'd been rehearsing with these three girls every day, and I knew they were scared of me, or jealous of me, or something. I didn't really care. I was nice enough to them and they kissed my ass and that was fine. They caught on to my energy and the group dialogue was snappy and fun, which was all it needed to be. They were just there to make me look good, anyway.

We were halfway through the script before I knew it—reading out loud made the whole thing fly. For one scene, the band's secret agent handler spent a lot of time talking about our mission to stop a spy ring at a nearby military base. He had a long monologue, so I risked a glance at Leslie Scott and Dave Quinn. He looked bored and was fiddling with his watchband. But Leslie was beaming, grinning, practically laughing out loud.

"It's going good," I wrote on the margin of my script. I pushed it toward Jonas. He read it and wiggled his eyebrows at me.

One more scene with Jonas, which we nailed. Then on to a scene at home with my family, then a band performance, then the final catch-the-bad-guys scene. I ran through them all in my head. I could see the end coming. Leslie was smiling. I was golden.

Until we reached the home scene. Lucie's little sister, Olivia, was supposed to complain about having to clean the litter box even though it was Lucie's turn.

"What if I let you wear my zebra-print skirt for dress-up?" I asked, turning in my seat so I could talk right to Madison.

But she wasn't looking at me. She was staring down at the script, holding it tightly in her little hands. Her face was pale.

The cool kid I'd met earlier seemed to have vanished.

"I don't wear dress-up," she said. Then she frowned. "Um, I don't *play* dress-up," she said, correcting herself. Madison looked rattled by the mistake, even though it was tiny. She didn't seem to realize that it was still her line. She stared at the script as if she'd never seen it before.

"Okay, then what do you want, Olivia?" I ad-libbed, trying to prompt her.

Madison's eyes shot up to mine, panicked, and I smiled at her. She was nervous, she needed to calm down. I took a deep breath, hoping it would give her the idea to do the same.

"I want . . ." She looked back down at the script for a second, then up at me. "I want to come to your next jig."

"Gig," I said, pronouncing it right. "And the answer is no."

Madison's cheeks were bright red, but she soldiered on. "Mom!" she called. "Lucie's not doing her chores!"

I had to hand it to the kid, she got the whiny-little-sister voice down perfectly. Maybe we could salvage the whole siblings-fighting scene after all.

"Kids, stop arguing, I need to work," said the actress playing our mom. Her name was Lynn McNamara, and she looked totally familiar even though I had no idea where I'd ever seen her before. Maybe in commercials, or maybe she just always played the mom in shows like this, I wasn't sure. One thing I absolutely knew, though, was that she was phoning it in.

"But Lucie wants me to clean Mr. Pebble's litter box and it's not my turn," Madison said. She got the cat's name wrong—it was supposed to be Mr. Pepper—but that hardly mattered.

"Lucie, you can't make Olivia do your chores. Mr. Pepper is your cat too," Lynn said, not even bothering to sound interested, let alone motherly. And if it had been me, I would've used the same name for the cat that Madison used, just to keep the scene sounding right.

"I'm sorry, I'm so late for my . . . rehearsal," I said. I knew Lucie meant "secret spying mission" when she said "rehearsal" so I made sure to emphasize it. But Lynn didn't pick up on that or anything else for the rest of the scene. Thank God the guy playing my dad was willing to make an effort. Once his character made an entrance, he and I managed to get the energy back up and get things moving again. Still, it felt like walking through quicksand just to get to the end of the scene.

"And we cut to live performance," Don said. "Cut back to scene, exterior military base, night. Lucie and Marsha hide behind their guitar cases."

I jumped right in, pumping as much sass into the dialogue as I could without exploding. Alexis, the girl who played Marsha, sassed right back. As we built toward the end of the episode, the other girls in the band matched our liveliness, and we worked it right up to the end of the scene.

"Fade out. End of episode one," Don said.

There was only a tiny second of silence before the

clapping started. The whole room erupted into applause, with a few hoots and hollers thrown in.

"You did it, Chloe," Jonas murmured in my ear. "That was fantastic."

I hardly had time to smile at him before Nika was at my side. Josh Golden kissed me, Diane hugged me, and Leslie Scott came over to chat personally. I glanced around the room, trying to find my mama in the crowd. Sure, she'd been on her best behavior earlier, but it was anybody's guess how long that would last. I spotted her talking to Dave Quinn, of all people. He was handing her his business card, they were both smiling, and Mama didn't look ready to topple over drunk or anything, but I knew better than to leave her alone with him for long.

"How'd ya like the show, Mr. Quinn?" I asked, walking right up to the big boss. He looked me up and down, checking me out as if I were a horse he wanted to buy.

"Cute," he said. Then he was gone. Leslie and Bo trailed him to the door.

Nika was practically vibrating with happiness.

"Dave Quinn said it was cute. Is that good?" I asked her.

"It's good. If he didn't like it, he wouldn't have said anything at all."

"It was good except for your mama," Mama said. "I think y'all should get them to cast me as your mama. Just like that Billy Ray Cyrus, he's on his daughter's show."

"Family photo!" Jude called, stopping me from strangling

my mama. Instead I looped my arm around her and smiled for the camera.

"Beautiful. That'll be on your fan site for sure," Marc said, taking in me and Mama. "Early, let's let Chloe get back to work."

"You call this work?" Mama rolled her eyes, as if she'd ever had an actual job in her life. But she let Marc lead her away to where Amanda was waiting.

"Two-hour break, then we start rehearsal," Don the first AD said, appearing out of nowhere. "Nice job, Number One."

"Thanks." I grinned. "Rehearsal so soon?"

"We're lucky they're letting us have lunch," Jonas joked, grabbing his script from the table. "They probably needed the time to recast."

Nika laughed, but I frowned. "What do you mean?"

"Lynn McNamara," Jonas said. "Didn't you see her with the casting peeps? They totally canned her."

"What? Already? When?" I glanced around the crowded room, but I couldn't see my TV mom anywhere.

"While you were schmoozing," Nika said.

"If you see the casting director approach after a table read, run," Jonas said. "It's like the coming of the Grim Reaper."

"Well, she deserved it," I said. "She barely even got out of a monotone. She almost ruined the whole thing."

"That's why she's never made it big," Nika said. "Poor kid, though."

I followed her gaze to little Madison Wills, who was sitting right at the table where she'd done her less-than-perfect read. Her mother stood behind her, talking to Gene from casting. Madison wasn't looking at them, but she knew what was going on—I could tell by her chin. It wasn't trembling because she wasn't crying. Instead, her chin was set, her jaw clenched, her eyes staring hard at the table. She was doing everything in her power to keep from crying. She didn't want to make a scene while they fired her.

Not many eight-year-olds have that kind of self-control. I know. I've been there.

"I'll be right back," I told Nika. Then I headed for the casting director. "Gene, hey!" I said cheerfully. "Hi, Mrs. Wills."

"Um . . . hi, Chloe," Madison's mother said. She had tears in her eyes, unlike her daughter.

"Great table read, wasn't it?" I said to Gene.

"Yeah. Sure," he said, looking confused. Gene had to be at least fifty, and he was the type of guy who probably chased little kids off his lawn. There was a permanent scowl on his face, and far as I could tell, he hated his job. Amanda said he was a disappointed man, but to me he just seemed bitter.

"I like Madison's name for the cat better than the writers'," I said. "Let's see if they'll rename him Mr. Pebbles, okay, Maddie?"

The little girl looked up at me, even more confused than

the casting director. I spotted Jude shooting a couple of the band members nearby. "Jude!" I called. "Get a shot of me and my TV sister!"

Jude turned and took a few snaps of me with Madison. The kid was a pro, she smiled for the camera even though her little heart was broken. The whole thing had Gene freaking out.

"Chloe, I need a minute with you," Gene said. "Outside?" He headed for the doors, but I leaned down to talk to Madison. "Don't worry. I've got this."

By the time I got out to the lobby, Gene was complaining to the Goldens and Nika was trying to mediate. There were lots of frowning faces and hushed voices.

"Hi, everyone!" I said, joining the group.

"Chloe, I'm glad you're here," Josh Golden said. "We've got a situation. You see, we were thinking . . ."

"We hate having to deal with these things," his wife put in. "But sometimes—"

"You want to fire my little sister," I said, cutting through the bullshit. "I don't."

"Clo, she messed up the read," Nika said.

"She was nervous," I said. "She'll do fine when she's acting with me. We understand each other."

"You only met her an hour ago," Gene said.

"Doesn't matter, I've got a feeling about her, and my feelings are usually right," I said.

"I've been doing this job since before you were born—I'll

take my experience over your feeling," Gene said dismissively. He turned away from me, completely ignoring me while he talked to the Goldens. "We all saw it. That girl isn't going to work."

I felt the muscles in my neck tighten up. I hate being ignored worse than just about anything. My daddy had spent most of his time ignoring me when I was little—Trav called it the Lonnie Gamble trademark. If you don't like what your kids have to say, just ignore them. Travis had always brushed it off, but I got furious about it. My mama hated my daddy because he treated her bad. Me, I hated him because he ignored me.

And the madder I got, the more he ignored me. That was the other Lonnie Gamble trademark—he was the only man in the entire world who I could never get the best of.

I stepped right in front of Gene, forcing him to look at me. "Who makes the call?" I asked him. "Who told you to fire her?"

Gene clammed up, and the Goldens looked a little pissed. "We make that call," Diane said.

Gene sort of sneered at me, and that was that. This man was no Lonnie Gamble, and there was no way he was going to win this time, Goldens or not.

"Guess I'll have to talk to your boss, then," I said.

I sort of knew that Nika was going to grab me, so I backed away really fast and made a beeline for Leslie Scott. She was talking to Dave Quinn near the outside doors. I got there before Nika could stop me, before the Goldens could catch up, and before I could think things over.

"Leslie, can I ask a favor?" I said. "I'm so sorry to interrupt y'all, Mr. Quinn, but I'm just so upset."

Leslie's smooth forehead wrinkled. "Upset about what, Chloe? The read was terrific."

"I know. I thought it was great! But I guess the casting people didn't like little Madison Wills very much, because they're trying to fire her." I put on the sad face I used to use in beauty pageants when they asked me a question about starving orphans or the pets abandoned after Hurricane Katrina.

"I see." Leslie shot the Goldens an annoyed look, but they didn't dare to say a word. I figured as long as I put the blame on casting, Josh and Diane wouldn't try to fight me in front of the big boss.

Quinn shuffled his feet, clearly impatient with this discussion. Leslie frowned, unhappy with his impatience. Perfect.

"Sometimes people aren't right for a role," Leslie said. "It's never pleasant when there's a child involved, but . . ."

"I don't know if I ever told you I have a twin? My brother Travis, he's supersmart," I said. "But it took him forever to learn how to read out loud. He just read so fast in his head that his mouth couldn't keep up with it, that's what our mama said." Actually, that had been my theory. Mama never even bothered to read the notes our teacher sent home.

Quinn was getting antsier by the second. I had to hurry.

"Anyway, when they made Travis read in class he got all nervous and that just made it worse. I think that's what happened to little Maddie in there," I said. "She'll do fine when it's just me and her filming a scene."

Leslie glanced at Quinn. Details like hiring and firing were too small for him to bother with, and soon he'd blow up about it. Leslie wanted me to go away—right now. She wanted this whole problem to go away. I kept the concerned-about-orphans-and-puppies expression on my face and waited.

"Fine," Leslie sighed. "We'll see how it goes."

Diane Golden turned and walked away. Josh just nodded. But I bounced up and down like a cheerleader.

"Thank you! Thank you both so, so much." I gave Leslie and Quinn a Texas wink and finally let Nika pull me away.

"Oh. My. God." My agent dug her nails into my arm as we followed the showrunners back toward the conference room. "What were you thinking?"

"I don't want them picking on a little kid." In the room, Diane was already talking to Madison and her mom. Madison was beaming. Gene, the casting director, was nowhere to be seen, which was just fine with me.

"What was that all about?" Hal Turman asked, wandering over with a muffin in his hand. Mama was hanging on his arm again.

"I saved that little girl's job!" I said.

"You let her talk to Dave Quinn about a casting decision?" Hal bellowed, turning on Nika. "The man's got companies to buy and senators to call and whatnot. He doesn't give a crap about casting."

"I call my own shots," I told him. "Don't blame Nika."

"Then you want to tell me why you pulled a stunt like that?" Hal said. "You might've just ruined everything."

"My Clo's always had a soft spot for kids," Mama said.

"Maybe that's 'cause nobody ever had a soft spot for *me*," I snapped. "And I didn't ruin anything. The table read was good, they all liked me. And I'm Number One. Why shouldn't I get a say in who plays my sister?"

"Because you don't run the show," Nika said. "Don't think for a second that Diane and Josh are going to forget this."

"I'll make nice to them," I said, waving it off. "Anyhow, it worked. Leslie gave me what I wanted."

"And now you're in her debt, big-time," Hal said. "Keep that in mind, *Number One*. If that kid fucks up now, it's on your head."

"And the Goldens will be the first ones to say so," Nika added.

"Nice goin', Clo." My mama smirked.

"Chloe! You're the best!" Madison came running over and hurled herself into my arms. "Thank you so much!"

"You're welcome," I said into her curly hair. She was

beyond happy. And that was worth it. She wouldn't mess up. Nobody would blame me.

I hoped.

E-mail from Travis Gamble

Coop! Sorry I've been AWOL, I had my San Diego gig this weekend and I was too busy hanging with models to check e-mail. You heard me. Models by the pool, models at the bar, models while I'm working! Gotta say, man, I thought catalog models were hot until I started getting the advertising jobs. But these chicks are beyond hot. Victoria's Secret–level hot. There should be another word for it.

Anyway, here's how much my life rocks right now—remember I said I was skipping a soccer match to go to this shoot in San Diego? I figured I'd come back to a whole shitstorm with Coach and Chloe. But there was a freaky monsoon thing here in LA—seriously, it's the first time it's rained at all since we moved here—and I guess it got pretty intense, it flooded the whole school parking lot and half the field, and there was a mudslide on the hill half a mile away. So anyway, the match was called for rain! Can you believe my luck?

I still didn't tell my sister where I went. She barely noticed I was gone, she was working all weekend—they made her band from the show do a gig on Saturday at this mall to make sure they could pull it off live. Chloe was mad that I didn't go, but I don't think she had a clue I was hundreds of miles away. Somebody filmed it, though— check it out on YouTube if they haven't yanked it already. Clo was incredible. She can even play guitar now. I just watch her and damn! Her life is cool.

I know you think I'm jealous but I'm not. I just want a cool life too. And soccer won't get me there. You know I'm good, but it's not like I'm Beckham. I won't be playing professional soccer and sleeping with Posh. So why shouldn't I be a model or an actor? Clo's got it all wrong. I'm not obsessed with the Hollywood thing like she is, but these modeling jobs and acting auditions are falling in my lap. Why shouldn't I do it? Make some money, have some fun, why would I say no to that? I don't care about school, I can always get a set tutor like Chloe has. Or not, who cares? I have only another year left anyway.

My sister wanted me to have a plan, and now I do. If they kick me out of St. Paul's for missing soccer, I'll just enroll at Hollywood High.

chapter three

**Nika Mays's Manuscript Notes:
Life and Work in Hollywood**

<u>Why not to date guys IN the Biz:</u>

1. They only want you for your contact list.
2. As soon as they get you into bed, they start looking for their next conquest.
3. They wear more product than you do.
4. They are more insecure than you are.
5. If your career hits a snag, they're gone in a nanosecond.

Why not to date guys OUTSIDE the Biz:

1. They don't understand why you're always reading the tabloids.
2. They don't understand why you're willing to take work calls in the middle of a date.
3. They don't understand why you can never take a day, or a weekend, off.
4. They don't understand why you're nice to people you hate.
5. They're boring.

My friend Marc and I were out for drinks one night (charging it to his PR firm, because we're both in the Business, so it wasn't getting sloshed with a pal, it was *networking*)—and the subject of our pathetic love lives came up. Neither one of us had any luck with men. So Marc suggested we stop dating guys in the entertainment industry. I suggested we *only* date guys in the industry. We made lists detailing why both options suck. And then we got even drunker.

The point is, I have no love life. That's why I was able to be so obsessed with Chloe Gamble's career. It was the one part of my life that gave me any kicks at all. Here's the thing: Men don't like me. Or they're intimidated. Or something. It's always been that way. In high school, I was in honors classes, so the guys I knew were geeks. And even they wanted to date cheerleaders, not smart girls. Then, in college, the guys all wanted to "experiment"—which is just a lame way of saying that they wanted to sleep around. That was okay, I didn't mind an experiment from time to time. But now, here in the real world, I couldn't even get that.

I'm pretty. I'm no Chloe, but I have eyes and I have a mirror. I know I'm hot. I can get a first date with anyone. But a strange thing happens during that first dinner or lunch or coffee. The talk turns to where you grew up, where you went to school, all that. And I say I went to Stanford. Then I watch as my date gets uncomfortable, as if maybe the fact that I went to a really good college means that I'm smarter than he is. Or that I'll be more successful than he will. Men may say they want an intelligent, successful woman, but my personal theory is that they're lying. They want somebody who they can feel superior to, somebody who will think that they're brilliant and wonderful. Not somebody who will realize when they're mispronouncing a word or messing up the percentage to leave as a tip at a restaurant.

Even the smart guys are like that. You'd think I could find a guy from Princeton or Harvard to stick with me—they can't possibly worry that I'm smarter than they are. But no. They want somebody . . . well, let's just say they want somebody who doesn't offer them any competition.

Marc thinks I'm full of shit. He says men don't like the Stanford thing because they think it means I'm too serious. That I'll want a *relationship*, and a ring, and a marriage and all the serious, grown-up stuff that most men are scared of. It's not true. Mostly I'd just like to get laid from time to time.

Anyway, that's my first problem—I'm smart and well-educated.

Then there's my second problem: the Business. Hollywood. It's the land of fantasy, the land of dreams coming true. It's also the land of broken hearts. You'd think with all the happily-ever-after movies we put out, we Hollywood types would know a thing or two about relationships. But no. Men in Hollywood are even worse than regular men. Here's what happens when you date a Hollywood guy:

Number one: You meet him at a party or a premiere or a networking brunch or, occasionally, at a business meeting. You cyber-stalk each other a bit. You ask around the assistant network to find out whether he's cool and single and straight. He does the same.

Number two: You set up a date. But it's not a regular date. It's a date masquerading as a business get-together. Drinks at Bar Marmont to discuss whatever his boss does and whatever your boss does. But you both know it's really a date. You get drunk. Maybe you dance. You might make out in a booth somewhere. But you do, in fact, talk about whatever his boss does and whatever your boss does, because that's how much work is life in Hollywood. You've got nothing to say for yourself, and neither does he. All you have is work. All you care about is work. But, hey! You've got so much in common, because you're both total workaholics!

Number three: For a week or two, you IM each other a lot during the day. You send gossip tidbits to him first, and he does the same. You help each other land a great meeting or find an up-and-coming actor or something. You talk about work all the time. It gets you both hot.

Number four: You finally give in and do the deed. The sex might be good, or it might not. But you do it, and you're psyched to be doing it. That lasts for another week or two.

Number five: You're out with him at a party or a premiere or a networking brunch or a business meeting, and you catch him flirting with somebody else. I'm African-American and I'm pretty. So usually my guys will be flirting with cute little blondes or with sultry Angelina wannabes or with hot Latina babes. Basically, things that I am not. It's not racist. They're just looking for another dessert at the buffet table.

And there you have Hollywood dating. This is the land of beautiful people. A guy in Hollywood would have a hard time finding a normal-looking girl, but he can find any kind of sexy, pretty, cute, sweet, curvy, skinny, *whatever* girl he wants. So once he's checked you—your type—off the list, he's looking around for the next type. He's done the pretty black agent. Maybe next he'll try a Midwestern blond publicist. Or a curvy Latina actress. Or a tattooed rocker girl from Florida. Why not? We're all just eye candy, and Hollywood is one big sweet shop.

Conquest. That's what men in the Business care

about. Landing the role, landing the big client, landing the next babe. And if I'm being honest with myself, the reason I recognize it in men is because I'm just like them. As soon as I've gotten what I want, I get bored with it. I want the next dessert.

That's my third problem. I want the conquest too. I want the biggest clients, I want them to get the best parts, I want them to make the most money. And I want to rise right along with them. I don't care about a sexual conquest. I care about my career. So as much as I hate guys in the Industry, and as horny as I get, I just can't bring myself to date a civilian.

Men who don't work in Hollywood just don't get it. They think movies are frivolous, they think TV is meaningless, they think the entire entertainment industry is as shallow as a puff of cotton candy. They roll their eyes or laugh when I complain about bad publicity or an actor losing a role. They think I'm blowing everything out of proportion because I act as if the world will end because I accidentally dropped one of my boss's phone calls. But the main thing that civilians really, really don't get is the work/life balance in Hollywood.

There is no work/life balance. Work and life are the same thing. If I'm having a drink with Marc, it's work. If I'm at the gym listening to a new song on my iPod, it's work. If I'm checking TMZ on my laptop at the office, it's work. If I'm having lunch or dinner or drinks or coffee or a walk or a run or a freaking shopping trip with somebody else, it's work. Everyone I know is in the Business and everyone is *on*, all the time. We're Hollywood types, we don't do meetings in a boardroom during office hours. Well, okay, we do, but that's only part of it. We also do meetings at bars and restaurants and hotels and on soundstages and film locations and in our cars. If I hear my cell ring when I'm in the shower, I turn off the water and answer it.

If I hear my cell ring when I'm in bed with a hot guy, I push him off and answer it.

Find me a civilian who will understand that.

So when Sean Piper asked me out at the studio commissary, I really wanted to say yes. He was an entertainment lawyer, he knew the Business. And God, was he hot. And God, was I horny.

"Just drinks," he said, fiddling with his cuff links. Agents and lawyers are the only ones in Hollywood who wear suits, and he wore his well.

"Drinks to discuss Chloe's contract?" I asked.

"No, that's what we're doing at this lunch," he said. "If she ever gets here."

"Rehearsal is running late. Chloe texted me," I told him. We'd already ordered iced teas and chatted about how hot it was. That's what you do at a business lunch while you're waiting for the star to show up. What you don't do is ask the other person on a date.

"So . . . drinks?" Sean said again. "Just us and some alcohol, no work."

He wasn't following the script. It threw me. Maybe since he was a lawyer, he wasn't exactly *in* the Business. Maybe he didn't know the rules. "What about Chloe?" I said.

Sean's eyebrows drew together in confusion. "Chloe is work. I said no work."

"Right." I chewed on my straw and tried to think over the pounding of my pulse. I liked Sean—a lot—but so did Chloe. She'd like to believe she's the most subtle person on earth, but in reality she's the exact opposite. Anybody with half a brain could see she had a crush on Sean. I honestly wasn't sure if she was even trying to hide it. "But Chloe likes you."

"Chloe is a child," Sean said.

"A child with a crush on you."

"And?" Sean said. "You think I'm into statutory rape?"

"No. But Chloe is my biggest client," I said, thinking out loud. "Her show's not out yet. Right now she's got huge buzz with no negatives. If she decided to jump ship, she'd have no problem finding another agent."

Sean stopped fiddling and sat back in his seat. "What are you talking about?"

"Chloe. If we went out, Chloe might be upset."

"So—"

"Chloe doesn't do upset," I cut him off. "She does anger, and she acts on impulse. If she's mad at me, she might just leave. And then I'm screwed."

"Are you turning me down because of Chloe, or because of you?" Sean asked.

"She's not just some client, she's my ticket," I said. I was almost surprised at my own honesty, but he'd caught me completely off guard. "She's going to be huge, and that will make my whole career. I can't piss her off."

"So no dates unless your client approves?" A tiny edge of annoyance had crept into his voice.

"You would do the same thing if it were a big

client at your firm," I snapped. "You wouldn't go screwing around if you knew it could ruin your career."

"Sorry, I thought I was asking you for a date, not 'screwing around,'" Sean said.

I just stared at him. I wasn't sure how to answer that. "I like you," I said, surprising myself. Sean leaned forward, but I backed away. "But I can't risk losing Chloe."

"That's how you're going to live your life?"

"Maybe." My face felt warm, and I was annoyed. Not sure at who, but I was definitely annoyed. "Maybe work is more important than life right now. I can't have both."

"I see." Sean didn't roll his eyes or tell me I was being shallow. He wasn't a civilian. He was just disgusted with me.

All Business

"Perfect once again, Chloe!" Norman, the director, said. "Ayala, sweetheart, I need you to stay on your mark."

Ayala played the drummer in my band, and she was a ditz just like her character. We'd been rehearsing this scene for an hour and she still couldn't hit her marks. "Sorry!" she chirped. "Sorry, Chloe."

I nodded. Every time she messed up, she apologized to me specifically. So did everyone else—sorry to the director, sorry to the star. *Me*. It almost made up for the fact that I was incredibly late for lunch with Nika and Sean.

"Once more, please," Norman said. He was tweaking a little today. We'd been rehearsing for three days and shooting started the next morning. It was all moving so fast that I felt dizzy, but I'd be happy to get the cameras rolling. Norman was nervous, though. Every time Diane or Josh showed up, which was pretty often, Norman got all high-strung. Nika had told me that the director on a TV episode wasn't as powerful as the director on a movie, and I guess it was true. Back when I was shooting that lame horror movie, *Ritual*, the director had been the absolute boss. But Josh and Diane were the bosses here.

I've got to get Nika to set up a lunch or something with them, I thought. The Goldens still seemed kind of pissed off at me about the Maddie situation. If I'd known how important they were, I might not have gone over their heads to keep the kid's job. But whatever. I'd work it out somehow. I had already convinced my acting coach, Alan, to coach Madison during my usual times. And I'd convinced Jonas to hang out with her and talk her through her nervousness, child star to child star. Now I just needed to appease the Goldens somehow.

"Norman, can you do this without me?" I asked, flexing a little of my star power. "I'm late."

"Oh. Sure, I guess . . ." his voice trailed after me as I walked away. I didn't need to wait for an answer. I was the star.

I made my way past the walls of my character's garage-slash-band rehearsal studio—the crew called it a "standing set," which meant it was always there on the soundstage and we would use it in every episode. There were other standing sets too—my family's kitchen, my bedroom, the hallway at school. And then there were sets that were in episode one but I guess they'd be knocked down when we moved on to shooting episode two. Past the sets, the soundstage stretched out around me, a huge warehouse-type building painted all black inside. One of the production assistants held the soundstage door open for me. I gave her a wink. "Aren't you sweet!"

"Have a great lunch," she said, her face lighting up. That's all it takes to keep the crew in your pocket, just a wink or a smile. I'd met a delivery guy here in Hollywood who told me that most actors don't even acknowledge the crew. I was never going to be like that. Who knew when I might need the crew on my side? It's worth a smile or two.

By the time I got to the studio commissary, I'd made a few changes to my outfit. I'd been wearing my school uniform—well, Lucie's school uniform—again. After the photos of me and Jonas at the Teen Dream party went up, with me in the slutty schoolgirl outfit, the wardrobe department had changed the uniform to make sure I looked young and sweet. It was a pleated plaid skirt and a white button-down. Lucie now wore the skirt just above the knee and the shirt untucked but buttoned. Well, Lucie was more of a prude than me—as I walked, I rolled my waistband under, shortening the skirt so that the bottom hit me mid-thigh. Then I unbuttoned the shirt most of the way, tied the ends together, and let my midriff show. I didn't have a belly button piercing—I didn't need one. My abs are perfect on their own, and I thought my hot lawyer could use an eyeful of them.

"Hi, y'all," I called. "Sorry I'm so late." Nika got up to kiss me hello, which everyone in Hollywood seems to do, and Sean just got up because that's what men are supposed to do when a lady shows up. That's what my mama always says, even though my sorry excuse for a daddy never did it even once that I can remember.

I kissed Nika on the cheek, and then I grabbed Sean's arm, stood on tiptoe, and kissed him, too. I felt his arm stiffen in surprise, but he didn't pull away.

"I've got to leave soon," Nika said, dropping back down into her chair. "Let's order."

"Okay." I barely had my butt in the seat before she waved the waiter over. I must've been later than I realized.

"You guys go first while I figure out what I want. Isn't it funny, I've never even been here before," I told Sean. "I always have lunch in my trailer or at the craft services tables. I like to eat with the crew sometimes, keep them happy."

"How very condescending of you," he said.

I just stared at him. Was he being sarcastic? I'd gotten so used to people kissing my butt that it took me a few seconds to realize that he was teasing me. "Did you just use an SAT word on me?" I teased back.

"Sorry." Sean met my eyes for the briefest second. "That was rude."

"It's okay, I know you were just playing," I said. But he wasn't listening. He was busy scowling at his menu while Nika ordered a salad. Sean got a burger. I went for a grilled fish thing, and then the waiter left and we all sat there while the tension settled around us like a blanket.

"Nika, I need to make nice with the Goldens," I said. "Should I take them out for lunch?"

"I'll send them a muffin basket from you," Nika said. "And then we'll both take them out."

"Great!" I smiled, but Nika and Sean didn't. They both sort of stared off at the other tables in the commissary, not looking at each other or at me. I let the silence stretch out long enough to be sure that something was weird.

"Okay, what the hell is going on?" I said. "You two are acting like freaks. Did my contract fall through or something?"

"No," Nika said, plastering a fake smile on her face. "I'm just tired. I was up late reading scripts. I'm trying to find a good teen romance for you to star in during hiatus."

"And that's much more important than sleeping," Sean put in.

"Yes. It is," Nika said.

"I'll say. We can sleep when we're old and rich," I agreed. "So what about my contract?"

"We're good to go," Sean said. "I've been back and forth with the network—"

"We both have," Nika cut in.

"And I've teased out the recording and touring into a separate deal which will be a rider attached to your contract," Sean said.

"How much?" I asked.

"Less than I wanted," he said. "But it's the best we're going to get. I had to agree to less compensation in return for including the performances. The network pushed hard on that one— they consider live shows to be promotion and so part of your original contract."

"But you won. You got it written up as a separate thing," I said.

"Yeah. And that's important—the fact that they gave in shows me how serious they are about you," Sean said. "They want you bad enough to let you push them around a little."

"I like it when people want me that way," I said, putting a little purr into my voice.

He didn't react to it. "If this is a hit, we'll be able to make an even better deal, get some real money for the live performances," he said, all business. "Enough that you can retire on it."

"Retire! I just got started." I laughed. "If it's enough for me to buy a big ol' mansion with a pool where I can skinny-dip, that'll do just fine for now."

"Let's not get crazy," Nika grumbled. "The show could be canceled after three episodes."

"Oh." The food arrived just then, and I stared down at my plate feeling like I might puke. I'd never thought about the show getting canceled. It seemed like every time I felt secure, there was another threat. Land the job, but I could get fired. Get the show on the air, but it could get canceled. "So when can I relax and enjoy myself?" I asked.

"When you find another line of work," Sean said.

"Well, I'm not doing that. And I'm not letting the show get canceled, either," I said. "I'm finally where I belong. No way I'm allowing this to stop."

"Hal would be proud of you." Nika gave me a real smile for the first time since I'd gotten here.

"Just don't expect to have any kind of life, with that attitude," Sean said.

Nika stood up. "I'm gonna go," she said. "Sorry, Clo, I've got a ton to do."

"You didn't even eat," I said.

"You guys get whatever you want. I'll give them my card." Nika gave me a quick kiss and stalked off toward the door.

"I'll be right back," I told Sean. I got up and went after Nika, catching her just as she stepped out into the sunlight.

"Hey. What's up with you?" I asked, grabbing her arm.

"Nothing." She didn't look at me.

"Did you and Sean have a fight or something?" I asked. "'Cause you're acting weird. Wait—did you have sex?"

"What? No!" Nika rolled her eyes. "Chloe, God."

"Sorry." I shrugged. "It makes people act stupid."

"Well, we didn't have sex. We're not going to have sex. We're just friends," Nika said. "We're colleagues."

"Colleagues can sleep together," I said. "My daddy slept with every single one of his receptionists."

"I'm not your daddy," Nika said. "And neither is Sean."

She headed off toward the parking lot, and I went back inside. Sean was waiting for me, and he seemed impatient.

"What's with Nika today?" I asked, sitting down.

Sean shrugged. "She's a busy woman." He was wolfing down his burger almost as fast as Travis does, and paying more attention to the food than to me.

"So do you think you might ever look at me?" I asked him.

"Not in that outfit," he said.

I laughed. "It's my wardrobe from the show."

"That's why the only men you'll find watching your show are perverts," Sean said.

"Then how about I change into something else and you take me out tonight?" I asked.

"Not a chance." This time, he looked me right in the eye.

"Why not?" I said.

"Because you're sixteen. It's not even legal."

"So? I don't care. My mama don't care," I said. "Who knows? Maybe I'll get myself emancipated and then it wouldn't even be illegal."

"I don't care if it's illegal, I care if it's immoral," Sean said. "Go find a boy your own age."

"I don't want a boy, I want a man," I said, dropping my voice down low.

Sean chuckled. "Okay, then go find a man. Any man but me."

I leaned forward so that he could see straight down my shirt. "You trying to tell me you don't want me? You expect me to believe that?"

"You're a beautiful girl, Chloe," he said. *"Girl."*

"I get it. You're a straight arrow. You do want me, but you're scared because I'm young." I sat back. "You'll get over that."

"I am scared," he said. "But it's not because you're young. I'm scared because you're such a predator even though you're barely out of a training bra."

"I'm not some little innocent virgin, if that's what you're worried about."

"Oh my God." Sean pushed his chair back. "I don't want to hear that."

"But you're gonna think about it," I told him. "Tonight, when it's late and you're all by yourself . . . you'll think about me."

"Maybe. But I'll never do more than think."

"We'll see," I said. "I don't give up so easy."

"Look, do you want me as your lawyer or not?" he asked.

"My own lawyer? Not just somebody doing Nika a favor?" I asked.

He nodded.

"Yeah," I said. "I want a lawyer."

"Then back off. I don't date clients," Sean said.

"Why not?"

"I sleep with you, it ends badly, and you fire me. Or my firm fires me. It's not worth the risk," he said.

"You're gonna choose work over getting with me? You crazy?" I asked.

He stared at me for a long moment without saying a word. Then he smiled. "Someone I respect once told me that work is more important than a love life sometimes," he said. "You can't have both."

He got up and left without even saying good-bye.

E-mail from Travis Gamble

Coop, big blowup here. Remember I told you about my soccer match getting rained out? I thought I dodged a bullet, but I was wrong. Coach didn't find out, but Chloe did. She came home from rehearsals and found my pay stub from the San Diego gig, and right away it was all about her, as usual. You'd think she might be too busy to bother snooping through my shit, but I guess not.

Chloe starts waving it in my face the second I walk in the door from school, and she's all, "What the hell is this? It has last weekend's date on it."

So I say yeah, I had a modeling job. Two days, eight thousand dollars. I grabbed the pay stub back, but it's not like I could storm off. The living room is my bedroom. I got nowhere to storm off to.

You know Clo—she won't back down. She's like, I know you had a soccer match last Saturday. And I say it got rained out, but she snatches the pay stub and shoves it in my face again.

She's like, the stub says Friday to Sunday. And there's no way I could know on Friday that my match was gonna be canceled on Saturday. So I'm honest with her, I say the whole point is that Coach didn't know I was gonna skip it.

And then Chloe starts yelling, big-time. She's all, "No, the point is we had a deal that you wouldn't even skip a damn practice for the rest of the year, forget about skipping a match!"

So now I'm mad, and I tell her the deal didn't involve her going behind my back to Nika.

Get this, Coop: All she says is, "Obviously Nika didn't listen."

That right there is the difference between me and my sister— Chloe catches me lying to her about going to a gig and I feel guilty. I catch Chloe stabbing me in the back with my own agent and she doesn't even blush.

I ended up calling the booker myself, BTW, because I can't trust Nika if she's just gonna do whatever Chloe wants her to do.

Even when I tell her that, though, Clo goes off on how it's all for my own good because I need to keep my scholarship.

You know what, though? It's bullshit. I don't care about the scholarship. This is all about Chloe. She's the one who wants me to stay in the fancy prep school. I'm willing to go to Hollywood High, even though Chloe says it's like a ghetto there.

So I tell her that, and she says, "No."

I'm telling you, Coop, if she wasn't a girl I would've hit her. Who the hell does she think she is, saying no to me? I don't even take that crap from my parents.

It's not up to her. It's my school and my work. She makes her own decisions, she doesn't make mine. Try telling Chloe that, though. She doesn't even listen to me, she just says, "I make the family decisions."

Well, not anymore. Not for me. We had this whole huge fight, I mean a screaming match like the kind my parents used to have. Chloe thinks I'm saying that I really want to be a model, and she doesn't believe that I want it bad enough. But that's not the whole story. I don't care about modeling, but suddenly there's an entire career falling in my freakin' lap. With money, and girls. So yeah, I do want that. Wouldn't you, Coop?

Anyhow, Chloe must've had a bad day or something, because she caved. I've never seen her do that before, but she just gave up all of a sudden. It's so not like her. I almost didn't buy it.

But then she's all, "You're the only person I love in the world, and you're the only person who loves me. I'm not about to let this come between us." Which is true. All we have is each other, that's how it's always been.

So I think we're done, and I'm going to Hollywood High. But no. Chloe's got this whole other stupid idea—she's going to drop out of St. Paul's and then we'll only have my tuition to pay. She figures she makes enough money to swing that.

Seriously, she can be an idiot sometimes, and I told her so. I mean, why is it okay for her to drop out but not me?

"Because I'm choosing to be a dropout. I'm doing it to myself," she says.

But I'm choosing it too. It's not always on her. I can make my own decisions.

There's no point in saying that to Chloe, though. I know her answer: "You wouldn't even be thinking about it if I hadn't dragged you here to Los Angeles." That's what she always says. She doesn't want to feel guilty for ruining my life. But it's my life! I wish she would just let me ruin it myself if that's what I'm doing. I tell you, Coop, it's too much pressure. I feel like if I do what I want, I'm letting her down. It sucks.

I just made eight thousand dollars. If I work more, I'll make more. So I tell my sister that she should worry about her own tuition and I'll worry about mine. She doesn't have to support us all by herself. I can help.

Know what she says? That I should save that money in case things go south. And in case I need to pay for college.

It's too exhausting to argue with her sometimes. She says she'll find a way. That we'll go to the admissions dean tomorrow and figure it out.

So that's it. I'm gonna be a model or an actor or whatever, and no more soccer. I should feel relieved, right? But instead I just feel like now Chloe's got one more loser to support. Whatever. When we go to the dean, I'll make it clear I want to pay my share. Chloe thinks she calls the shots, but she doesn't. Not for me.

I'm taking control of my own life now.

chapter four

Nika Mays's Manuscript Notes:
Power Plays

"The line goes around the block!" Chloe sounded astonished to see the people waiting on the sidewalk outside the studio gate, but personally, I wasn't even surprised. Teen shows don't always get a ton of attention, but every so often there's a star who hits a nerve. Miley Cyrus. Hilary Duff, back in the day. And now it was Chloe Gamble. She'd been on Perez Hilton's site for four days in a row now. Her mini-interview with *Extra* had aired last night. Anyone who was paying attention knew about *Cover Band*—and knew that today was the first day of shooting.

"And that's just for the taping," I said as I pulled up to the gate. "They're going to let another fifty people in for the live performance later."

Chloe was practically vibrating in the seat next to me, she was so excited. "I can't wait," she said. "I cannot *wait* to finally get started!"

Later on, the LAPD detective on the Gamble case told me he found Chloe to be "scary," and I laughed at him. But the truth was, she could be a little scary sometimes, and I think that was the exact moment that I first realized it. The tone of her voice, the look in her eyes . . . She was like a coiled spring just waiting to release. The girl had been in Los Angeles for three months and she'd already become an Internet star, shot a horror movie, and landed the lead role in a TV show. But she still felt as if she hadn't even gotten started.

"Stop the car!" My friend Marc appeared from the crowd of people, jogging over to open Chloe's door.

"Marc! You spending the day on-set with me too?" Chloe asked. "Cool!"

"I wouldn't miss Day One," he told her. "But you should get out here and walk in to the studio."

Chloe shot me a confused look, but I laughed. "There are paparazzi out here, and they're not allowed inside the gates."

"Okay. Don't have to ask me twice . . ." Chloe was already halfway out the door.

When she stepped out of the car, there was a strange noise—a sudden silence, followed by a loud rush of sound. People cheering, people yelling for Chloe's attention, photographers calling her name, footsteps as paparazzi and security guards all rushed toward Chloe. The flash of cameras almost blinded me. I had no idea how Chloe could even see enough to make it over to the line of people, but somehow she did. I got a glimpse of her signing autographs, and then the security guard waved me through the gate.

I left the car with a valet and went back out to the sidewalk. It was mayhem. I couldn't even see my client through the group of fans and photogs.

Finally Marc emerged from the knot of people, his arm around Chloe. "Fantastic—we'll have pictures of Ms. TV Star all over the Internet in an hour."

I glanced at Chloe, who was still waving to people as the security guards ushered them back into line. "Hey, y'all, can you get a shot of me

Ed Decter

with my agent and my publicist?" Chloe called to one of the paparazzi.

"Whatever you want," he said, snapping away as she looped her arms around me and Marc.

"E-mail it to Slade PR," Marc called while Chloe blew the guy a kiss. She was good. The best way to make sure the paparazzi don't sell hideous shots of you to the highest bidder is to make sure the paparazzi like you. And today, she'd made them like her.

"Chloe, look. You literally stopped traffic," Marc said.

It was true; the cars waiting to get into the studio were backed up in the street because there were too many people milling around.

"Well, hey there!" Chloe suddenly cried, waving like a prom queen. I followed her gaze to one of the cars, a sleek green Jag. Inside were Josh and Diane Golden, the showrunners of *Cover Band*. Diane waved back, and Josh smiled. But their eyes weren't really on Chloe. Their eyes were on the line of fans.

We couldn't have planned this better, I thought.

The Goldens were the only dark spot in Chloe's bright life right now, and I wasn't sure that

Chloe even realized how much of a problem that could be. In television, writers have a lot of power. The Goldens had created this show, they'd written the pilot and shepherded it through the entire process of getting made—from initial pitch to today's shooting—and they were the ones ultimately responsible for its quality. Sure, they were the head writers, but they were also the executive producers. That meant they hired everyone on the show from the production assistants to the director, and it meant, obviously, that the Goldens were everybody's boss. TV showrunners are bigwigs. They're powerful. They're in charge.

But they still answer to their overlords, just like everyone else.

The cast and crew of a show report to the showrunners. But the showrunners work for the studio, and the studio works for the network, and the network honchos work for whatever corporation owns them, and the corporation answers to its shareholders. In the military, it's called the chain of command. But in Hollywood, it's more like the chain of fear. The cast and crew are afraid of pissing off the showrunners, because the showrunners can fire them. But the showrunners are afraid too. The Goldens created *Cover Band*, but if they got on Leslie Scott's bad side, she would replace them with different showrunners. Of course, Leslie was afraid of Dave Quinn. And Dave Quinn was afraid of his board of directors. And I'm sure they were afraid of somebody too. We all have to please our bosses if we want to stay employed.

In a normal situation, Chloe's job would depend on keeping her showrunners happy. And at the table read the other day, she had done the exact opposite.

But as I watched the Goldens watching Chloe—and her crowd of fans, and her paparazzi squad—I felt the power dynamic shifting. This line of people here to see an unknown actress, that wasn't a normal situation. And the Goldens knew it. To have a star powerful enough to bring in her own fans was good, it was something that Leslie Scott and Dave Quinn would be very happy about. If it came down to a choice between the showrunners and the star, well, the star might win.

I had a feeling that Josh and Diane Golden were thinking that exact thing right now.

"Did you set up a lunch with them yet?" Chloe asked me.

"I was going to do it today," I said.

"Maybe you don't have to after all." Chloe sounded very pleased with herself as she headed toward the studio gate. I couldn't blame her. But now I think it might have been better if that moment had never happened, if Chloe hadn't seen how much power she suddenly had. It was too much, too fast—another thing Detective Lopez told me, later.

Right then, though, it was fantastic.

"I have a feeling this is going to be a good day," I told my client as Marc and I escorted her inside.

"Those people love me," Chloe said.

"That's nice, but it'll be even nicer when we can capitalize on it," Marc said. "If this show takes off, we'll use your fan base to land you endorsement deals."

"Endorsement? You mean like I do an ad for perfume or shoes or something?" Chloe asked. "You can get me one of those deals?"

"That's what PR is, Chloe Gamble," Marc said. "Prove you've got fans hanging on your every move, and companies will throw cash at you just to walk around carrying their product."

"I hear those gigs pay crazy money," Chloe said. "How many can you get me?"

"Whoa!" I shook my head. "Let's not put the cart before the horse, people. Chloe needs to concentrate on doing a good job on the show today."

Both of them stared at me. "Did you just say 'cart before the horse'?" Marc asked.

"She looks like Nika. But she is turning into Hal Turman a little more every day," Chloe said. "Tell me more about the money." She towed Marc off toward the trailers.

My BlackBerry rang before I could follow, and Sean Piper's name popped up on caller ID. I glanced at Chloe, then headed off toward a bench along the walkway. Chloe didn't need me, she had Marc. And things were weird enough between me and Sean without Chloe hanging around, asking me a ton of questions.

"Sean, hi," I answered the call.

"This a bad time?"

"For you? Never," I said, dropping my voice to a purr. Then I caught myself. That had sounded flirty, and I had to stop flirting with him. "What's up?"

"We need to talk," he said. His voice sounded a little strained, just like my own did.

"Is there a problem?" I asked. Was he going to bail on me now because I'd turned him down? I didn't give him a chance. "Is it the contract? If we don't get Chloe paid soon—"

"It's all through, she'll get paid next week," he snapped.

"Oh. Good."

There was a little silence.

"It's not about Chloe, for a change," Sean said. "I've got a proposal for you. You have a minute to talk?"

"Um . . ." Yes, I did. Chloe and Marc had completely left me in the dust, and shooting didn't start for another half hour. "Not really. But why don't you come to the studio? *Cover Band* is shooting today." I frowned, annoyed at myself the second the words left my mouth. Seeing Sean in person was dangerous, because the more I saw his face, with its weirdly sexy dimple, the harder it would be to keep my hands off him. But I couldn't help it. I'd told him we couldn't date, but that didn't mean I actually *wanted* it that way.

"I'm booked all day," he said.

"Then come tonight. Live performance, then an after-party," I said. "We can talk then."

He hesitated for a tiny second. "You don't do anything without Chloe, do you?" he said. "Fine. I'll see you later."

When I hung up, I wasn't sure whether I felt nervous or excited to see him. It hardly mattered, though, because the main thing was that he wasn't bailing on me. He was handling Chloe's contract.

I headed for her trailer to give her the good news. Nothing ever made Chloe quite as happy as hearing that she was getting paid.

The trailer was packed when I got there. Marc was inside with Chloe, and so were Josh and Diane Golden.

"—totally right about Madison," Josh was saying. "She's done fantastic work in rehearsals."

"Oh, I'm so glad y'all noticed!" Chloe chirped. "I asked my very own personal acting coach to work with her, and I think he's done wonders. She's hardly nervous at all anymore."

Diane gave me a little wave. "We were just telling your client how happy we are that she convinced us to keep Madison Wills," she said. "They're adorable together. I think she wishes Chloe was her real big sister."

"It was a good call, Chloe," Josh said. "Maybe we should make *you* the casting director from now on!"

Everybody laughed. We were all fake-laughing, and we all knew it. But that's Hollywood.

"Anyway, we just wanted to say sorry," Diane said. "We'll let you get ready now. It's your big day!"

"Thanks so, so much for stopping by. Y'all don't know how much it means to me," Chloe said sincerely. "I never meant to step on any toes with the Madison thing. I just truly believed she'd do a good job, and I always follow my heart."

"That's one of the things we like best about you," Diane said.

"But I won't mess up again. Next time I'll go through proper channels," Chloe promised as the showrunners headed for the door.

"You just concentrate on having fun today," Josh said. "We'll see you all on-set."

I held the door for them, said my good-byes, and then climbed into the trailer. Chloe and Marc were both giggling.

"I guess that muffin basket really worked on the Goldens," I said, starting to laugh.

"Muffin basket my ass," Chloe said. "They saw people lined up to see me and they came running to make sure I wasn't mad at them!"

"That was a thing of beauty," Marc said. "Nika, you didn't even see half of the butt-kissing. The Goldens are freaking out!"

"Still, Clo, you did the right thing," I told her. "You were very gracious."

"I'm the one with all the power. I'm the one with the fans," Chloe said. "I can afford to be gracious, right?"

"Yup," I said. "You've got the power, Chloe Gamble."

Day One

"Here we go!" the first AD called. "*Cover Band* episode one!"

The lights were hot. I'd been sitting in the set for my character's kitchen, and the lights were really hot. Madison, across the table, had been complaining about it too. But the second Norman the director called "Action" I forgot about the lights.

I forgot that Madison was Madison and just thought of her as my sister, Olivia.

I forgot about the bleachers full of people watching. I forgot about the world outside and I forgot about my jerk of a daddy and my drunk of a mama and about Trav and our school troubles and about every single bad thing that has ever happened to me.

I forgot about everything in the world except for those cameras ten feet away. Pointed at me. Recording my face, my voice, myself. It felt like a million eyes pointed at me, and it felt like heaven.

Alan always says I should forget about the audience and just focus on my character. But he also says to relax. Here's what he doesn't get: It's the audience that relaxes me. People's eyes on me, their attention on me . . . That's all I want in the world. As soon as I felt the camera, everything in my whole life just clicked right into place.

Before I knew it, my scene with Maddie was over and we were on to one with the new actress playing my mom. I stood staring into the fridge and pretending to tell her about my school day, lying the whole time because Lucie's parents don't know she's a secret agent. Lying to my mama is second nature to me, but having my mama ask about school, well, that part took some serious acting on my part. Then the kitchen scenes were finished and me, the cameras, and the crew all moved over to the next set, my bedroom. The girls who played my bandmates showed up for this scene, and it was lots of fun, lots of energy, and lots of corny jokes. We'd spent tons of time in rehearsal, planning out which girl would sit where during the scene—the director called it blocking—to make absolutely sure we would all be in the frame. I guess it's hard to fit a lot of people on camera at one time. Ayala messed up on the first take, but after that it was smooth sailing, and we were on to the next scene.

Things were going so fast that I felt a little light-headed. Nika appeared by my side.

"You okay?"

"I can hardly believe how fast this all goes. I always thought there'd be about ten takes for every scene. But we've only done a couple each."

"That's because you're so good, Clo."

"I'm not complaining. I love this!"

Jonas came jogging over. "We're on the phone for this next scene. You want me to read it with you?"

"I kind of figured you would," I said.

"Usually I'd be off in my trailer and the script supervisor would read," he said. "But since I just can't stay away from you, I might as well help out."

I grinned up at him, and he leaned over and kissed me. I heard some gasps from the audience in the bleachers, and I laughed. "Putting on a show, are we?"

"Always."

I looked over toward Norman, Josh, and Diane, who were all sitting in director's chairs behind the cameras, and they were smiling at me in the same way the pageant judges would smile when I was awarded the tiara—like I was the daughter they had always wanted.

That was my life. Every single thing was so damn perfect, I could hardly wait for more!

"So?" Jude asked me as soon as I stepped out of the soundstage after the taping was done. "How did it go?"

"Let's see . . ." I pretended to think for a moment. "The phrase 'better than sex' comes to mind."

Jude laughed, and so did the girl next to her. She was wearing a headset and had a clipboard in her hand, so I figured she must be a PA. She was also standing a little too close to Jude and I wondered if there was some kind of girl-crush going on.

"Sorry, did I interrupt something?" I teased them.

The girl's cheeks flushed. "No. I was just . . . I'm stationed at this door in case anyone needs to get in between scenes," she stammered. "But I guess the taping is done, so . . ." She backed away and fled through the door.

"She's cute," I said to Jude.

"Yeah, so don't frighten her like that."

"How could *I* frighten her?"

"She's a production assistant. You're the *star*."

I thought of that weird thing Hal had said to me. *Heavy is the head that wears the crown.* It sort of made sense to me now.

"I need some shots of you in wardrobe for the website— they want to do a diary of the first day of shooting. I've got it set up right here; it'll only take five minutes."

I followed her across the walkway and over to a grassy area with a fountain. The tripod was set up to shoot me sitting on the edge of the stone basin with the water playing behind me. As soon as I perched on the edge of the fountain, Jude held a light meter in front of me.

"After you get what you need, you want to grab something at craft services?"

"Can't. When I'm finished with you I have to grab Jonas."

"You leave him alone, he's mine," I said, expecting Jude to smile or smirk. But she just kept working.

I stuck out my tongue and flipped her the bird, but Jude just kept shooting. Finally, I put a finger up my nose.

"C'mon, Clo."

"No, *you* come on," I said. "You're being all ultraprofessional and weird."

"Clo, I *need* this job. I *love* it. I can't do anything to fuck it up. I'm still on probation."

"Okay, so after Bob Lavett gives you the gig full-time, then you can use my trailer for booty calls with that PA," I said.

Jude didn't even crack a smile.

"Kidding."

"Yeah, for now. But people get famous and then they get . . . bipolar or something," Jude said. "I can't tell you how many people I know who have been slapped down by their friends once their friends make it big. So when we're here, at work, I can't be your friend. I'm just one more person who's got to be good enough that you don't fire me."

"No way." I jumped down from the fountain and went right over to her. "Look, don't you get all weird on me. Everyone else walks around here treating me like I'm some kind of princess. But you know I'm just an idiot who tried to crash a network test."

"You're an idiot who *did* crash a network test," Jude said.

"Thank you! Keep making fun of me, please," I told her. "You might be the set photographer, but your real job is to keep me being *me*. The day you start acting like I'm your boss instead of your friend, that's the day I'm leaving Hollywood."

The cute PA stuck her head out the door of the soundstage and called my name, her voice nervous. "Front gate just sent your mom in, Chloe. She asked them to let you know she's here."

"Uh-oh," Jude muttered. She slung her camera over her neck and grabbed the tripod. "I guess we're done here."

"Come with me. You can get a shot of the fake stage mom Mama's turned into," I said. I waved back to the PA. "Thanks!"

As she disappeared back inside, Jude shot me a look. "Her name's Kelli."

"That might be a little too perky for you," I told her.

Jude gave me a playful shove, but I couldn't enjoy it, because my eyes fell on the one thing I had never expected to see. Kimber Reeve. Right here on my own studio lot. With venti Starbucks in her hand and a smirk on her face.

"Well, well, if it isn't Chloe Gamble," she said. "Hi, Jude."

"Hey, Kimber," Jude said, her voice curt.

"What brings you girls here?" Kimber took a sip of coffee and I imagined all that caffeine going straight to her face and wrinkling up her perfect skin.

"*Cover Band* shoots here. You know, *my* show," I said.

"Today's our first day of production. I guess if you only just got here you were too late to see my fans lined up outside the lot."

"I guess so." Kimber yawned. "I've been so exhausted from working on *Virgin* that I slept as late as I could this morning. Todd Linson has us doing take after take, until he's got every emotion he could possibly want. You know these Oscar-winning directors! Totally meticulous, even when they're working in television."

"Sounds brutal," I said. "But at least you don't have to carry the whole show by yourself, since you're just a supporting role. I'm in every single scene of my show."

"Oh, right, sort of a little Hannah Montana rip-off, isn't it?" Kimber asked.

A thin guy in a headset appeared at Kimber's elbow, "You're in makeup in five, Ms. Reeve."

"Sorry, gotta run," Kimber said. "I'd say we should get lunch tomorrow, but I'm off to a press junket in New York right after we wrap. The network has a private jet taking us, isn't that so sweet of them?"

"Sure is," Jude said, grabbing my arm. "C'mon, Clo, you've got to get ready for your live performance."

She dragged me away before I could say anything else to Kimber. I guess she was scared that we might drop the nice act and start a real catfight right there on the studio walkway. But she was wrong. I had nothing else to say to Kimber Reeve. She had a part on an NBC show, with a famous movie director and private jet rides. And I didn't.

"What is she doing here?" I hissed as Jude pulled me toward the trailers. "This is *my* studio! Her show is on NBC."

"It doesn't matter. Shows shoot all over the place, not just on their own lot," Jude said. "You'll find ABC shows at the NBC lot, and Fox shows at Universal. *Virgin* must be shooting here for some reason."

"Yeah. To piss me off," I muttered.

Jude jogged a few steps ahead of me, then turned around and snapped a picture.

"What the hell?" I said.

"Don't worry, it's not for the diary. It's for your biography in ten years." She smiled. "We'll call this shot 'The Moment Chloe Decided *Cover Band* Was Not Enough.'"

E-mail from Travis Gamble

Hey, Coop. I figure you're hanging in the cafeteria about now, chowing down on Spurlock High's famous "cheese" burgers with the all-grease fries on the side. (I miss those fries!) Gotta tell you, bro, you better get your butt out here as soon as summer break starts. Because while you're at lunch, I'm hanging on a Hollywood studio lot! Sounds glamorous, right?

Totally not. I've been sitting in Chloe's trailer for like an hour and I'm freakin' bored. It's the first day of Clo's big new show and

Mama wanted to come watch. She's on some whole kick where she's pretending to be all interested in our lives—well, Chloe's life. She went to a table read last week and got to see my sister in action with all the crew people kissing her butt, so now Mama wants some of that for herself. That's what I think, anyhow. It's all bullshit, though. It's not like I could wake her drunk ass up to come in this morning for the actual taping (where they film all the scenes from the plot), but she feels mighty proud of herself for getting here to see the rock concert Chloe's band is giving tonight. I mean, how hard is it to jump up and down and dance at a rock show? Whatever.

Anyhow, apparently the lighting crew is running behind setting up the big stage outside, so we're all stuck here twiddling our thumbs in Chloe's trailer. My sister is so psyched about this damn trailer, like it's such a big deal that she's got some luxurious pad. But, dude, it's just an RV. Farting around in an RV ain't glamorous, whether you're in Hollywood or just camping out in a Walmart parking lot.

I told Chloe that this place is almost as small as our apartment at the Oakwood, but she just laughed. She says at least here she gets her own bed.

Mistake. Because then my mama gloms onto that like Chloe is trying to be disrespectful to her. She's all, "Chloe, anytime you want to start sleeping here at night is fine with me. Least that way I'd get some sleep without you snoring all night."

Clo is awesome, though—she says, "Mama, that's yourself you hear."

I don't know what those two are complaining about. I'm the one that has to sleep on the couch. I told them that, but it just made things worse.

Mama starts bouncing up and down, clapping her hands. She's like, "Well, what are we being so stupid for? We don't need to be in no Oakwood anymore, not now that Chloe's a big star!"

She thinks we can move into a mansion now or something. Chloe's all, "We don't have enough money." But my mama has no clue, she figures Chloe makes plenty of money so of course we can afford a three-bedroom place somewhere, and we'd all have our very own private rooms.

But Chloe's on top of things. If Clo says we don't have the money, then we don't.

My mama isn't having any of that, though. Once she gets an idea into her head, you can't talk her out of it. She starts whining that we're being cheap and she knows how much Chloe's fancy show is paying, blah blah.

Chloe's all, "But the show could get canceled after two episodes, Mama, and then we'd be shit out of luck."

And my mama says, "So poor Trav has to keep sleeping on the couch?" As if she gives a crap.

Tell you what, though. I'm gonna buy an air bed. Maybe I'll even set it up outside on the balcony. Least out there I could think straight. I might be starting to lose my mind a little living with these two women all the time.

IM

COOPERMAN: Hey. Whine much?
GAMBLEGOAL: Piss off.

GAMBLEGOAL: But thx for the IM. Gives me an excuse
to get outta the trailer.

COOPERMAN: That's what I'm here for. You on a movie
set now?

GAMBLEGOAL: Nah, the trailers are all set up in a roped-off
part of the parking lot. Hollywood's only glam from the
outside.

COOPERMAN: Still better than Spurlock.

GAMBLEGOAL: No shit.

COOPERMAN: Got some news for you.

COOPERMAN: Trav?

COOPERMAN: Duuuuude! You there?

GAMBLEGOAL: Sorry. Just ran into Nika.

COOPERMAN: Hot lesbian?

GAMBLEGOAL: No, hot agent. She went by the trailer, but
Clo sent her to talk to me out here so my mama
wouldn't listen in.

COOPERMAN: What's up?

GAMBLEGOAL: Audition for a commercial.

COOPERMAN: Selling what?

GAMBLEGOAL: Who cares? It shoots in Barcelona. Some
famous movie director is making it. I'd get to go to
Spain for two days!

COOPERMAN: You suck.

GAMBLEGOAL: I know. Hope I get it. I'm not sure if it's
acting or modeling.

COOPERMAN: Don't sweat it. You can't do either one.

GAMBLEGOAL: HA!

COOPERMAN: I have news. My dad just had your dad fix the AC in his office yesterday.

GAMBLEGOAL: Don't care.

COOPERMAN: My dad told me he asked Lonnie about you. Lonnie said he knew you were in California cause he got some phone bill a while back with a bunch of Los Angeles area codes on it.

GAMBLEGOAL: Shit. Chloe's BlackBerry bill.

COOPERMAN: Just wanted you to know he knows you're there.

GAMBLEGOAL: Yeah, not like he's bothered to call even once. Nice father. Doesn't care if we're dead or alive.

COOPERMAN: Sorry, man.

GAMBLEGOAL: No worries. It's nothing new. Long as me and Clo stick together, we don't need parents anyway.

Rock Star

"Just look at it, Clo," my mama whispered. "This here's everything you ever dreamed of."

She was right. The sun was just going down, but it was still light enough for me to see every single face in the crowd of people, all there to watch me. Sure, there were three other girls in my band, but they weren't the stars. I was the star. I held the black curtain at the back of the stage open for another moment, scanning the faces in front. Nika was out there, Travis too. They were both young enough and hot enough that we could risk their faces getting on camera—I'd cleared that with the Goldens, just to play the good girl. But I hadn't expected to see Sean. He was there with Nika, looking a little out of place in his dark suit and tie.

"Who's the Ken doll?" Mama asked, peering over my shoulder.

"That's my lawyer."

"Mmm. Corn-fed and cute," Mama purred.

"And too young for you," I said.

My mama laughed. "And too *old* for you."

"No such thing," I said, letting the curtain fall closed. Sean might say he wanted nothing to do with me, but he was lying. Why would he come to see me perform if he didn't care? Everybody knows that when you watch a rock star, you get all weak in the knees. Strap on a guitar, step up to a microphone, rock out . . . and nobody can resist you. It's about power. The one in the spotlight, the one with everyone's attention focused on her, that's the one with the power. Tonight, at the after-party, Sean was going to be putty in my hands.

"Ready for the big show, Chloe?" Leslie Scott asked, coming up behind me.

"Born ready," I said. "This is the easy part—I love to sing."

"We just can't shut her up at home," Mama put in. "Not

that we'd want to. Why, she's better'n half the people on the radio."

"You must be very proud of her," Leslie said.

"You can't even imagine, Ms. Scott." My mama wrapped her arm around my shoulders. "To see such talent shining out of your own child, well, it's just humbling. I truly feel blessed."

Leslie beamed at her, and my mama beamed right back. I wanted to laugh. Mama had never felt humble or blessed in her entire life, unless you count sloppy drunken confessionals. But damn if she wasn't pulling off the sweet Girl Next Door again. I'd forgotten how good my mama was when it came to acting. If only she hadn't gotten herself knocked up with me and Trav, maybe she could've been the star of her own TV show too.

"Well, I'll let you get warmed up. Break a leg," Leslie said.

"Ms. Scott, you wouldn't happen to know where a doting mama is supposed to sit during the concert, would you?" Mama asked. "I know that's not your department, but if you could just point me the right way . . ."

Leslie smiled. "Why don't you come with me? Dave Quinn and I are watching with the director and I'm sure we can find you a seat."

"Quinn is here?" I asked, surprised.

Leslie nodded. "There's a lot riding on this show, you know. The parent company's having trouble, laying people off, you know how it is."

Mama nodded like she had a clue.

"You don't mean they're going to run out of money for the show?" I said.

Leslie chuckled. "Not at all. I just mean it's more important for the show to do well, so you're getting all the executive attention you can stand."

"I like attention," I said.

"Well, sugar, we wouldn't be here if you didn't!" Mama said. "Now you sing your heart out, you hear?"

She turned to leave, but just about the last thing I needed was my mama schmoozing with my bosses while I was on-stage. I grabbed her arm and dug my nails in, but she just leaned over and gave me a kiss, like she didn't understand what I meant.

I watched her walk off with Leslie Scott. What could I do? Far as my bosses were concerned, Mama was a pure delight.

Which meant for me, she was a ticking time bomb.

But none of that mattered when the crowd hushed and Norman called, "Action." It was my character's name that they were all shouting, but it was *me* they wanted. Me who stepped out onto the stage, waving into the blinding lights. Me at the microphone, fingers strumming the guitar I was getting pretty good at, voice bouncing back at me from the buildings surrounding the stage set.

I couldn't see the people out there, but I *felt* them. The energy of the crowd poured into me, kicking my song up another level. The three other girls in the band seemed to feel it too—we'd never sounded so tight.

We were supposed to do two songs, then stop. Then we'd do it all again, to make sure we had everything we needed for the show. But I didn't want to stop. When we got to the end of the second song, I grabbed the microphone off its stand.

"Thanks for coming to the first day of *Cover Band*!" I called. A wave of applause and screaming came back at me. "You're our first audience and we love you!"

More cheers. Off to the side of the stage, I saw Jon and Duane talking furiously into their walkie-talkies. Probably Norman was telling them to stop me. I wasn't supposed to ad-lib, and I damn sure wasn't supposed to use the crew's time doing stuff on my own. But it was a gorgeous evening, the crowd was excited, and my band was on fire. I could do whatever I wanted, and I knew it.

"You want to meet the band?" I called. Everybody yelled and clapped, and I waved my bandmates forward. No better way to get them on board than to stroke their egos a little. "This is Lizette on bass, Alexis on guitar, and Ayala on drums. And I'm Chloe Gamble!"

The crowd went crazy, whistling and cheering, and I laughed out loud. My bosses might not like this, but they still had the lights on me, and the mike was live in my hand.

"We're going to shoot that whole concert one more time, and I want y'all to be just as great as you were before," I told the crowd. "But I thought I might sing you one of my own songs first. Would you like that?"

More screaming.

I stuck the microphone back into the stand and grabbed my guitar. The first song I'd taught myself was my own song, my YouTube hit. "I could care, but I don't . . ." I sang.

Lizette joined in, jamming along on her bass. And by the time we'd reached the first chorus, the whole place was singing along with me. They knew the words. They knew my song. They knew *me*.

Mama was right. This here was everything I'd ever dreamed of.

"Where's Mama?" I asked Trav the second I walked in to the club.

"I thought she was with you," he said. "I came here straight from the studio, with Nika." He nodded toward my agent, who was at the bar. She had a plastic wristband on, showing she was old enough to drink. This was a posh nightclub, but it was a strictly age-appropriate party, no booze for the under-21s, at least that's what Jon the AD had announced just after the taping ended. A show for teens with a cast of teens equals guaranteed ID checks at the after-party.

"I saw Early before I left," Amanda said, stopping on her way to the door. "She said she was going to call a cab and go back to the Oakwood. Too much temptation in a place with an open bar." Amanda fished a cigarette out of her giant purse. "I guess she didn't want to risk showing her true colors to the powers that be."

As she headed outside for a smoke, I turned back to Travis. "That sound like Mama to you?"

He shrugged. "Maybe Mama's truly turning over a new leaf."

"Or maybe she's got a date with the porn producer," I said. "But you know what? I don't care. Long as she's not here to make a fool of herself, I'm gonna have me some fun!"

"Jonas has a flask," Travis said, holding up his glass.

"Yeah, so does every single member of my band," I told him, grinning.

"I did not just hear that." Sean's voice floated from the darkness behind Trav. I looked over my brother's shoulder to see a cushy circular booth with a little RESERVED sign on the table. Sean was way in the back, his tie undone and a drink in his hand.

"Is this my table?" I asked.

"They're certainly not reserving it for me," Sean said.

"Trav, you want to go get me a drink?" I asked my brother.

"A real one or a kiddie one?" Travis asked.

"Kiddie one is fine with me. I don't need to drink to have a good time," I said, sliding into the booth beside Sean. "I like to be aware of every delicious sensation."

He picked up his glass. Scotch, neat. "To success," he said, downing it. "You have fun. Make sure you drive home, since you're the only one not sneaking booze."

"Where you goin'?" I asked as he slid away from me.

"Home."

"You came all this way to have one drink?" I said. "I don't buy it."

"I came to talk business with Nika. We talked, I'm done." He stood up. "Nice show tonight."

"Thanks. What's the business?" I said, leaning forward to show off my cleavage.

"My firm's got a client who needs an agent. I'm recommending Nika, since she's got a way with child stars."

"I know you don't mean me. I'm no child," I said. But he'd thrown me off my game. Nika was taking on another client? "She as hot as me? This new child star?"

"Relax. It's a boy, and he's only twelve." Sean smiled. "But he's good, he can act. It's my first big client hookup, and it's thanks to you."

"So you owe me one?" I said.

"I negotiated your contract for free. We're even," he said. "Believe me, I'm never going to get into debt with *you*. I'd never get out."

"You got that right," I said. "Sure you don't want another drink?"

"Oh, I'm sure." He gave me a little wave and took off.

"Where's he going?" Nika asked, coming over to the booth with her drink.

"Home. He's scared of me," I said.

I was joking, but my agent didn't seem to notice. She gazed after Sean, chewing on her lip. "I need to talk to him for a sec," she finally said, taking off toward the door.

I leaned back against the booth and took a deep breath. The place was crowded, and everyone here worked on my show. *My* show! How many people in the world get to say something like that? So why were Sean and Nika and even Mama being all weird?

"You're the most important person in the room, what are you doing alone?" Jonas asked, dropping down next to me.

"I was just wondering the same thing," I said.

He reached for the bottle of sparkling cider on the table and poured us both a glass. Then he pulled a silver flask from his pocket and poured some in.

"What is that?" I asked.

"Vodka. Goes with anything." He grinned. "I've been to a lot of these parties. I know what I'm doing."

I took a sip. It was basically disgusting, but whatever. I took another sip.

"What's with you?" Jonas asked.

"I've been hitting on my lawyer for days now and he keeps shooting me down," I said. "I don't get shot down. Not by anyone."

Jonas began to laugh.

"It's not funny," I said.

"It's totally funny." He shook his head. "You have everything in the world, and you're busy being pissy about the one thing you can't have."

"I'm not pissy," I said. I looked around the club again. My party. My show. "Okay, I'm a little pissy. I should be enjoying this more," I admitted.

"You don't need that lawyer guy. I saw you up onstage tonight, singing your song like a rock star." Jonas slipped his arm around my shoulders and leaned in to whisper in my ear. "You totally got off, right up there in front of the crowd."

I closed my eyes and pictured it again. The music all around me, the hot lights, and the adoring eyes of the crowd. A delicious warm feeling spread through my body. "I definitely did." I opened my eyes and looked at Jonas. "God, I wish we could tape a show every single day!"

"Pace yourself. It's a long season," he teased.

"I know. I just love it," I said. "Thank you for talking sense into me. Who needs a man? I've got a TV show!"

"I'll drink to that." He took a swig of vodka and held the flask out to me.

I shook my head. I'd had enough to drink. "Let's go dance."

"We should go chat with the Goldens," Jonas said. "Get the business out of the way."

"Screw that. They'll come talk to me." I grabbed his hand and hauled him out of his seat.

By the time we got to the dance floor, half the crew was out there grooving. The girls from my band seemed to be fighting over Travis, who had clearly forgotten all about getting me a drink. And Jude had her camera around her neck, but she wasn't working. She was dancing close with Kelli the PA.

Everyone cheered when Jonas and I stepped onto the floor, and I wrapped my arms around him and just danced. Nika came back and Travis was there. Jude took some pictures, the Goldens watched with huge grins on their faces. Even Amanda got out there and shook her big booty. I pulled Jonas's flask from his pocket and took another swig, but I didn't need it. I was high on life. No more cheatin' daddy, no more drunken mama, no more Chloe and Travis fightin' our way to the top.

I had a TV show.

Trav had a modeling career.

If I could stay on this dance floor forever, I'd die happy, I thought.

Turned out, I didn't need to drive home. Nika called a car to take us all back to the Oakwood at two in the morning. Which was just as well, because Travis was drunk and Amanda was half-asleep, and Jude went home with Kelli. The next day was a workday, call time at 9:00 a.m.

I stumbled into the dark bedroom and kicked off my shoes. I was too tired to bother getting undressed. "Move your butt over, Mama," I said, climbing into bed.

But the bed was empty.

Mama wasn't there.

chapter five

E-mail from Travis Gamble

Coop! Remember how I told you my mama was acting weird, like a good mother or something? Well, that shit's over. She's gone again. Said she was going home, but there's not a trace of her anywhere. Chloe even called that country singer she took off with last time, but his wife answered the phone so Clo hung up.

Her timing sucks, too, though I guess that's normal for Mama. Today's the day we went to meet with the dean about my soccer scholarship—to say that I'm ditching it. Chloe thought we could bring Mama in her new "responsible parent" mode, but so much for that idea. I think Mama would've found a way to mess it up, anyhow. Chloe and me do better on our own.

So we go in to the office, and the secretary looks like she's got something up her butt. (She always looks like that.) But Clo just takes one glance at her computer screen and calls her on it—she's totally reading TMZ! Seriously, this chick has to be at least forty but she's got it up and it's on a page about Chloe! So the secretary reads what it says, some whole thing about how Chloe's band rocked the world last night at their first performance for the show—which they totally did, BTW. And you can tell the secretary's impressed, even though she's all "When do you have time to do your homework?" Yeah. Like that's ever been a problem for my sister.

Anyhow, we go in to see Dr. Cardillo—he's the dean—and he's all serious. You gotta know, Coop, Chloe had to do some major heavy lifting to get him to agree to take us on. As soon as we sit down I start having second thoughts. Like, why do I need to be modeling boxer briefs? Chloe's supported us for years, and all she wants is for me to play soccer and be normal. Why am I gonna ruin that? I have a good life at St. Paul's. I can't believe I'm making my sister come back here and undo everything she did to get us in here. Cardillo is a scary guy.

So I'm ready to just bolt and forget the whole modeling thing, but Chloe is super calm. She's all, "I'm afraid I have to ask you for another favor, Dr. Cardillo. You see, my brother here has been missing some soccer practices."

Cardillo doesn't even flinch, dude. He just comes right back at her and says that Coach Ibanez told him I've missed scrimmages, too. He gives me the stink-eye, which totally works on me, but Clo ignores it.

She starts in with how I'm missing soccer for a good reason, because I've been working. I've gotten a lot of modeling work, and even some acting jobs, and stuff like that as if she's actually proud of me. Seriously, Coop, the girl can act. She thinks my jobs are for shit, but she totally sold it to Cardillo. And then she says, "I'm sure you remember that we're in a bad situation, family-wise. We need all the money we can get, just to keep a roof over our heads."

It sounds like she was playing drama queen, right? It's all pretty true, though. Anyhow, the dean wasn't having any.

He's all, it was clear from the start that Chloe would be pursuing a career in Hollywood. But everyone expected me to be a star player on the soccer team. That's why they gave us both a scholarship.

I felt like a turd. I wasn't planning on anything else, I totally thought I'd be playing soccer. So I say that, and Cardillo doesn't care. I'm like, "These jobs fell in my lap. And the pay is really good."

But the guy doesn't even crack a smile. Then Chloe starts in again, talking about how neither of us ever thought this would happen, and that we never meant to jerk them around. And then she says, "I have my own TV show now so I'm earning money, and maybe I can pay tuition for Travis and me. If you'd just keep us on at the school, I'll find a way to swing it. We don't want to give up on our education."

And Cardillo just says that their tuition is somewhat expensive. Yeah, like, INSANELY expensive. I was pretty much ready to give up, because the guy wasn't budging.

But Chloe's still all serious and grown-up, and she says she's asking him to be patient with her because she only gets paid one episode at a time, and there's her agent and the Coogan account, and our mama gets a percentage for expenses, and then we've got our rent. And while she's talking, I'm thinking that there is no way in hell Chloe can ever afford to pay tuition. But instead she's like, "I'm hoping you'll let me work out some kind of payment plan."

Like a monthly fee or something—it's a good idea, right? So I jump in with, "And I'll put some of my money toward it too." Chloe doesn't want me doing anything like that, but I figured why the hell not? If I put it out there right to the dean, she couldn't stop me.

Cardillo does this thing where he looks you straight in the eye and strokes his chin, like he's judging you. You'd think he would look at Chloe, right? But instead he stares at me. I gotta tell you, Coop, I was squirming!

"Am I to understand that you won't be playing soccer at all anymore?" he asks.

So I told him the truth: I want to play. I love it just like always. But sometimes there are work conflicts.

Cardillo pulls out the big guns. He says Coach Ibanez will be very upset by this.

It sucks, Coop. I love Coach. I think I would've caved right then, but Chloe jumps in. She's all, soccer is important, but right now we're just trying to make sure we can stay in school at St. Paul's because our only other option is Hollywood High.

She cracks me up sometimes. Here Cardillo is trying to play the guilt card by talking about Coach Ibanez, and Chloe totally out-guilts him by bringing up the ghetto school he's going to force us to go to!

Chloe's like, "We would hate to have to go to Hollywood High."

And Cardillo says that we're both such excellent students, it would be a shame to see us go there.

So it seems like maybe he'll agree to let us pay in installments. Which is really cool. But then it gets a whole other level of weird. Cardillo starts talking about how Chloe has taken a lot of responsibility onto herself. He's all, "Ms. Gamble, no one your age should be expected to work full-time, go to school, and manage the family finances."

That's true, you know. You'd think he might try saying that to our mama. Oh, wait, she took off on us!

And THEN . . . Coop, he's like, "Let's not worry about the tuition for the rest of this year." As in, he'll waive tuition. Because there are only a couple of months left in the semester, and me and Chloe have enough pressure in our lives with our jobs and all the time we must put in to get such good grades. And he's all, "I don't want to add to the burden."

I'm still trying to process all this, and Clo gets all teary and grabs my hand and starts saying how she just can't even express how much that means to us, because we don't get much help. . . .

You remember how she used to act whenever your mom caught us all skipping school or something, and Chloe would turn it around and make it seem like a cry for attention because our parents suck so much? It was kind of like that, like she was just so overcome with emotion. I'm no actor like Clo. But it doesn't matter, nobody looks at me when she's doing her thing.

Cardillo gets all puffed up and he's beaming like he just did a good deed, he's talking about how he'd hate to see smart young people kept from an education because of something like money, and Chloe's all grateful and putting on her act. It was craziness, man.

And I was like, "Wait. So we don't have to pay *at all*? Even though I'm off the soccer team?"

Cardillo says they can afford to extend a needs-based scholarship to good students because they have a large endowment at St. Paul's. I'm thinking, no shit, your soccer stadium is world-class. And then he starts in about how they just happen to be holding their yearly fund-raiser next month, some kind of dinner that a bunch of the really rich parents and alumni go to so that they can kick in more money to the school.

And then he turns to Chloe and he says, "You know, they might like it if you'd come and sing a song or two, Chloe. I'm sure they would be happy to meet the beneficiary of their generous donations."

Chloe goes, "Do they write you their checks at the dinner?"

And he says yes. Or they send checks shortly after the dinner.

So I'm not a genius, but I get the feeling there's something going on here that I don't know about, because all of a sudden my sister has dropped the gushy, poor little girl act. And Cardillo has gotten all wordy and businesslike. And he's never called my sister by her first name before, BTW.

Chloe says, "You just let me know what night the dinner is and I'll clear my schedule."

And Cardillo says that's wonderful. And then they actually shake hands!

Then Chloe grabs me and we walk off down the hall, just like that. Still in our fancy prep school, only now it's free and I don't even have to play soccer in return.

I couldn't even process it. I mean, what just happened? So I say to Chloe, "Are they giving us a free ride just to get you to sing at that fund-raiser?"

Chloe's not thrown at all, though. She says, yeah, they want her to sing and they're psyched that she's getting famous. And, BTW, she says they're psyched that I'm getting famous too. We make the school look good.

So we begged our way in, and now they're jumping through hoops to keep us.

As soon as we're away from the office, my sister starts laughing, so I do too. I guess we're not the Beverly Hillbillies anymore.

The Other Woman

When Trav and I got home from school, Mama was back.

"Well, hey there, sugars!" she said, waving from the couch. She was pretending to be casual, but all she wanted us to do was see the bracelet on her skinny wrist. Diamonds. Probably fifty of them, all on that one platinum band.

"Where the hell have you been, Mama?" Travis said. He probably hadn't noticed the jewelry, guys don't see things like that. And I definitely wasn't going to give her the satisfaction of mentioning it.

"Oh, you know, here and there," my mama said in a weird singsong voice.

Travis shot me a look. Whenever Mama did not want to

talk about her bad behavior, she put on the little girl voice and acted as if she were so cute that she could get away with anything.

"Fine, Mama, keep your secrets," I said. "But go take a shower. You stink like a winery."

Mama was a little huffy about it, but eventually she wandered off into the bedroom to get herself cleaned up. Being sexy is the one thing she cares about, even more than she cares about drinking. And smelling bad ain't sexy; even Mama knows that.

Soon as she was gone, I grabbed her purse off the kitchen table.

"What are you doing?" Travis asked me as I plopped down on the sofa and started riffling through Mama's bag.

"You up for a little field trip?" I asked him, holding up the black velvet box I knew I'd find in her purse.

"Do I really have a choice?" he said.

"Nope. Give me two minutes to change clothes," I said, heading for the bedroom while Mama showered.

Travis didn't bother asking me where we were going, but he did shoot me a few sideways glances in the Escalade. "Want to tell me why you're dressed like a model for J. Crew?" he asked as we pulled up to a valet on Rodeo Drive.

"Nope," I said. "But give me your Bluetooth." Travis handed over his headset and I tucked it behind my ear. I grabbed a clipboard from the backseat, one with a *Cover Band* call sheet on it to make it look official, tucked it under my arm, and climbed out of the car. Trav followed me through the heavy glass door into Harry Winston, jeweler to the stars.

"Who are we being today?" he murmured.

"You just browse through the pretty jewelry," I told him. "I'll only be a minute."

I spotted it almost immediately. The exact same bracelet my mama had been showing off. I crouched closer to the jewelry case to see the price tag: $32,000. I felt myself gasp.

Almost immediately, a rail-thin blonde with overly plump lips approached; her smile frozen by the Botox. "Welcome. What can I do for you today?"

I held up a finger and pretended to be listening to somebody on my headset. "Okay. The two-toned ones *and* the red ones? Got it. Shoe store is my next stop. Your dinner is at six-thirty, the car will pick you up at six. Bye!" I ignored Trav's confused expression and turned to the saleswoman instead. "Sorry! My boss can't decide which Manolo Blahniks she wants." I rolled my eyes.

The woman laughed. "Who can?"

Perfect. She thought I was one of the thousands of personal assistants running around Los Angeles, which meant she'd do whatever it took to be on my good side. If you keep the assistants happy, you keep their wealthy bosses happy.

"I'm hoping you can help me," I said, stepping closer and dropping my voice. "On the DL."

"We're very discreet," she said.

"My boss just got this incredible Harry Winston bracelet." I pulled out the velvet box I'd found in my mama's purse and set it on the gleaming counter. I lowered my voice to a conspiratorial whisper. "But there's a problem."

The saleswoman's brows knit in concern. Harry Winston customers don't have problems. Not when you pay thirty-two thousand dollars for a diamond bracelet. "What type of problem?"

"My boss was on a press junket in Europe when the bracelet was delivered, and"—I made sure to pause to emphasize the enormity of the problem—"and . . . there was no card. Someone, someone here at Harry Winston forgot to include the card."

The saleswoman looked puzzled for a moment, but then the clouds of confusion cleared. She realized that my "boss" was probably some famous A-list starlet who had *so many* wealthy admirers that she didn't know which one of them sent the thirty-two-thousand-dollar Harry Winston diamond bracelet! This was a huge problem.

"Maybe I should speak to a manager?" I said.

"No need for that," the rail-thin blonde said, "I'm sure I can help you." I noticed her Botoxed lips were quivering slightly. Maybe she was imagining how quickly she would be fired if it was discovered she had forgotten to include a card from a very important client to a very important star.

I tapped the jewelry case and indicated the bracelet in question. The saleswoman almost looked relieved.

"Ah, the sunflower bracelet. I sold that myself! I can print you up another copy of the card. Won't take more than a minute."

"Do you have a business card? I want to make sure my boss knows who to thank."

A huge smile stretched the Botox across the saleswoman's face. "I'll bring you one."

Two minutes later Travis and I were back on Rodeo Drive and I opened up the cream-colored envelope the rail-thin saleslady had given me. "Holy Goddamn."

"Who's the bracelet from? That porn producer?"

"Nope. Turns out Mama is movin' up in the world," I said.

"Well, are you gonna tell me?"

"Mama is sleeping with Dave Quinn. My bosses' boss's boss."

"Great." Travis dropped down onto a wrought-iron bench in front of one of the posh boutiques lining the sidewalk. "Quinn, the guy everyone is scared of at your show?"

"Yeah, he's the guy that can fire everyone, but no one can fire him. But that's the least of our problems."

"There's a bigger problem?"

"There is. He's married. To Connie Liu."

"That newslady?"

"Yeah," I said. "But she's not just a newslady, she's a network anchor."

"So Mama's the other woman. Again."

"Yeah, but this time she could end up on the cover of *People*."

He frowned. "Clo. You don't think Quinn would tank your show, do you? I mean, if Mama goes even more crazy than she is now?"

"I doubt it. He'd have to explain so much, it would be bound to come out in the press. If the show is a hit."

"So what do we do? Just keep quiet?" Travis asked.

"I don't know. Mama was awfully proud of that bracelet," I said. "But I guess if he keeps giving her stuff, she'll keep her mouth shut, at least when she's sober. I can't see Quinn putting up with the sloppiness the same way Lester Orcutt did." I'd been watching the rich people and the tourists strolling by on Rodeo Drive, but suddenly I focused on something else.

My own face, staring back at me from the side of a bus kiosk. And a guy and a girl standing about ten feet away, looking back and forth between the real me and the poster of me, whispering to each other.

"Oh my God, that's me," I said.

Trav busted out laughing. "That jeweler lady could probably see it through her window! You're gonna have to stop lying to people, Clo! You can't pretend to be some assistant once you're famous."

"You're right," I said. "Which means I've got to solve my Mama problems ASAP."

* * *

"Morning, Ms. Gamble," the guy at the security gate said. "When you gonna get your own car?"

"When my show's a huge hit, Eddie. I ain't stupid," I told him as he buzzed me through the pedestrian gate. Travis had dropped me off on his way to some big audition, and he was too late to do more than pull up to the curb so I could jump out of the Escalade.

Eddie chuckled. "Most girls like you would have a fancy convertible before they even got their first check."

"Most girls aren't like me," I said, walking on into the studio lot.

"Walk by the tank today. They've got it filled," Eddie called after me. "It's worth seeing."

I veered off the main walkway and headed toward the tank, which was a big concrete field about four feet below ground level. They usually kept equipment there, and half of it was used as a parking lot. On one side of it was an office building, but the side that faced the tank had no windows, and the wall was painted blue. Amanda said they used that blue wall for exterior scenes sometimes, because the blue in the distance looked like the sky.

It wasn't just the wall that was blue today. The whole tank had been cleared out, and it was filled with water. I stopped walking and just stared. It was bigger than any swimming pool I'd ever seen, and the way it ran up against the big blue wall, it looked as if the water went on forever. The guy at the gate was right—it was worth seeing. Somehow I'd never realized that when they called it the "tank" that meant it could be filled up like a fish tank. I laughed out loud. Only in Hollywood could a parking lot turn into a gorgeous lake overnight. Out in the middle of the water was a yacht, and around it were smaller boats with cameras, huge lights on stands, and two different cherry pickers waiting to swoop overhead and film the decks.

I didn't know the tank could be used like that, but I knew this much: That there was a big-money shoot.

"Got to get this area clear, love," somebody said behind me. "They're starting in five."

I turned around and saw a PA standing there. Jeans, T-shirt, baseball cap, clipboard, headset. The standard PA uniform. But this guy was staring at me as if I were some sort of annoyance, his eyebrows raised, his foot tapping impatiently.

"I kind of work here on the lot," I said, pointing to the huge billboard of me above my soundstage.

The PA wasn't fazed for a moment.

"You're not Matthew Greengold, and that's all I care about," the PA said.

"Matthew Greengold's here?" I asked. The guy had directed pretty much every movie on the top-ten list of all-time highest grossing movies.

"He's on his way, and that means no lookie-loos, even big TV stars," the PA said with a smile.

There was no way in hell I was clearing out if the most famous director in the world was about to make an appearance, and I was about to tell this guy so, but Kimber Reeve beat me to it.

"Don't be so rude to my friend Chloe!" Kimber called cheerfully. My rival's hair was in some complicated twisty updo. She was wrapped in a plush robe, carrying a steaming mug of tea, and for some reason was wearing rain boots on her feet. Two other PAs flanked her as she walked toward the tank. She was loving the attention. "Chloe's the star of one of the little teen shows that shoot here. I'm sure she was just coming to wish me luck in my scene."

"Your scene?" I said.

Kimber nodded. "On the yacht. It's the cliffhanger for our last sweeps episode. Todd Linson got the network to cough up some serious cash because there's such buzz for the show. It's going to be amazing." She began walking again, and I was obviously supposed to go with her like we really were friends. I knew I should leave, but I was dying to get the dirt about Matthew Greengold. So I went along with her little game, for now. "Anyway, Todd invited Matthew to come watch today. You know Matthew produced Todd's last film. They're tight."

"So nobody's even allowed to walk by? Wow. That's a lot of security just to visit a friend on-set," I said. "Even if he is so famous."

"The security's not just for him. He's got Anne Lynch with

him. She's the star." Kimber looked so smug that I wanted to punch her.

Anne Lynch was the best actress in the world, and everyone knew it. She'd won two Academy Awards, one playing an American attorney and the other playing a Polish war refugee. She had been nominated for four more, had countless Golden Globes, and basically was about a million times more talented than anybody else in Hollywood.

"The star of what?" I said as if I barely cared.

"*Frontier.* Matthew's next project, haven't you heard about it? It's based on the novel? Won the Pulitzer?" Kimber furrowed her brow, as if she were truly concerned about my lack of culture.

"I don't have much time to read. I'm too busy working," I said.

"Right. Well, it's a multigenerational epic, Oscar bait for sure," Kimber said. "They're casting the character of Anne's daughter. Todd told them about me, so they're here to take a look."

"At you?" I was so horrified, I couldn't even play my usual Texas bitchy-sweet role with Kimber.

"Mm-hmm. Todd is such a big fan of mine, he's just loved everything I've done on *Virgin.*" Kimber stared me straight in the eye, totally rubbing my face in it. She had a big network show with a wad of cash, and she had the best director in the world there to watch her. With the best actress in the world, just as a bonus. Kimber's show had buzz and so did she, and now she was in the running for a part in a huge Oscar-caliber movie.

She won. And we both knew it.

"They're calling for you, Ms. Reeve," one of the PAs said, listening through her earpiece.

"Wish me luck," Kimber said.

"Luck," I said as sweetly as possible.

There must have been boards just under the surface because Kimber Reeve literally walked on water off toward her expensive yacht on that incredible lake, where Todd Linson and Matthew Greengold and Anne Lynch were waiting for her. As for me, I walked toward my trailer.

My trailer. Where I got ready for my show, which I was the star of. Where I got to act and sing and play the guitar. Where everybody kissed my ass. Where I did the world's coolest work and got paid crazy money to do it.

It wasn't enough. I wanted the big director and the acting legend and the role in a Best Oscar Film. Some lucky rich girl from Connecticut shouldn't get that life—I should get it!

I slammed open the door of my trailer, pulled out my BlackBerry, and dialed.

"Max here," Kimber's ex-boyfriend answered on the first ring.

"It's Chloe Gamble," I said. "Don't talk, just listen."

"Oookay." He sounded amused.

"You told me once that we should cut a single together,

remember? You said it would piss off Kimber Reeve. You still interested in that?"

"Which part? The single, or Kimber?" Max asked.

"Both."

"Sure."

"Good," I said. "Because I am going to sit down this very second and write a hell of a song, aimed right at Kimber's heart."

Nika Mays's Manuscript Notes: Everybody Rises

Work breeds work. How many times had Hal Turman told me that? It was his second favorite bit of agent wisdom, right after the Don't Do. I used to roll my eyes at my boss when he'd trot out stupid clichés, but now I was starting to think of them less as clichés and more as solid advice.

Here's what I always used to think when Hal announced that work breeds work: If that's true, then how can the Don't Do ever succeed? Because if you say no to work (the Don't Do), then it can't breed more work.

I pointed that out to Hal once, and he told me I wasn't as smart as I thought I was.

Chloe Gamble had a job on *Cover Band*. I'd gotten

her the job by doing the Don't Do. I said no to the first offer, and I said no to the second offer. It went off perfectly. Now she had work, but she also had an iron-clad contract that prohibited her from taking any other roles while the show was shooting. So her work couldn't possibly breed more work.

Except that Amanda had a new job. And so did Jude.

"You'll never believe who I'm meeting for dinner!" Marc sang as he sat down across the table from me at lunch. "Darren Gerson of Glitter Publicity."

"For a job interview?" I asked.

"Thank you, Chloe Gamble." Marc clinked his water glass against mine in a toast. "The girl oozes PR opportunities out of every pore—I barely have to do anything for her! And yet my phone is ringing off the hook."

"Did they make you an offer?"

"No, but they're going to tonight," Marc said. "And I think I'm going to take it. I've been an assistant at Slade for almost two years. I'm done."

"Don't take it. Glitter is second-rate," I said. "But use it. Tell your boss about it and make her give you a promotion or you'll walk."

"And if she says no?"

"*Then* take the job at Glitter," I said. "But she won't say no. Especially not if you tell her that Chloe will follow you."

"Will she?" Marc asked.

"Count on it." I smiled. "Ask me my news."

"Tell," he said.

"Travis Gamble just booked a huge commercial. It's for *Chanel*."

"No!"

"Yes. And Javier Bronn is directing it." I laughed out loud. "Can you believe he landed that? Little Travis!"

"Honey, his important parts aren't little," Marc said. "And he's got a famous sister. If they can't get her, they'll take him."

It was true. Work breeds work. Chloe's job made work for Amanda and Jude, and now Marc and Travis. And mo.

"I've got more." I leaned in closer to him. "Sean Piper brought me a new client; he told me about it at the *Cover Band* party."

"You mean a non-Gamble client?" Marc asked.

"Mm-hmm. Josh Andrews. This kid has been on two different soaps in New York. He's been acting since he was preverbal," I said. "The mother had him using an entertainment lawyer there. And she's the manager."

"Mom-ager." Marc made a face.

"Yeah. But now little Josh is twelve and he's decided to move to LA," I said. "His lawyer works at the New York branch of Sean's firm, and they figured they'd just switch him over to somebody out here."

"No way. He needs an actual agent if he wants to do anything besides soap operas," Marc said.

"That's what Sean told them," I said. "And he's very convincing. So is Chloe's meteoric rise to success. Sean's boss got into it with the mother, telling her how huge Chloe is going to be and how I could do the same for Josh. He'll have the 'Chloe Team' of me and Sean, blah blah blah. So now Josh has a lawyer and an agent."

"And no need for the mom-ager. Clever." Marc eyed me suspiciously. "And you have an even tighter bond with Sean."

That was maybe my favorite part of the whole thing. I tried to look casual, but Marc knows me too well.

"You really can't sleep with him now that you're in bed together, career-wise," Marc said.

"I wasn't going to sleep with him anyway," I said, not even sure if I was lying or not.

"Here's your consolation prize: publicity!"
Marc grabbed his BlackBerry and began typing.

"What are you doing?" I asked.

"E-mailing Nikki Finke about the hot new team
in town, Nika Mays and Sean Piper." Marc hit
send, and I knew there would be a blurb about
Sean and me on Nikki's blog tomorrow. Every
executive in the Industry reads that blog, and
now they would all know my name. And who knew?
Maybe I'd get some more clients out of it. Maybe
Sean would.

All because of Chloe and her job on *Cover Band*.
Work breeds work.

Freedom

"Kimber has Dame Anne Lynch coming to see her!" I
practically screamed at Nika as we sat in traffic on Hollywood
Boulevard. "She's up for a part in Matthew Greengold's new
movie!"

"I read that script; the part is tiny," Nika said.

"I don't care, Nika!" I cried. "It's a real movie, it's not just
some kids' TV show on a cable network."

"You know who has a kids' TV show on a cable network?
Miley Cyrus," Nika said. "I promise you, everyone in Hollywood
takes Miley a lot more seriously than they take Kimber."

"Matthew Greengold," I said. "The most famous director on earth."

"Yes, Matthew Greengold is looking at Kimber for a bit part, because she has a supporting role in a TV show that his friend is making." Nika sounded exasperated. "Yes, that makes Kimber smug. And yes, that makes you mad; otherwise you wouldn't be Chloe Gamble."

"There are no famous directors coming to see me," I said. I knew I sounded whiny, but I couldn't help it. All I really wanted was to smack Kimber Reeve's self-satisfied smile off her face. All I wanted was to show her once and for all that I was better than her, even though I didn't have the rich daddy and the fancy schooling.

"Clo, you're in this for the long term, right?" Nika said.

I nodded.

"Then first you have to do one thing—*one thing*—that makes money, and it doesn't matter what it is. Once you've made somebody ten million dollars, they have to take your calls. Once they've bought a house in Pacific Palisades with money that *you* earned for them, they have to keep giving you work. Forever."

"Once Kimber wins an Oscar for a Matthew Greengold movie, she'll get work forever too. And she'll be taken seriously," I said.

"I thought you wanted money. Where did this 'serious actress' thing come from?" Nika asked, glancing sideways at me.

I thought about that. "It came from hearing that Kimber might get a part in *Frontier*," I said.

Nika laughed. "At least you're honest."

"It's not just about money, it's about . . . I don't know, fame," I said. "I want the money, but I want the Oscar, too. I want people to stop and stare if they see me on the sidewalk. I want my face on billboards that are as tall as entire buildings. I want Kimber to be jealous and I want all the movie roles, every single one, so that she doesn't get any. So that nobody gets them but me, I want first pick. And I want people in, like, China to know my name. I want little girls to dream about growing up to be *me*."

Nika was silent for a moment. I stared out the window at the palm trees blowing in the wind, flowery vines twining around their trunks. Ever since I'd walked away from Kimber that morning, I'd felt like my veins were filled with lava instead of blood. I wasn't even sure if I was furious or humiliated. Maybe both.

"Okay," Nika said. "Let's do that."

"I'm not kidding."

"Neither am I, Chloe. You want to be a supernova. I want you to be one too."

I frowned. "Of course you do. If I get big, you get big."

"So what? Yes, I want you to be the next Reese Witherspoon because that will make me the hottest agent in town. It doesn't mean I'm not your friend. I'm just your agent first."

Nika turned into a driveway that plunged underground below an office building, pulling to a stop in front of a valet stand set up by the garage elevator. She climbed out of the car and so did I, and by the time the guy drove off with the car, I'd cooled down a little.

"It's still amazing to have my own TV show," I said. "I do realize that, you know."

Nika nodded.

"But I'm impatient. It's moving faster for Kimber."

"That's not always a good thing," Nika said. "Trust me—as your agent *and* your friend. As impatient as you are, be patient enough to make this show a hit. And then you can write your own ticket."

The elevator arrived, and I took a deep breath. "First things first."

Travis was waiting for us upstairs in the lobby. "You ready?" he asked me.

"Born ready," I said.

Nika signed us in at the front desk, then turned to us. "Let's do it." She led the way down the hallway, which was more like a carpeted path between what must've been fifty cubicles. Standing up, you could see the entire floor of the building in one glance. I guess when you sit down at a desk in a cube, you don't realize that you're basically in a big ant farm.

"Why is everyone looking at us?" Trav asked as we followed Nika.

I shrugged. Everyone always looks at me. But now that he'd pointed it out, I had to admit that it wasn't just me they were watching. Every cubicle we passed, some guy in a suit turned to check me out, and to check Nika out, and lots of times they even seemed to check Travis out. Occasionally there was a woman in a suit, and they were all watching our butts, too.

"Seriously," Travis murmured. "You think they might jump us?"

"You brag about being a fashion model, Trav. Well, walk the walk," I teased him.

"In here," Nika said, pulling open a glass door into a conference room with glass walls. Through the glass, I could see the suits still gawking at us.

"Nika! What is up with this place?" I asked.

She wiggled her eyebrows. "Why do you think I wanted to meet here? It's good for my ego."

"LA is weird," Travis said.

"Why's that?" Sean Piper asked, buzzing through the door with a stack of papers in his arms. He dropped them on the big wooden table with a thud.

"Every single person in your law firm just checked us out, all of us," I told him. "I don't even get that much attention from you one-on-one."

"Lawyers are horny," Sean said, avoiding my eyes. "As a group."

Trav busted out laughing.

"I mean it. Other people get to do stuff. We just do paper-work. All the time," Sean said. "A couple of hot girls walk in, everyone wants to watch them."

I opened my mouth to say something about helping him with that horniness problem. But then I noticed something strange. He wasn't looking at me when he talked about us being hot girls. He was looking at Nika.

"These my official papers?" Travis asked, completely miss-ing the tension. He lifted a document off the top of the stack on the table and started reading.

"Yup. You sign those and I'm your lawyer," Sean said, pull-ing a pen from his suit jacket. He waved for me and Nika to sit down as Travis signed, and then Sean took the papers and stuffed them into a manila folder. "I guess I'm the Gamble family lawyer now."

"Not the whole family," I said. I reached for the rest of the forms he'd brought in.

Sean put his hand on mine, sending a jolt of electricity through my whole body. He'd never touched me before, not voluntarily. "Why isn't your mom here?" he asked. "She needs to have a say in this."

His tone of voice was older brother, or concerned teacher, or sympathetic reporter. It was *not* 'I've got to have you now.' I snatched my hand away, leaving him with the papers.

"We've got a . . . situation," Nika told him.

"And that situation is that my mama is having an affair with Dave Quinn," I said. This time when I looked Sean in the eye, he looked straight back at me. But he was still just concerned. Not *interested*, not like I wanted.

"You're sure?" he asked.

"He gave her a sixteen-carat diamond bracelet. I'm pretty sure," I said.

Sean leaned back in his chair, and his gaze went to Nika. "This is bad," he said.

She nodded. "We've got to move fast."

Sean sighed. "Okay. One set for Chloe, one set for Travis." He slid some forms across the table to my brother and me.

"What's this?" I asked, looking it over. "I thought we were signing legal contracts."

"It doesn't work that way. This is just the first step, a petition for the court. You're going to need a judge's order, and you'll need to jump through hoops," Sean said. "More hoops than I expected, now that your mother's not in the loop."

"You're sure about this, guys?" Nika asked. "It might get ugly."

Across the table, I met my twin brother's eye. Was he nervous? "It's just you and me, Trav," I said.

"Same as it's always been," he told me.

Same as it's always been, I thought.

"We're sure," I said. "We're going to divorce Mama once and for all."

Chapter six

From Nika Mays's Manuscript Notes: Emancipating a Minor

Emancipation. It's a powerful word. Its literal meaning is "liberation." Setting free. That's a beautiful thing. Unfortunately, here in Hollywood it's generally more about gaming the system than freeing anybody. There are all kinds of stories about child actors divorcing their parents, and usually people assume that it means the parents are monsters who abuse their kids or at the very least take their kids' money and spend it all on themselves or their drug habits.

That's true. Sometimes.

But most of the time when teenage actors get emancipated, their parents are completely in favor of it because it's a good career move. There are pesky things known as child labor laws that make hiring a minor a nightmare of paperwork and regulations for producers. And that's *before* the kid even starts working. Once all the work permits are requested and approved, the educational requirements have to be followed, and those requirements severely limit the amount of time the teen actor is allowed to work. When an actor is only allowed to work six or even nine hours a day, it puts a crimp in the shooting schedule, because the average Hollywood workday is twelve hours long.

Then there's the money. Every time a producer hires a minor, there has to be a Coogan account set up to put money away so the kid's parents can't touch it. That's another whole mountain of red tape. And then there are the parents themselves. They're legally required to sign every contract, every work permit, every single piece of paper that the teen actor needs to get hired. So the producers have to negotiate not only with the kid, but with the parents. And parents can be really demanding and stubborn and, well, annoying. But most parents—most stage parents, anyway—know that about themselves. They realize that the producers would be much happier if they didn't have to deal with stage parents. They realize that their kid stands a better chance of landing that next big movie if there is no mountain of red tape in the way. They realize that if a Kimber Reeve is emancipated and a Chloe Gamble is not, all things being equal, the part will probably go to Kimber Reeve.

So those parents take their kids to a lawyer and get them emancipated. It's a simple process of petitioning the court, proving that the teens make enough money to support themselves, proving that their parents are okay with it, and voila! Emancipation.

But Early Gamble was not most parents. Early couldn't have cared less what was good for Chloe's career—not unless she could be sure of profiting from it herself. And what I'd come to know about Chloe's mother was this: Early was selfish, and Early was an alcoholic, and Early had earth-shatteringly bad judgment, but Early was *not* stupid.

"The instant she finds out about this, she's going to go ballistic," I told Chloe and Travis as we left Sean's office.

"So what? She can't stop us," Chloe said. "Sean says we have to prove we've got income and prove we can support ourselves. Well, I just deposited a damn big paycheck yesterday, and Trav's fancy commercial in Barcelona is set to pay pretty good too."

"And Chloe's money has been paying the rent ever since we got to Los Angeles," Travis said. "Mama doesn't contribute anything."

"Now, Trav, she does amuse us from time to time," Chloe said. "Like when she was so drunk she spent twenty minutes banging on the neighbor's door because she thought it was ours and she'd left her keys in the taxi."

"Yes, you two are financially fine," I said. "But the court also requires that your mom allow this emancipation to happen. She doesn't have to be totally in favor of it, but she has to *allow* it. She can't fight it."

"Well, she will fight it," Travis said. "Tooth and nail."

"Can't we have her declared an unfit parent?" Chloe asked.

"It'll take forever; you'll be eighteen before you even get a court date," I said. "Besides, if you do that, they might want to bring your dad in so he can have custody."

I've never seen anyone's face change so fast as Chloe's did at that moment. She went from mildly annoyed at this crimp in her plans to flat-out furious so fast that I took a step back.

"No," Chloe said. "Not happening. Not ever. I'd kill that man before I let him have control of Trav and me."

We were at the elevators now. I pushed the down button and we waited in silence. Chloe's face was pale and her hands were clenched into fists. But Travis just looked thoughtful.

"We'll wait," he said suddenly. "Sit on the papers for a while before we file them with the court. Mama is bound to do something stupid and then we can use it to make her go along with it. Just like the way we got her to sign our Coogan account paperwork."

"She was so wasted, she didn't even know what she was signing," Chloe pointed out.

"I think the chances are good that that will happen again," I said.

A slow smile spread over Chloe's face and she relaxed. "Then once we get the court order that we're free, we'll kick Mama out of our lives for good."

"You don't have to do that, you know," I said.

"Emancipation only means that your parents aren't obligated to support you anymore. It doesn't mean they're not still your parents."

Travis snorted. "Mama hasn't supported us, ever. We support her."

"We've been the grown-ups all along. Now it'll be official." Chloe led the way into the open elevator, bouncing as she walked. "I hope Mama fucks up soon. I don't want to wait."

"Clo, you'll still have to follow the child labor laws. You have to go to school and you can't work long hours," I said. "The only thing that changes is that we don't have to involve your mother in career decisions."

"Sean said there was a test, to make me an official high school graduate," Chloe said.

"Yes, it's given in June." I had wanted to smack Sean when he brought that up. Nobody should leave high school early. Colleges don't like anything other than an honest-to-God diploma. The California High School Proficiency Exam would give Chloe a certificate that meant, legally, she was a high school graduate. But that was not a diploma, and as far as I was concerned, that was not an option. "You're not going that route, Clo."

"If I'm a graduate, I can work adult hours. The

child labor laws don't apply anymore," Chloe said. "That's what Sean said."

I opened my mouth to argue, but Travis just laughed. "Okay, I'll do that too."

Chloe's eyes blazed. "No way in hell. You are graduating. For real. And applying to college and all that normal stuff."

"So I guess that special certificate doesn't really count, then," Trav said.

I bit my lip to keep from smiling. Travis knew how to play Chloe better than I did. "It's fine for me, just not for you," she muttered. But she didn't mention it again for a while. She was already almost done with sophomore year. Maybe I could find a way for her to graduate early for real. And in the meantime, just getting her legally separated from her time bomb of a mother would be enough.

It took less than a week.

"You're kidding me," Sean said when I called him five days later.

"Nope. Early is missing again—"

"*Again?*" he cut me off.

"This is the third time she's taken off since I've known Chloe," I said. "She's been gone for a couple of days."

There was a little silence on the other end of

the line, and I could tell that he was shocked. Part of me wanted to tease him for it, the nice boy from Michigan being here in the big, bad city where a mother could be drunk and missing and it was no big deal. Sean had obviously never seen a family like the Gambles, and I couldn't tell if he was disgusted by them or if he felt sorry for them. But honestly, I was no better. Everything about Chloe's home life shocked me. Sometimes I think that was why I closed my eyes to the danger involved in Chloe's naked lust for money and fame, why I never let myself worry that she'd go too far . . . not until it was too late, anyway. Because I got it—no place was ever going to be far enough from Earlene and Lonnie Gamble and their house in Spurlock, Texas. Chloe wanted to forget her past, and I wanted that for her too.

"Did you call Child Services?" Sean asked.

"God, no, and you won't either," I said. "Chloe and Travis can take care of themselves. That's why we're emancipating them, remember?"

"I've never thought that was a good idea," he said. But he didn't sound very certain at the moment.

"File the petition now and note that the mother can't be found to sign it," I said. "I'll vouch for that and so will Amanda. And so will the dean at Chloe and Trav's school, for that matter. If the parents are AWOL, you can get a judge to issue the court order for emancipation, can't you?"

"It's not the cleanest way to do things," Sean said.

"Look, I haven't told Chloe this, but I think I know where Early is," I said.

Sean sighed. "Where?"

"I have a friend from Stanford who's in the training program at EdisonCorp, and she says there's a huge summit in Tokyo all this week and next," I said. "If it's about EdisonCorp, Dave Quinn will be there."

"Hold on, you think he brought Mrs. Gamble to Japan?" Sean said. "Wouldn't his wife find out about that?"

"How? She's too busy working," I said. "Japan is a world away."

"This is ridiculous," Sean told me.

"Chloe's show premieres in two weeks. If word leaks out that her mother is sleeping with the guy who's paying for the show, how is that going to look?" I pressed him. "Bad. It's going to look bad."

"She didn't get the job because of this affair," Sean said.

"Right. And everybody cares about details like that when there's a huge sex scandal," I said sarcastically.

"So you're telling me I have to convince a judge to give Chloe and Travis special treatment immediately, or else . . . what?" Sean asked. "If the media finds out about Quinn and the mom, it'll still look bad."

"But at least we can try to separate Chloe from it," I said. "We can let Early take the fall by herself." It was a long shot, and I knew it.

But it was the best chance we had.

Alone

"I've got a new one," I told Max as he tuned his guitar. "It just came to me in the shower this morning."

"There's a nice thought," he said, shooting me a smile.

I laughed. "Behave. You're not here to flirt, you're here to help me write."

"I can multitask," he said, but I could tell he wasn't offended. He didn't seem to care if I was in a flirty mood, or if I was in a bitchy mood, or whatever. We'd gotten together three times in the week since I'd run into Kimber at the studio, and so far the bitchy moods were probably winning, but how could I help that? Between Sean Piper ignoring me and Kimber getting so much attention and Mama taking off again, I was pissy.

And now Trav was gone too. I'd dropped him off at the airport this morning, and he was probably halfway to Spain by now. I'd planned to head straight home, but somehow I found myself driving down Sunset Boulevard to Silver Lake, where Max lived. It was Sunday, so I had the day off, and I couldn't face going home to the Oakwood all alone. Not that I really cared if my mama came back. But I'd never been all by myself before. I'd always had Travis.

"Let's hear it," Max said. "Or do you want to work on the bridge for 'Lucky Bitch' first?"

I shook my head and started strumming my own guitar. I still didn't know how to really write songs with an instrument—all I'd ever done before was come up with a melody and sing words to it. That's what I'd done with Max on the Kimber song, I'd shown up and sung out a whole rant about how smug and entitled she was. And Max had just started right in, playing some kind of harmony to the tune I was singing.

It wasn't as good as 'I Could Care' . . . yet. But it would be. No rush. I wasn't so mad at Kimber today. I was mad at my mama. That's who I wanted to sing about.

"I'm not sure these are the right chords," I said. "But that's what I had in my head."

Max began playing along with me, copying the chord progression. And then I started singing:

So get out
Move along
Don't clutter
Up my song

Clean out your stuff
Give back my car
Don't make this rough
Leave the guitar

Let me lay this out for you
There is no maybe, baby
There is nothing you can do
Because you and I are through

And . . . it's not me—it's all you

When I got through the first verse and the chorus, I stopped. "That's all I got so far," I said.

"Cheerful," Max said, sarcastic.

"I'm not cheerful about my poor excuse for a mama, and you wouldn't be either," I said.

"So let's see. You've got a song about how your father sucks, a song about how Kimber sucks, and now a song about how your mother sucks," Max teased. "At this rate, you're going to run out of material pretty soon."

"No way, I got a lot of things I'm mad at. People, too," I said.

His eyebrows shot up, but he just shrugged. "Then I guess we'll just have to call the album *Chloe's Revenge*."

I laughed out loud. "That's perfect!"

"Might be better if we also had some stuff you could dance to," Max said. "Or some nice gooey love songs?"

"Nope. Love is for idiots," I said.

"Love is the fuel of life," he said, and he didn't even roll his eyes while he said it. "Don't you get tired of writing angry songs?"

"Not as long as they're all good."

"They are, and you know it," Max said.

"Besides, I write the songs and the anger goes away," I told him. "And then I can relax and enjoy myself, cause I got everything in the world to be happy about. And it's only getting better. Soon enough there'll be no Mama to manage and I'll make all my own choices. Finally."

"If you think your agent and your bosses and all your 'people' are gonna let you make your own choices, you're living in a dream," Max said. "No such thing as thinking of yourself once you're a meal ticket for somebody else."

"That won't stop me. Just watch," I said. I scrolled through the contacts on my BlackBerry until I found the number I wanted, then I hit dial.

I got a guy's voice on voice mail. "Hey there, TJ, it's Chloe

Gamble, remember me?" I said after the beep. "You did sound for my YouTube video and I think you said you've got a friend with a recording studio. Well, I would just love to see that studio, maybe lay down a few tracks with you as engineer. Give me a call if you're interested!"

I hung up, knowing full well that TJ would be calling the second he got that message. Max was staring at me, eyes narrowed. "Who's TJ?"

"Somebody who won't tell my agent and my bosses that I'm recording songs I wrote," I said. "The Snap Network owns any music I write while I'm on *Cover Band*."

"So you're just going to lie to them?" he asked.

"I'm just going to not tell them. When I'm ready to release an album, my lawyer will figure it out. That's what he's there for," I said.

"Yeah, I'm sure he'll love that," Max said, shaking his head.

"Whatever. It's his job to do what I want," I said. At least in my career. And if my music created some big legal problem, well, that just meant I'd need more face time with Sean. And he'd give in to me eventually. All guys do, and that's a fact.

"Thanks for driving me, Mandy," I said on Tuesday morning as Amanda whizzed down the empty freeway toward Hollywood. My call time was at six in the morning, and traffic didn't get heavy until six fifteen. It was the one good thing about getting up at that godforsaken hour.

"No problem, sweetheart." Amanda took a drag on her cigarette and blew the smoke out her window.

"Why didn't you just take the Escalade?" Jude asked from the backseat. When she'd heard I was going in with Amanda, she'd decided to tag along for some girl time. I knew what it meant, that she and Mandy thought I might be lonely and wanted to distract me. They were right, but I wasn't about to admit to it. Never admit a weakness.

"That damn car is too big for me," I said. "I can't even see over the front of it."

"Says the girl from Texas," Amanda said. "I'm willing to bet you learned to drive in a pickup truck."

"Doesn't mean I liked it," I said. "I might've been born *in* Texas, but I was born *for* Hollywood."

"So you need a Bentley," Jude said. "No problem."

I grinned. "Just give me a couple more years!"

Amanda tossed her butt out the window. "Any word from your mama, sugar?" she asked.

"No, and there won't be," I said. "Not unless she needs me to bail her sorry ass out of jail." I rushed on so they wouldn't try to give me any pep talks or act all sympathetic. "I got a text from Travis, though. He's in some swank hotel in Barcelona; he says he can't get to sleep at night on the bed because he's been staying on a couch for so long."

Jude and Amanda laughed.

"His big commercial starts shooting today and he's all

worried he'll do something wrong," I said. "But really, how hard can it be to stand around looking all moody?"

"With Javier Bronn calling the shots, there will be more involved than standing around," Jude said. "I can't wait to see it."

"They can make it as artsy as they want, it's still just a perfume ad," Amanda said.

"Not for Trav," I said. "For Trav, it's a free trip to a bigger world."

When we got to the studio, Amanda headed straight for the wardrobe trailer to start things up for the day, and I went to makeup. The second episode of *Cover Band* was shooting on Friday, and this time instead of a live show we were doing a video. Nika said the Snap network wanted to shoot the video for this episode's song and then do another video with the show's theme song. They were going to use the theme-song video for ads on other networks. All in all, it came down to a day of me singing and dancing in about six different outfits, which was fun. And then an easier shooting day on Friday, because it would just be the stage sets and not a concert. The Goldens seemed annoyed about it, though, and they kept saying how every episode was supposed to have a live performance. Nika said that was too expensive.

I didn't know whose side I was supposed to be on, and I didn't care. I listened to the Goldens complain and I bitched right along with them. And then when Bo Haynes from Snap came by to visit, I listened to him pretend that the videos were a hot new idea and I totally agreed with him. Long as nobody catches you playing both ends, you can keep everybody happy.

I got out of makeup with a face full of glitter and sparkly gems on my eyelashes, which my mama would say was a little much for seven in the a.m., but Keesha said made me look like a hot angel. I knew I looked amazing, so who cared? Jude was waiting on set, talking to Bob Lavett, the photo guy from the network. We'd never met, but I knew who he was because Jude was always trying to impress him. He'd already extended her probation through the end of the month, but right at that moment I decided I'd had enough of it. Jude was my best friend and she was a kick-ass photographer and she knew enough not to try to make me sit around crying about my MIA mama and brother. She knew enough to just be there, and that meant I owed her one. I practically skipped over and flung my arms around my friend's neck.

"Jude! Are you shooting us while we do the videos?" I said. "Because look what an incredible job they did on my makeup!"

Jude laughed, pulled out her camera, and shot away while I posed. Well, fake-posed. I could do beauty queen poses and I could do model poses, but what Snap wanted was sixteen-year-old-girl poses, sort of silly and fun and totally fake. Whatever. I could pull it off.

"Those'll be great," Bob Lavett said.

"*Everything* that Jude does is great!" I said. "But you know that, Bob, you see every shot, don't you?"

He looked sort of stunned that I knew his name. "Um . . . yeah, I do."

"I bet it's not easy, just looking at pictures all day," I said. "You probably have to wade through a lot of crap to come up with good shots, but every time I go to the Snap website, we all look incredible!"

"You give me good material to work with," Bob said, actually trying to flirt with me.

"No, Jude does. She's my secret weapon; she always makes me look good," I said. "I don't know what I'd do without her. I'm kind of shy about getting my picture taken usually, but not with Jude. She makes me feel safe."

I could almost feel Jude's embarrassment, so I didn't look at her. I kept my eyes locked with Bob's.

"Trust is important in this business," Bob said.

"Exactly! See, I knew you and I were kindred spirits!" I said, "Anyway, I absolutely need Jude on-set. If it was anyone else I'd just freeze up and look all weird. And I know you really helped her out to get this job, so thanks, Bob. Really."

By now he was turning red, so I just gave him a wink and took off toward Jonas, who had just come sauntering through the door. "You're happy," he said.

"I'm feeling my power," I told him. "Bet you ten bucks Jude has a permanent job by lunch."

"I'm not dumb enough to bet against you," he said.

My BlackBerry buzzed, and I checked the text. It was from TJ the sound guy and it said: "Any time you want, we'll make it work." I smiled.

"Secret admirer?" Jonas asked.

"Not an admirer. But definitely a secret," I told him. "What are you doing here?"

"I've got that one scene in the second video. They must think my ugly face will attract the canine viewers."

"Don't even try that crap with me. You know you're gorgeous," I said.

"Sure, but I'm not egotistical enough to *say* it. That's why I fish for compliments," Jonas said.

"It ain't ego, it's just truth. I'm the hottest thing on this studio lot and that's a fact," I said. "But maybe you come in second."

Jonas laughed. "You up for clubbing tonight? There's a party at Uber."

I wrinkled my nose. "That gay bar?"

"Gays throw the best parties." He shrugged.

"You ever gonna come right out and tell me that's your thing?" I asked.

Jonas didn't even flinch. "I don't have a thing. *This* is my thing." He gestured around the soundstage. "Who needs sex when you've got fame?"

"Amen to that."

"Besides, if I show up at a gay bar with a hot girl, that means I'm straight, right?" he said.

I had to laugh. "Sometimes I think you're just using me," I joked.

"Did somebody say Uber?" Jude asked, coming up behind us. "I'm in."

"Gonna bring Kelli?" I said.

"Probably. I'm celebrating." She gave me a huge, crooked grin. "Official set photographer!"

"I knew it!" I cried. "Damn, that was fast. I thought it would at least take an hour or so."

"With the way you were laying it on? Please." She turned to Jonas. "You should've heard Chloe sweet-talking Bob Lavett. I was embarrassed for her."

"But it worked!" I said.

"Number One, we're ready for you," Jon the AD called. I gave my friends a little wave and ran over to the stage. Who cared about my mama taking off, or Trav being oceans away. I had the best job in the world, and I had the pull to get my friends the best jobs in the world. Not a thing was going to ruin it for me.

E-mail from Travis Gamble

COOOOOOOP!!! Here's something I bet you thought you'd never hear me say: Suffering through Señor Garrido's Spanish class was

TOTALLY worth it. In Spain, I can land scorching señoritas just by saying *Hola, me llamo Travis*. Scorching. Babes.

Dude, I am e-mailing you from Europe. How outrageous is that? I'm across the ocean! I'm in Barcelona! I gotta tell you, I used to think it was fun to skip school and go pool-hopping. Well, skipping school has nothing on this.

First. I get off the plane and there's a guy there with my name on a sign, so already I'm feeling swank, right? Then he takes me to the hotel and it's right on the freakin' beach. On the Mediterranean. Coop, I've never even managed to get to the Pacific Ocean since we've been in LA but now I've gone swimming in the Mediterranean! So then Javier shows up, he's the director. Chloe says he's famous, and you know who he is—remember that movie *Destruction*, that French action flick we saw on the Austin soccer trip? He made that. I don't know why he's doing commercials, but I guess Chanel is a big-money client so it's worth it. Nika said there's buzz about this ad, like who gives a flying fuck about a perfume ad, but whatevs. Anyway, he kisses me hello. Not in a gay way, but just me holding out my hand for a shake and instead he grabs me and kisses my cheek. O-kay. So I'm trying to be all professional like Chloe taught me, and I'm asking about rehearsal times and crap like that, and Javier just starts laughing in my face. He's all, 'We don't need to rehearse, we need to relax,' and he sends me off to the beach for the rest of the day.

With Monserrat. Who is 28. And drop-dead.

So we get to the beach and she takes off her top, and she's naked underneath. Then she takes off her skirt and she's got on a thong. And that's all. So there's me, lying on the beach in Spain with this smokin' woman who's basically naked. I try to make small talk in Spanish, but the most talking I've ever done in Spanish is trying to buy beer from Juan down at the 7-eleven in Spurlock, you know? Finally she just puts her hand over my mouth and starts speaking in English. She's telling me all kinds of stories about how Javier is such a genius and I'm thinking maybe she's sleeping with him, so I ask, and she's like, "No, I'm the casting director for all of his films."

Weird-ass place. It's like, at home you'd go to the office to meet somebody new at work. And in Hollywood, you go to a restaurant and have lunch or dinner but it's really just a work meeting. Well, I guess in Spain you go lie around naked on the beach and that's a work meeting here.

So then Monserrat brings me back to the hotel and I get changed and there's a party in the bar for everyone in the commercial, except they keep calling it the "mini" as in "mini-film," because that's how Javier sees it.

Just for the record, nobody even brings up the idea that I might be too young to drink.

Monserrat introduces me to Jacinda, who's from England but lives in Madrid. She's another one of the models in the ad. She's got this outrageous red hair and those freckles, you know, the little tiny ones just on her nose. I know, my man, SO not my type. But she had me upstairs in bed within an hour. Dude.

But then the next morning everyone was razzing me because I missed half the party. AND I missed meeting Sasha. That's right, Sasha Powell. (I'm glad we're not having this convo in person because I know you'd hit me right now.) Somehow Nika forgot to mention that Sasha Powell was starring in this commercial. I texted Chloe about it and she was all, "Duh. Sasha Powell is the new face of Chanel." Did *you* know that?

Anyway, apparently Sasha and Javier are besties, so she recruited him to make this fancy "mini."

We shot most of my part today, and then I do another half-day tomorrow, and then I'm on a plane back home. Sasha's shooting for two more days after that but I guess that's just her alone. In my part, I'm dressed in this Italian suit—damn! You should see this thing, Coop. I look GOOD. And I'm chasing Sasha down an alley. And then I'm kissing Jacinda's neck. And then Sasha's slapping me. And then I AM MAKING OUT WITH SASHA POWELL!!!

So on the list of reasons that my life is unbelievably cool, we've got:

1. I had sex with a British model last night.

2. I kissed Sasha Powell about twenty times today.

3. During lunch, I went to this park in the middle of Barcelona and there was a pick-up soccer game. So I joined. Coop, imagine it—I played soccer in Spain on my lunch break!

4. One of the production assistants, this girl named Luz, just asked me to go skinny-dipping with her in half an hour.

5. I kissed Sasha Powell about twenty times today!!!!!

I don't think Chloe's TV show is anything like this. But I'm starting to get why she's so obsessed with being an actress. This life is beyond anything you can even conceive of in Spurlock, Texas. I'm not playing, Coop, I think you need to come out to LA when school ends. Here's the deal: I got this job because of Chloe. I mean, I got the audition because she's famous and because of her I get on the gossip blogs sometimes too. So people want her, but they can't get her, so they take me instead.

Point is, now that I'm getting my own work, maybe I can get you work too. Maybe if I keep doing a good job I'll get better and better roles and then I can tell them you need to be my personal assistant or my manager or something. And they'll pay you to do it!

Javier told me today that he loves my "presence" and he might have a part for me in his next film. If I get an actual movie role, Coop, I need my wingman with me. Keep me humble, you know. Think about it.

IM

CHLOE: Trav?

GAMBLEGOAL: What up?

CHLOE: Busy?

GAMBLEGOAL: Nah, just e-mailing Coop. Chilling on the
beach with my new friend Luz.

CHLOE: Hot?

GAMBLEGOAL: I'm not talking to my sister about this.

CHLOE: Nika called. Sean set up a hearing for us with a judge.
About emancipating.

GAMBLEGOAL: Cool. When?

CHLOE: Tomorrow when you get back. You land at 4, meeting's
at 5:30. Nika says we need to hurry before Mama shows
back up.

GAMBLEGOAL: We're divorcing Mama while she's MIA?

CHLOE: That a problem?

GAMBLEGOAL: No. For you?

CHLOE: No.

GAMBLEGOAL: Clo? You okay back there?

CHLOE: See you tomorrow.

My Own Voice

"Okay, Travis is in," I said, sticking my BlackBerry back in my bag. I sat back against the cushy leather of the guest chair in Nika's office. "We just better hope his plane is on time."

"The judge will wait, for a little while anyway. It's a favor to my boss," Sean said from the chair next to me.

"Well, tell him thanks for me," I said, trailing my fingers along the arm of his chair. "Couldn't your boss just ask for the court order without having to meet us?"

"No, because that would be illegal." Sean frowned at me. "The whole point of this is to make sure that your interests— and your brother's—are best served."

"Our interest is in being free of our drag of a mama," I said. "Our interest is in being able to use our own money and not have it tied up in a Coogan account."

"But you're kids, Clo, whether you want to hear it or not," Nika said. "The court needs to feel that you're able to take care of yourselves. Not just with money. With responsibility."

"I can take care of myself in every possible way," I said, my gaze on Sean. He had his tie undone and his shirt open a couple of buttons, and he'd never looked better.

"This is the argument. Your mother can't be found. She routinely leaves you and Travis alone. That means, we'll say, that she believes you can be trusted to live on your own," Sean said. He was looking at a spot maybe on my forehead, maybe on the wall behind me. Anywhere but at my face. He was afraid to meet my eye, and that meant I was getting to him. Well, good.

"There's no way my mama would admit to that," I said.

"If she can't be found, it's an *implied* admission," Nika said. "She may not approve of you being on your own, but she is tolerating it. That's the legal requirement."

"Just so long as she's AWOL, she's agreeing? That there is a beautiful piece of legal stupidity. You really go to school for this stuff?" I asked Sean.

"For years," he said. "And you should be glad I did, because it takes serious chops to make an argument like this one. I'm not sure it will work."

"I trust you," Nika said.

"I do too," I told him, leaning forward to put my hand on his. With Nika there, he couldn't smack me away without it looking strange. So he tried to ignore me, and I left my hand there. "And don't worry, if you need backup, I can sell anything. The judge won't be able to resist us."

"I've asked Amanda to tag along, and Jude, just in case," Nika said. "They can attest to the fact that Early's been gone for weeks and that she's done it before."

Sean stretched and yawned, dumping my hand. I smirked at him. "I'm supposed to go to some party at Uber tonight with Jude and Jonas. You want to come?"

"No, we'll be working late on this," Nika said, even though I hadn't exactly been talking to her. But Sean didn't say anything, and I guess that was my answer.

"Okay." I stood up to go, and they both just sort of waved at me. As I wandered back through the office to the lobby, I noticed a lot of empty desks. It was late, most people had gone home, and I should have been getting ready to go out. But my place at the Oakwood was empty and boring, and Sean didn't want to hang out with me, and neither did Nika. I could go to Uber, but I knew it would be Jude and her crush and Jonas checking out other guys while he was dancing with me.

And no Travis to talk to.

And no Mama to worry about.

I pulled out my BlackBerry and texted back to TJ. Then I dialed Max.

"Chloe?" he answered.

"Can you meet me in the Valley? Half an hour?" I asked.

"You serious?"

"You know it," I said. "And bring your guitar."

It took me more than a half hour to find the recording

studio; it was so in the middle of nowhere that I felt like I'd gone back to Texas. But when I pulled the Escalade into the tiny parking lot, I saw two other cars there.

Inside, Max was tuning his guitar and TJ was firing up the equipment in the booth. "Here she is," TJ said, coming over to shake hands. "Thanks for calling me, Chloe. I appreciate the business."

"You kidding me? Thanks for coming out on such short notice!" I said. I noticed a woman in the office, settling a sleeping baby down in some kind of portable crib. "Oh my gosh, I didn't mean to drag little Daisy out so late!"

TJ looked astonished that I remembered his daughter's name, but what can I say? The first thing my mama ever taught me about winning beauty pageants was to remember every name you hear. People like it when you call them by name, it makes them feel special. And people *really* like it when you call their kids by name. People with kids would like to spend all day talking about their kids, so if you can hook into that, they'll love you for it.

"It's no problem, she can sleep through anything," the woman said, pulling the door slightly closed behind her. "She's got musician parents, she's got no choice."

"Hi there, I'm Chloe Gamble," I said, offering my hand.

"Sharon, TJ's wife," she said. "I'll be running the mike for you tonight, Chloe."

"Oh. I didn't know it was a family business," I said.

"My cousin owns the place, but we use it whenever we need to," TJ said.

"It's a nice setup," Max put in. "I think Optional Blueberries recorded here last year. My buddy's the drummer."

"Yeah, my cousin engineered that one," TJ said. "I'm afraid Chloe's stuck with me."

"Stuck with you? Why, you're part of why I've got my own show on TV," I said. "You helped me make my YouTube video and that's the whole reason I've got any kind of career at all."

"*You're* the reason, Chloe," Sharon said. "I saw that video, and TJ told me you were even better in the room. You've got it. You're lucky."

"That's a fact," I said with a wink.

"What are we doing first?" TJ asked.

"Same thing as last time. 'I Could Care,'" I said. "Only now it's got Max's fantastic guitar, too. And if he wants to get fancy producing it, I'm open to suggestions."

Max smiled. I don't think he understood until that moment I'd wanted him to produce the songs. That's how I like to deal with guys—keep them off balance.

"You and a guitar, that's all you need," Max said. "Your voice is strong enough without any big orchestrations."

"That's what the YouTube video proved," TJ said as he fiddled with a bunch of dials. "Just you belting it out. Not everyone can do that."

"I sang at every beauty pageant I ever won, just me and no

accompaniment," I said. "But I always sang famous songs, not my own stuff. I can sound like anyone."

"Must be why you're a good actress," Sharon joked.

"You got me there," I said. "Every pageant crown I got, I was being a different person in order to win it. You got to give the judges what they want."

"You don't need to sound like anybody else these days, Chloe Gamble," Max told me. "Your own voice is all you need."

He was strumming his guitar as he said that, not even looking at me, one dread hanging forward over his face as he watched the strings move. He wasn't making any big statements or trying to be all meaningful or anything. But suddenly I choked up.

My own voice. That's what I'd be recording here tonight, with these nice people. These normal people. I didn't need to be out at some club to be happy, and I sure as hell didn't need to be home alone missing my brother, and I didn't need to be throwing myself at some damn lawyer who didn't want me.

I just needed to sing. In my own voice.

When I got back to the Oakwood, it was after one in the morning and I was just as drunk as I would've been if I'd gone to the party at Uber. Except this time I was high on music. We'd recorded all three of the songs I wrote, and Max had come up with an incredible bridge for the one about Kimber, right on the spot.

Travis would be home soon, later that very day. And by the time we came home again tomorrow, we'd be free, court-ordered, emancipated minors.

I went into the bedroom and stopped short. There she was, snoring away in bed like she'd been there forever.

Mama was back.

Ed Decter

chapter seven

IM

GAMBLEGOAL: Guess where I am.

COOPERMAN: Paris? In a Speedo?

GAMBLEGOAL: Fail.

COOPERMAN: Playboy Mansion?

GAMBLEGOAL: Fail.

GAMBLEGOAL: Though I'm going to a party there next week.

COOPERMAN: You suck.

GAMBLEGOAL: Ditch school, hitch out to Cali, and come with.

COOPERMAN: You kidding? My mom would murder me.

GAMBLEGOAL: Tell her hi for me.

COOPERMAN: So where are you?

GAMBLEGOAL: In a freaking mansion in the Hollywood Hills.

Can see the whole city from the hot tub.

COOPERMAN: Hot tub?

GAMBLEGOAL: Seats six. But I like it better with just two.

COOPERMAN: ??

GAMBLEGOAL: Me. And Sasha.

COOPERMAN: ?????????????????

GAMBLEGOAL: Sasha Powell. My GIRLFRIEND.

COOPERMAN: In your dreams.

GAMBLEGOAL: In my BED, dude!

GAMBLEGOAL: Well, in her bed.

COOPERMAN: Details. Now.

E-mail from Travis Gamble

Coop, I am not shitting you. I was back from Spain for three days when
I get a call from Sasha, and she's all "Come over to my place in the
Hills so we can pick up where we left off in Barcelona." And I'm like,
Chloe must've gotten some friend of hers to punk me. No way is it
really Sasha Powell. But what the hell, I go to the address she gives
me. And there's Sasha, and she's all, "I'll give you a tour of the house."
And then she is dropping a piece of clothing in every room she shows
me. I'm not even kidding. By the time we get out to the back—where
there's this pool and a Jacuzzi with this little waterfall thing—she's
totally fucking nude. And she goes under the waterfall, and I'm thinking
maybe I actually died in a plane crash coming back home from Spain,

because this is not real. I'm not watching the most gorgeous movie star on earth do a porno just for me.

So, yeah. Sasha Powell. And we've been at it like rabbits ever since. No more details than that. I might not be a gentleman, but I'm also not my asshole daddy bragging about his latest bimbo to his drinking buddies. (Okay, I'll say this: Remember we saw her in that super-short lace robe in the Woody Allen movie Chloe dragged us to? When I woke up this morning, she was walking around in that robe. You can punch me later.)

Anyway, you gotta see this house. It's at the top of one of the hills overlooking Hollywood, and from the back deck you see all of Los Angeles on one side, and the whole Valley on the other side. Sasha's got a telescope, I'm talking super-expensive equipment (She says it was her old boyfriend's. Is she talking about Kanye, you think?). I pointed it toward the Oakwood, and I could see the pool! I even saw that porn producer lying around like he always does. Wish it was a sniper rifle instead of a telescope!

But Sasha doesn't even consider this place to be her actual house. She says it's a crash pad for when she's partying in town or working late on-set. Her real house is in Malibu, I haven't seen that one yet. But apparently it has eight bedrooms and two pools and a tennis court. Oh, yeah, and then there's a penthouse in Manhattan.

I'm making her sound spoiled. She's not. She's completely cool and funny and normal. Okay, not NORMAL, but for somebody who gets nominated for Oscars, she's normal.

So she's off at a meeting with Tom Hanks right now, and I'm

chilling in the Hills house. Sasha might not think it's much of a house, but I'd settle for a single room of this place. I'd like to just move right in. I'd even settle for sleeping on the couch here. Because the one place in all this world I do not want to be right now is at my own home in the Oakwood. Not since Mama got home.

Chloe and me were supposed to be signing our papers to get free of Mama, and right at that very second Mama shows back up. It's like she's got a sixth sense or something. We had to skip our meeting with the judge and pretend everything was normal until Chloe figures out what to do. And it's not like Mama's gonna notice anything weird going on, because she's too busy throwing a freaking tantrum about her boyfriend.

Get this, Coop: Mama went off to Japan with this super-rich business guy. Who is MARRIED. Loser. Anyway, he goes to some weeklong meeting in Tokyo and takes my mama with him. Then he takes her on a tour of Asia for another two weeks—she got to walk on the Great Wall of China! And he bought her a buttload of jewelry and four suitcases worth of fancy clothes. Hell, even just the suitcases probably cost as much as a car. And she won't admit it, but I think she got Botox or something, because she looks younger. That's what Clo says, anyway.

You'd think my mama would be happy with that kind of haul, right? Nope. She's all pissed off that her stupid boyfriend made her fly back to LA by herself. First class, BTW. She thinks he should've come with her, but he had to fly to NY because that's where he lives. With his *wife*. Mama's busy pouting and crying like she just got dumped by her one true love or something. Or else she's drinking. Or both. Then yesterday she started talking about how she could ruin his whole life just by making one call to the media, because his wife is some big newscaster and he's this famous billionaire.

Thing is, he's Chloe's boss.

So now Chloe is ready to kill my mama and Mama's crying and making threats, and it's a big ol' nightmare.

I'm thinking that right about now is a good time to spend the week at my famous, beautiful girlfriend's gated house in the Hills. Hell, maybe I'll just stay here forever.

Nika Mays's Manuscript Notes: Stage Mother Management

As soon as I got off the phone with my hysterical client, I went straight into Hal's office.

"You never taught me how to deal with the mother," I said. Hal was in a meeting with Bonnie, but I didn't care. I ignored her and her outraged expression. Bonnie's biggest client was angling to get a guest spot on *Cover Band*. Compared to me, right now, Bonnie was nothing. She could kiss my ass.

"What are you talking about, first thing I ever teach anyone is stage mother management," Hal said, also ignoring Bonnie.

"Not this kind of stage mother," I said. "Early Gamble is planning to go public on her affair with Dave Quinn."

"Jesus," Hal said. "She's sleeping with Quinn?"

"He's finished with her, so now she wants to ruin him. Chloe's literally thinking of tying her up so she can't get to a phone or a computer."

"Nice. The apple doesn't fall far." Bonnie sniffed.

"Shut up, Bonnie," Hal said. "This is a situation."

"How do I deal with it?" I asked.

"Buy her off," Hal said.

"Chloe's already paying her," I told him. "And Quinn spoiled her too. I don't think it's about money this time, I think she just wants to make a scene."

"Back in my day, we'd let Quinn handle it. It's his problem," Hal said.

"Quinn is the money for Chloe's network. It's everybody's problem," I said. But Hal's eyes were watering and he looked sort of . . . old. Suddenly I realized that he might not have an answer to this one. Early wasn't the kind of pushy, selfish stage mom he was used to. She wasn't out to get what she could for Chloe. She was only out for herself. "Never mind, Hal," I said. "I'll handle it."

But I still wasn't sure how to do that by the time Marc and Sean arrived to meet with Chloe and her mother.

Earlene had stomped into my office like an angry two-year-old and thrown herself down on the couch. She was staring out the window, sulking, while Chloe just sat there with her arms crossed. It struck me funny, right then, how backward their relationship was. Earlene was the spoiled kid and Chloe was the frustrated parent. I doubt she ever got the chance to be a child, not with parents like hers. I tried to tell the cops that, later; I tried to convince them that Chloe must've had it bad all her life. But I don't think they cared.

"Where's Travis?" I asked.

Chloe shrugged. "I texted him."

"He's at Sasha's house," Marc said, coming in with Sean right behind him. "I just leaked a photo of him walking her dog this morning. It's adorable!"

"Guess he ain't coming, then," Early said, shooting a triumphant look at Chloe. "He's minding his own business."

"You and Quinn *is* my business, Mama," Chloe snapped.

"It's true, Early, Quinn is in charge of Chloe's network," I said. "You were playing with fire when you got involved with him."

"He hit on me," she said, like that mattered. "He wouldn't take no for an answer. It's very exciting, to have a powerful man come after you like that." Early gazed at Sean as she spoke, inviting him to come after her too.

"And then he dumped you," I said brusquely. "You must've known he was married."

"He told me he don't love her. He said she's frigid," Early said. "He's a lying bastard, and I'm gonna make him suffer for it. You're a publicist, right, Marc? Maybe you can get a bidding war going for my story. His wife is famous, ain't she?"

"If it gets out that Chloe's mother was sleeping with Chloe's boss, it will look like that's why Chloe got the job on *Cover Band*," Marc said. He talked slowly, as if she were a child who didn't understand. "It will look like that's why the show got picked up by the network. It could ruin the show before it even premieres."

"That's what I've been telling her," Chloe grumbled.

"If the show is hurt, and Chloe loses her job, that means you won't be getting your percentage of her earnings," I pointed out.

Earlene waved her hand dismissively. "Clo will get another job."

"Early, you got a nice trip to Asia out of the whole thing. And look at that dress you're wearing," Marc said. "I'm betting Quinn bought it for you, right?"

"So that makes it okay that he ran back to his wife?" Earlene snapped. "'Cause he bought me nice stuff? I am not a prostitute, you know."

"You sure about that, Mama?" Chloe said.

Earlene jumped to her feet. "I have had enough of your mouth, young lady! I am your mama and you will show me some respect!"

"Once Chloe is legally emancipated, that argument won't work anymore," Sean put in.

My throat tightened. Marc cringed. Chloe and her mother both shut right up. Chloe turned white. Early turned red. And we all stared at Sean in horror. Chloe hadn't told her mother about getting emancipated. We'd all agreed that we wouldn't tell Early until we could figure out what to do.

Every bit of attraction I'd ever had to Sean

vanished instantly. How could he be so stupid as to bring this up now?

"What is he talking about?" Early hissed.

"It won't work with Travis, either," Sean added. I wanted to smack him. Marc had his hands over his mouth, his eyes wide as he watched the show.

"What is he talking about?" Early practically screamed. "Chloe! What in the hell—"

"You are *so* fired," Chloe snapped at Sean.

"Sorry, but she's got to know what's happening," Sean said, unfazed. "We were going to file for a court order while your mother was missing, but now that she's back, we'll need her approval."

"I am not approving *anything*," Earlene said. "Just what the hell do you mean, 'emancipated'?"

"It means that me and Trav would be in charge of ourselves, we wouldn't be saddled with you anymore," Chloe said.

"What, like you're divorcing me?" Early cried.

"Yes!" Chloe said.

"No," Sean said. "That's a different process. Legal emancipation would allow Chloe—and Travis—to sign their own contracts, not need Coogan accounts, and be financially responsible for themselves. There would be no financial tie to you anymore."

Early's eyes narrowed. "So Chloe wouldn't have to pay me my share?"

"So you wouldn't be responsible for supporting her anymore," Sean said.

"She don't support me now. She's never supported us," Chloe said.

"Who taught you how to sew your dresses and win all them pageants so you could make money?" Early said. "Who drove you all over the goddamn state of Texas so you could be Miss Cow Festival?"

"Who cashed all my pageant checks and drank half the money away?" Chloe yelled.

I glanced at Marc. He was inching toward the office door as if he might try to escape, and I was tempted to join him. This was not the kind of conversation that should be happening in a place of business. I couldn't believe how out of hand it had gotten. But Sean looked completely calm, as if he didn't even realize the can of worms he'd opened.

"No! She's not getting emancipated and that's final!" Earlene yelled at Sean. "You can't do it without me agreeing."

"When you decided to take off for three weeks without telling your children where you were, I filed a petition to the court to emancipate them because you clearly didn't think they needed their mother to care for them." Sean was still speaking calmly, but now there was an angry edge to his voice that took my breath away. His eyes never left Earlene's as he went on. "You came back before we met with the judge, but that doesn't change the fact that you left your children to fend for themselves, and you've done it before. I will argue that that means you think Chloe and Travis are adult enough to live by themselves and support themselves. I will argue that you have already essentially agreed to emancipate them. And I will win."

Early stared at him, speechless. Then her lower lip began to tremble, and a tear ran down her cheek. Usually I'd feel sympathetic, but Chloe had trained me to see her mother as the consummate performer that she was.

I'd seen Earlene's Girl Next Door. I wondered what Chloe called this little act.

Early let out a sob, wrapping her arms around herself. "You must think I'm a horrible mother," she whispered, glancing up at Sean through her eyelashes.

"Yes, I do," he said.

Early recoiled as if she'd been slapped. Then

she grabbed her purse and ran for the door. Chloe went after her, shooting a furious look at Sean as she left.

Marc and Sean and I were all left there, shell-shocked.

"I cannot believe you did that," I finally said. "Sean, what were you thinking?"

"Yeah, I thought we were trying to solve the Dave Quinn problem," Marc said. "If I'd known it was going to be trailer trash family feud, I wouldn't have come."

"I *did* solve the Dave Quinn problem. Early is so busy freaking out about the emancipation that she's forgotten all about Quinn," Sean said. "You're welcome."

My mouth dropped open in surprise. "You did that on purpose?"

Sean shrugged. "Earlene was going to find out about the emancipation. We actually do need her to agree to it. I simply chose the best time to tell her about it, and that time was when she was about to do something really stupid. Now she'll spend her time fuming about Chloe and Travis, not about Quinn."

And just like that, all my attraction to Sean reappeared, times ten. If not for Marc, I probably would have jumped Sean right there on my office couch.

"You," I told him, "are so *not* fired."

Premiere

"Where's your brother?" Jonas asked me as we waited in the limo.

"He's coming with Sasha," I said, my eyes on the crowded sidewalk outside the club. There was a line of people out there waiting to get in to the party for *Cover Band*'s premiere. Snap had decided to do a big splashy thing for the first airing, because the show had gotten so much buzz, mostly thanks to me and Jonas and our hot fictional affair. "You think there's enough paparazzi yet?"

"There's never enough paparazzi for you, Clo," my mama said from the other seat. She'd been drinking nonstop ever since the limo picked us up at the Oakwood, and I'd just about stopped apologizing to Jonas for bringing her. If only that moron Sean had kept his mouth shut about the emancipation, Mama wouldn't have even bothered coming along. But she thought she had to watch me like a hawk now, like maybe I would sneak off and get myself emancipated when she least expected it.

"There's the Goldens," Jonas said, pointing to the showrunners as they headed into the club, "and the rest of your band is already inside. It's all about us."

"Unless your brother shows up with his famous girlfriend. Then it's all about *her.*" Mama laughed.

I grabbed Jonas's hand. "Let's go." Outside, the flashes started going off the second we stepped onto the curb. People from the line screamed and yelled my name and sometimes Jonas's name.

"Chloe, can I have your autograph?" one girl called as Jonas led me toward the door of the club.

"Inside, okay?" I called back. "I'll get you all when we're inside! Thanks for coming!"

Everyone cheered. I blew them a kiss. They cheered louder.

"How 'bout some sugar, guys?" one of the photographers called.

Jonas wrapped his arm around my waist and pulled me in for a kiss, and the cameras exploded, shooting us from every angle.

"Y'all ever do that when you're not on film?" my mama's voice cut through the noise, pulling me right out of the moment. Forget about kissing—Jonas hadn't even been hanging out with me much lately, not since I stood him up for the Uber party. Turned out, he hadn't been too happy about showing up at a gay bar alone after all.

I stepped away from Jonas and grabbed Mama, digging my nails into her arm. "You behave yourself, Mama."

"Chloe, is that your mom? Smile!" a paparazzo yelled.

Mama and I both smiled. Jonas smiled. Cameras went off, shooting three people who were really not happy at all.

"Whose dress is that?" somebody called.

"You'll have to ask my stylist, Amanda Pierce," I called back. I knew the designer's name, but I liked to give Mandy shout-outs sometimes.

"Oh, lord, *she's* not coming, is she?" Mama whined as we headed inside.

"'Course she is, Mama, somebody's got to babysit you while I schmooze," I said.

The instant we stepped inside, I noticed two things. Number one was that Travis and his movie star girlfriend were already here. And number two was that Dave Quinn was here too.

"Just what in the hell does *that* bastard think he's doin' at your party?" my mama shrieked. Her eyes went all wide and crazy, and I thought she might just hurl herself through the air at Quinn. I guess my twin thought so too, because he rushed over and got right in Mama's face.

"Mama, hey. Meet Sasha," Trav said. He took Sasha Powell's hand and grinned like an idiot. "Sasha, this is my mama."

"Early Gamble," Mama said, as sweet as pie now that she was talking to an honest-to-god star. "My Trav has told me all about you."

"Nice to meet you, Mrs. Gamble," Sasha said. "I—"

"'Scuse me," Mama cut her off. "There's a man here I got to see."

Trav and me exchanged a look, and Travis took off after Mama. He steered her toward the bar, because that was the only place she'd be willing to go other than directly to Quinn.

"Hi, I'm Chloe Gamble." I stuck my hand out to my brother's girlfriend. "Sorry I've been so busy working that I haven't met you yet."

"Hey, Chloe, how are you?" Sasha Powell shook my hand and didn't bother to mention that she'd been hogging my brother for the last week and he'd barely been home to the Oakwood even once. *That* was why I hadn't met her yet. "Hey, JoJo," she added.

"Sasha." Jonas kissed her on the cheek.

The last thing I'd ever do is let somebody catch me being surprised. But right then, I was shocked. "How do you two know each other?" I said.

"We both did a stint with the Mouse back in the day," Jonas said.

"Oh." I was a little annoyed that he'd never mentioned knowing her. I'd been complaining about how Sasha Powell was taking over my brother's life and he hadn't said a thing. "I can't really picture you in Mickey ears," I said.

Sasha laughed with her famous puffy lips and rolled her famous bedroom eyes. "I did not wear them well. JoJo did, though."

Jonas gave her a wink.

"How early did you and Trav get here? We didn't see you outside," I said to Sasha.

"Oh, I came in through the back door. I didn't want the paparazzi to see me," Sasha said.

I just stared at her. She didn't seem to realize that she was insulting my brother. Or maybe she was insulting me. Did she not want photos of her and Travis, or did she not want the world to know she was at a party for a kids' show? Either way, screw her.

"Clo, you have to come say hi to Quinn," Nika said, appearing through the crowd. "Tell him thanks for flying in just for the party."

"No way," I said. "Him being here means I can't have a single second of fun at my own damn premiere."

"What? Why?" Jonas's perfect eyebrows were drawn together in confusion, and I suddenly realized that he didn't know about Mama and Quinn. I'd gotten so used to having him around that I forgot he wasn't really part of my posse. For a split second, I considered telling him the truth, but then I noticed Sasha listening too, and that decided me. The fewer people who knew about my mama's indiscretions, the better.

"I get nervous around the money people," I lied. "I'm always scared they'll pull the plug on the show."

Jonas smiled. Sasha yawned. I pulled Nika aside.

"I'm not talking to that cheating son of a bitch, and he oughta know why," I said through clenched teeth.

"He pays the bills," Nika said.

I looked over her shoulder at Dave Quinn. He was drinking wine with Bo Haynes, but his eyes were on the bar. "He's staring at my mama," I hissed. "That's why he's here. He don't care about *Cover Band* even a tiny little bit."

Nika turned to check it out. "Jesus, you're right," she said. "It's like babysitting a couple of twelve-year-olds. We cannot let them get into a scene here, there's too much press."

"I'll ask Jude to take Mama home," I said.

"She won't go, not when she's got Quinn's attention," Nika said.

"'Scuse me, *JoJo*," I said, turning back to Jonas. "I have a little family situation to deal with. D'you think you and Sasha could go say hi to Mr. Quinn? I don't want him to think we're ignoring him. . . ."

"Sure," Jonas said quickly. There was no downside for him to talking with the big honcho. And Sasha didn't seem to mind either. The second they were on their way, Nika and I made a beeline for the bar.

"You let go of me, sugar, or I am gonna start yellin'," Mama was saying.

"You just want to go throw a drink in Quinn's face," Travis said. "And I will not have you making a fool of yourself in front of Sasha."

"Or in front of my cast and crew," I said, frowning at my brother. His priorities were screwed up, and he needed to realize it.

"You two do not tell me what to do. I am your mama, and I make the decisions," Mama snapped. "Y'all ain't emancipated yet!"

"Let's take this over to the VIP Lounge," Nika said.

"No. Chloe's fan club should hear about the kind of person she really is. A cold-hearted girl who wants to dump her own mother." Mama raised her voice and managed to bring a couple tears to her eyes.

"I'll tell the bouncers to keep the fans out for a few," Nika said, heading for the door.

"Look, Mama, we're not trying to cut you off," I said.

"Darlin', I'm no idiot. You wait till I'm outta town and then you take yourselves off to your cute little lawyer and try to get independent?" Mama smirked. "You are absolutely tryin' to cut me off. And I will not have it."

"Fine. Then I'll make you a deal," I said. "You behave yourself and I'll buy you out. Okay? We'll get ourselves emancipated but we'll still give you your percentage of our earnings, long as you play your part and act nice."

"I ain't got to say yes," Mama said, crossing her arms and pouting like a kindergarten kid. "Y'all can't make me agree to this."

"You ain't heard the rest of my deal," I told her. "If you keep acting this way, if you make a scene with Quinn or get yourself in the news for sleeping with him—"

"If you ruin Chloe's career. And mine," Trav put in.

"—then we *will* cut you off," I said. "I'll go to the gossip blogs and spill my guts about how you're an awful mama and a drunk, and I'll move out of the Oakwood and stop paying the rent and you'll have to go crawling back to Daddy."

"You hush up, now. I ain't ever goin' back to that good-for-nothing man," Mama said.

"Then behave. Get your bag, go out to the limo, and go home," I said. "No hooking up with Quinn, no throwing your drink in his face. Don't even look at him."

"That gentleman did not do right by me." Mama pouted.

Travis rolled his eyes. "What's it gonna be, Mama? I want to get back to Sasha."

"I want a raise," Mama said. "A bigger percentage."

"No," Trav and me said at the same time.

Mama stuck her chin out and made a big show of leaning over so she could see Quinn over my shoulder.

"Tell you what, you can have an allowance," I said. "Every week the three of us will sit down and figure out if you acted like a mama enough to earn some extra cash."

"How much?" Mama said. But people were pressing close around us now, fans trying to move in on me, waiting to catch my eye and get an autograph. Nika must've gotten to the bouncers too late.

"Here comes Quinn," Travis murmured in my ear. Sure enough, that jerk was on his way over, his arm around Sasha's waist as if she needed his protection to get through a crowd of tweens here to drink soda and watch a show about high school spies.

"If you leave right now, I'll give you five hundred dollars," I said. "And we'll talk about the allowance later."

Mama has an excellent sense of timing—she's the one I got it from. She waited until Dave Quinn was close enough to lock eyes with her, close enough to get a good view of her deep neckline and her short skirt . . . and then she turned her back on him. "Travis, you walk me out, sugar. There's an ATM across the street so you can get my money before I go home."

For a split second, I thought my brother was going to refuse. Not because he didn't like bribing his own mama, but because it meant walking away from his famous sexpot girl-friend. His gaze went to Sasha, and he hesitated.

"Trav!" I snapped.

"Fine." He grabbed Mama's arm and practically jogged her toward the door.

"Chloe! Where's your mom off to?" Dave Quinn asked, as if nothing was weird, as if he hadn't taken my mama on an adul-terous tour of Asia only two weeks ago, as if he didn't know that a single hint of their affair could ruin my show and my career.

"I think she's got a date," I said. "But thanks so much for coming to support the show, Mr. Quinn."

"Of course," he said, watching my mama's ass as she walked out of the club.

"Where's Jonas?" I asked Sasha.

"Oh, he's off in the bathroom doing some X," she said.

"I didn't hear that," Quinn said. "Excuse me. Congrats, Chloe."

I gave him a fake smile and waited until he went off to join the Goldens near the bar. Then I frowned at Sasha. "What kind of joke was that?"

Sasha laughed. "Don't worry, Quinn doesn't care."

"About what?"

"The ecstasy," she said. "He knows how Jonas is."

My mouth dropped open, but I had nothing to say. Jonas was in the bathroom doing drugs? Really?

"Ooh, but I guess *you* don't know." Sasha made a face. "It's not like he's an addict or anything, don't worry. He just likes to have some fun at parties."

"You know that from being on a Disney show with him?" I asked.

She shrugged. "We've known each other a long time. It's no big deal."

"It is to me," I said. "It's number one on the list—don't get sloppy drunk. I think that applies to drugs, too."

"You have a list? Cute." Somehow Sasha made everything sound boring. I couldn't tell if she was trying to be bitchy or if she was just actually bored. Maybe when you become an international sex symbol at the age of eighteen, you *are* bored with everything by the time you're twenty-one. I was definitely going to find out.

"The Don't Do list. I think 'don't ignore your fans' is on

there somewhere," Max said from behind me. He was teasing, as usual, but right that second I didn't care at all, I was just so happy to see him.

"Well, hey there, sugar!" I cried, throwing my arms around him. "I wasn't sure you'd come."

"I wasn't sure they'd let me in," he said.

I'd put his name on the guest list—TJ and his wife's, too—so I knew Max was just being self-deprecating. That was his shtick, and it worked for him. His other shtick was keeping me honest. He was right; I'd been so busy worrying about my mama and Trav's girlfriend that I'd forgotten to get to the kids who were here just to see me.

"Hi, y'all!" I called to the group of girls standing about ten feet away. They were watching, waiting, afraid to interrupt me, as if I were some important person who they didn't dare talk to. "I've got a few minutes before the show starts. Let's take some pictures!" I walked over to them and was surrounded in a split second. Kids hugging me, pens and paper shoved in front of me, people snapping photos and telling me how much they loved my YouTube song. Through the blur of faces, I saw the Goldens watching me, along with Quinn and Bo Haynes. I saw my bandmates looking a little pissy, and Sasha Powell hiding in the VIP area with Travis.

Then suddenly Jonas was there next to me, his arm around my waist and his eyes a little weird-looking. I tensed up when he leaned in to whisper hello. If Sasha hadn't told me about the drugs, would I have even known? Did I really know anything about Jonas? I'd pegged him as a friend right away, but I'd never bothered to find out anything beyond the fact that we had great chemistry.

"Are you guys together?" one girl asked.

"Are you in love?" somebody else squealed.

Jonas laughed and kissed my cheek, which would have seemed perfect yesterday. But something was off tonight. Travis was wrapped around his girlfriend's finger, and his girlfriend was way more famous than me, and Mama was a constant threat to my success, and I was mad at Sean for telling her too much even though Nika said it had been a "tactic." And now Jonas wasn't just a nice guy who wanted publicity with me, he was a kid who had grown up rich and famous and who used drugs when he wasn't even legal to drink yet.

The lights went down, and I felt a rush of relief. I couldn't tell what was bothering me, because everything was bothering me, and even the little speech Josh and Diane Golden were giving didn't make me feel any better.

I moved away from Jonas, shaking his arm off my waist, and he didn't seem to notice.

"Geez, Clo, relax." Max handed me a glass of water. "It's your show, on actual TV. It's all good."

I looked up at the huge screen, which was showing an ad for the Snap Network. It was a live TV feed, so people around the country were seeing this exact same thing on their televisions. "I'm stressed," I said.

"No point in stressing, there's nothing you can do now but hope it's a hit," Max said.

I laughed. "Thanks. That's real encouraging." But I actually felt better, not because of what he said, but just because in this whole club, for this whole weird night, Max was the only normal thing.

The screen went dark for a second, and then the sound of my voice filled the air, singing the *Cover Band* theme song. The club went wild, everyone yelling and cheering. Then the show started and there I was, on screen, being Lucie Blayne. Acting in a TV show. Right this second there were complete strangers looking at me and deciding if I was cute enough and funny enough to bother watching for a half hour. Right this second, I was on TV.

"Breathe," Max said.

I took a gulp of air, then another. I'd been holding my breath for God knows how long, and I hadn't even noticed.

"My show's on the air," I said, reaching for Max's hand. He twined his fingers through mine and right away all the weirdness of the night vanished like a puff of smoke. Max nodded toward the big screen.

"Here you go, Chloe Gamble."

"Here I go."

Snap, Chloe Gamble is a star!

The Snap Network's "Cover Band" struck a chord with audiences Wednesday, garnering an astounding ten share, a record for a cable premiere. The skein was expected to fare well with the kiddie set, but it also pulled great numbers with the all-important teen demographic thanks to star Chloe Gamble's pull.

"Cover Band" launches the net and makes Snap prexy Leslie Scott a hot player. Biz watchers have her heading out to the Coast for meetings with all the major producers. Showrunners Golden & Golden are also golden, as Snap has snapped up the rights to their next pilot as a possible companion piece.

chapter eight

Fame Montage, Scene One

"My trailer just got twice as big," I said on Wednesday morning. "Look at it! It's like a double-wide."

Next to me, Jude laughed. "I think they're expecting your ego to get twice as big too, Ms. TV Star."

"I ain't complaining," I said.

Jude went off to meet with Bob Lavett, and I went into my shiny new trailer. Jonas was waiting on the couch. "Nice digs."

"Thanks," I said. Things were awkward between us, but he acted like he didn't notice it.

"You're the shit now, Chloe. How do you like it?" he said.

"It's what I was born for," I told him. "But it's fast!"

"What is?"

"Everything. It's like nothing happened at all before the show premiered, and now it's been on the air exactly two times and my whole world has changed." I picked out a tea bag from the huge selection someone had put in my kitchen. "What's that thing they do in movies?" I said. "You know, where it all moves kinda fast and time passes. Lots of little scenes where the ugly girl gets pretty, or, like, the two friends fall in love or something?"

"A montage," Jonas said.

"Right. That's my life now. A montage where I go from nobody to big star." I grinned. "I hope it never ends!"

Fame Montage, Scene Two

"I wasn't sure we'd see you again, now that you're so famous," TJ said when Max and I pulled into the parking lot of the recording studio. The place was deserted, as usual.

I climbed off the back of Max's motorcycle and took off the helmet he'd gotten for me as a congratulations present when the ratings for *Cover Band* came out. He said I could get my own bike when I made my first million.

"You kidding? Chloe can't live unless she's misbehaving," Max said. "And recording her own songs is *bad*."

"After tonight, we're almost done with 'Lucky Bitch,'" I said. "And that feels pretty good to me."

TJ laughed and unlocked the studio door. "Then let's get to it."

"What on God's earth is that?" my mama asked, her voice hoarse from another hard night of drinking. She'd been with Alex the porn king, even though she claimed she was just out shopping.

"Gifts for Ms. Gamble," the guy at our door said. "Your agent said to bring them here, unless you'd rather I drop them at the studio?"

"Gifts from who?" I asked, checking out the pile of boxes and bags in the hallway.

"Callaway clubs!" Trav cried, rushing over to grab a leather bag full of golf clubs. "I call these."

"Somebody sent me golf clubs?" I said. "Why?"

"Ooh! This here is the biggest bottle of Chanel I've ever seen!" Mama was already ripping through the packages as if they were for her.

"You're from the Turman Agency?" I asked the guy. "Do you know who sent me all this?"

"Here's a list." He handed me a printout with an itemized list of goodies and the companies that had sent them. "Ms. Mays said to tell you that your publicist will handle the thank-yous; you should just enjoy."

He moved the boxes inside just as my mama pulled out a Balenciaga bag. Free, for me.

Just because I was famous.

COVER BAND takes the stage

Snap Network's signature series, "Cover Band," continues to gain in the ratings, and the network announced today that episodes would be repurposed to air on sister network CBS during the summer. It's a huge win for Snap brass, and a promising start for stars Chloe Gamble and Jonas Beck.

Snap announces that the "Cover Band" band's summer mini-tour of West Coast amusement parks sold out within a day, and the net is in talks to expand the tour to traditional venues.

Meanwhile, publishing partner Simon & Schuster is planning a line of "Cover Band" graphic novels, and a script-based novelization of the first season of the show, featuring an exclusive interview with star Gamble herself.

Fame Montage, Scene Three

"Look at my new business card!" Marc cried, handing a bunch of cards around the table on the patio at The Ivy, the most famous restaurant in Beverly Hills.

"'Marc Duval, Publicist,'" I read aloud.

"You got the promotion!" Nika said.

"Congrats," Sean added. "You deserve it. I can't even open a magazine without seeing Chloe or Travis plastered all over it."

"Thank you, thank you," Marc said. "I owe it all to Nika and her genius career advice."

Sasha Powell cleared her throat.

"Right, and to Travis for being hot enough to score a hottie like Sasha," Marc said.

"And to me, for being me," I said.

"And to Chloe, for not being modest," Jude agreed.

I winked at her. "Modest girls don't end up stars."

IM

> GAMBLEGOAL: Coop, it's almost summer, you coming to LA or what?
>
> COOPERMAN: My mother's worried I'll fall in with a bad crowd.
>
> GAMBLEGOAL: WTF? You'll be with me and Chloe.
>
> COOPERMAN: . . . crickets . . .
>
> GAMBLEGOAL: Shut up. Your mama loves me.

COOPERMAN: Dad says she's scared if I see Hollywood,

    I'll never come back to Texas.

GAMBLEGOAL: She might be right.

GAMBLEGOAL: Dude, come on, I can introduce you to Sasha Powell.

COOPERMAN: Yeah, but I got no chance with Chloe anymore.

GAMBLEGOAL: You never had a chance with Chloe. But get

    yourself out here and maybe I'll find you a hot model.

COOPERMAN: Okay, when school's over, I'm there.

Fame Montage, Scene Four

"How come Travis didn't come tonight?" Jude asked. "I thought he loved The Ruffians."

"He does, but Sasha wanted him to visit her on-set. She's doing that cameo in the Will Ferrell movie." I smeared on some lip gloss in the vanity mirror while Jude circled the block in Silver Lake, looking for a parking spot. Her girlfriend, Kelli, was in the backseat, and she hadn't said a word since we left the Oakwood. I guess I was being rude to make her sit back there, but I always get shotgun. That's just the way it is.

"Just do valet, I want to see Max before they go on," I said.

"Valet is so expensive," Jude grumbled.

"It's on me," I told her. "Except they won't make me pay. I haven't paid to park even one time since the show premiered."

"Well in that case . . ." Jude hit the gas and pulled back

around to the front of the club. One of the valets ran over to open my door, and as I climbed out I saw his eyes go wide.

"Hey, it's Chloe Gamble!" somebody yelled. Three or four guys with cameras came rushing toward me, snapping every move I made.

"What are you doing here, Chloe?" one of them called.

"I'm here for The Ruffians," I said. "They're my favorite band."

Kelli was already at the door, and Jude grabbed my hand. "Ignore them," she said, pulling me away. But the cameras kept going, even when I wasn't looking at them.

From the H METER blog

—**Buzzing Up:** KIMBER REEVE, star of the upcoming NBC series *Virgin*, is said to be thisclose to landing the role of Young Anissa in Matthew Greengold's film version of the bestselling novel *Frontier*. Reeve beats out Scarlett Johansson and Megan Fox for the part, a small but pivotal role in an important film. Is this Reeve's next step on the ladder to credibility?

—**Buzzing Down:** PINKBERRY. Paris Hilton reports that she's "bored" with the brand and looking for new culinary thrills. Panic at Pinkberry HQ.

—**Buzzing Up:** Internet rumors have CHLOE GAMBLE in early talks to play April West, teen daughter of the famous treasure-hunter Nat West, in the next installment of the West franchise.

Fame Montage, Scene Five

"I'm thinking I may have to stop coming for a while," I told Alan, my acting coach. "Nika and Marc have me scheduled for every spare second this next month. Did I tell you I'm doing the voice for my character in a *Cover Band* video game?"

Alan just steepled his fingers like he does and frowned at me.

"What? I'm acting," I said. "Your job is done, you taught me everything. You saved little Maddie's career."

"So that's it? You're done learning your craft?" he asked.

"I'm living my craft," I said.

"Video games and movie openings and photo ops?" Alan said. "Listen, Chloe. You can be a teen sensation . . . You *are* a teen sensation. Or you can be more, you can be a real artist. A real actor."

"How?" I said.

"Keep coming to me. Keep working. Treat our sessions as a private thing, something you do for yourself, to work on your own inner actor. It's not for *Cover Band*. It's for Chloe."

For me, I thought. *Just like my music.*

"Okay," I said. "I'll do it."

Fame Montage, Scene Six

"I've been talking to the people at Disney about a hiatus project for you," Nika said. "It'll be tricky because the company is a direct competitor with Snap, but it's not as if Snap does features."

I wrinkled my nose. Disney is boring. "What about that Nat West movie?"

"They don't even have a script yet," Nika said.

"The Disney thing would be perfect," Sean put in.

"I don't want to make a kid movie," I said

"You're never going to just admit that you're a kid, are you?" Sean asked, teasing me.

"There is nothing childlike about me," I told him. "I keep telling you to come over and find out for yourself."

"How do you like my new office?" Nika cut in, frowning at me. She never liked it when I hit on Sean so openly. But what choice did I have? The man kept ignoring me. One of these days I was just going to have to sit myself down on his lap and force him to pay attention to me. But not in my agent's new office.

"It's outrageous. Three times bigger than your old one," I said. "What happened?"

"I told Hal I needed it since I'm running New Media *and* I'm the biggest earner in the last two months." Nika sounded mighty pleased with herself.

"You're welcome," I said.

"It's not just you," Sean told me.

"Right, it's me and my brother."

"And the three other new clients Nika and I have signed." Now Sean sounded pretty self-satisfied too.

"It's mostly me, though," I said.

Nika laughed. "It is definitely mostly you."

Fame Montage, Scene Seven

"Do we get to keep these clothes?" I asked Jonas while the photographer's assistant did a lighting check.

"If you ask, they'll say yes," he told me.

"Well, I'm asking." I sat up and stretched, trying to loosen up my shoulders. We were sitting in a rowboat tied up to the dock of Lake Balboa in the Valley, and it was as hot as hell—as hot as Spurlock, Texas.

"You don't have to wear Abercrombie. You can just call up Armani and ask *them* for free clothes," Jonas said as the spritzer girl came over and sprayed our faces with water to keep us cool.

"But we're advertising for Abercrombie," I said. "Aren't we supposed to actually use the thing we're selling?"

Jonas shrugged, closing his eyes and tilting his head back so the sunlight hit him evenly.

"Ready, guys?" the photographer called.

"Born ready," I said, putting myself in the same pose as Jonas. Just a couple of bored, sexy kids draped all over each other on a hot summer day—in skimpy Abercrombie & Fitch clothes. I closed my eyes and thought about the way we'd look in a glossy magazine spread, four pages long and filled with me and Jonas and nobody else. Marc said it was advertising for *Cover Band* and for Abercrombie, but I knew what it really was.

It was advertising for Chloe Gamble.

COOPERMAN: Holy crap, dude, I just saw a picture of you with Tiger Woods!

GAMBLEGOAL: I know, he was practicing at this course in Santa Barbara where me and my buds were hitting a few.

COOPERMAN: Tiger Fucking Woods!

GAMBLEGOAL: Chloe got these sweet clubs for free, Callaway just sent them to her in case she felt like playing a round. Yeah, like that's gonna happen.

COOPERMAN: So you took them.

GAMBLEGOAL: Damn straight. Clo's publicist—I guess he's mine, too—says companies send her shit so that maybe she'll use the product and get photographed with it. Free advertising.

COOPERMAN: Not free if they have to cough up a set of premium clubs.

GAMBLEGOAL: Yeah, and all they're gonna get is a picture of me and my friends shaking Tiger's hand!

Fame Montage, Scene Eight

"Invites!" Marc sang, throwing himself down onto a lounge chair near the pool at the Oakwood.

"Anything good?" my mama asked, not even bothering to open her eyes.

"Turn over, Mama, you've been out here for two hours already," I said. She made a face at me, but she turned.

Fame Montage, Scene Nine

"Premiere party for the new *Twilight* movie," Marc said.

"Yes," I said.

"Launch party for the new Super Humpty track shoes."

"Ugh, no," I said.

"Premiere party for a new Internet show?"

"I'll go to that one," Travis said, climbing out of the pool where he'd been doing laps.

"Museum benefit for the Getty," Marc said.

"Am I supposed to care about art now?" I said.

"Jude would probably like it," Trav pointed out.

"Fine. Say yes for me and Jude. And Kelli," I said.

Marc nodded, making a list of my yeses and nos. "The next one is a must-do," he said. "Get this. Will and Jada want you to come play with their kids."

"What?" I said. My mama snorted.

"The kids love the show. So Will wants you and Jonas to go to their place and hang out for a few hours." Marc frowned at Mama. "Do not underestimate the impact this could have on your career."

"Is Will Smith going to be there?" I said.

"Don't know. Doesn't matter."

"Okay, you get Jonas to go and I'm in."

"Girl, please, Jonas will go anywhere. The boy's a professional."
Marc made a note on his BlackBerry. "Playdate with destiny!"

From the H METER blog

—**Buzzing up:** NIKA MAYS and SEAN PIPER. This new
H-wood team is shaping up to be Child Star Central. In addition
to white-hot CHLOE GAMBLE, the agent-and-lawyer duo reps
JOSH ANDREWS from the NY soap world, and has just signed
CEECEE GRAY, age 10, who is in talks to play the daughter in the
reimagined "Family Affair" TV show in development.

—**Buzzing down:** Huge family-based reality shows. Seems
the American public wants to call social services on these
camera-ready "families."

Fame Montage, Scene Ten

"Got your fake ID, Trav?" I asked my twin as he pulled the
Escalade up to the front of The Ivar.

"I'm not coming in. I have to get Sasha at her trainer's
first," Travis said. "Maybe we'll meet up with you later."

I rolled my eyes. "You haven't said a sentence in three
weeks that wasn't about Sasha Powell. Are you her boyfriend
or her personal slave?"

"Jealous much?" Trav asked.

"Nope. I have a scorching hot career. How about you?" I
opened the door and climbed out, leaving Trav to think that one

over. I knew for a fact that he'd skipped two auditions recently just because Sasha had something else planned.

"Chloe!" yelled a voice.

"Chloe, over here!" someone else called.

"Hey, where's your brother going? Travis!"

I stood on tiptoe to look over the heads of the paparazzi that had surrounded me the second my Jimmy Choos hit the sidewalk. There, near the club door, a huge black guy in a dark suit. He met my eye and nodded. Instantly, two big bouncers waded through the photographers, clearing a path for me. They escorted me to the door and hustled me inside.

"Straight to the VIP Lounge, Ms. Gamble?" the guy in the suit asked. He was obviously head of security here.

"Sure, thanks." I followed him through the club with my own personal bouncer squad still on either side of me. We got to an alcove off the dance floor, and he opened a velvet rope for me.

"You have fun now," he said, and vanished into the crowded club. I turned around—and walked right smack into Zac Efron. He grabbed my arms to steady us both.

"Scuse me! I am just such a klutz today," I said.

He laughed. "No worries, Chloe. I'll see you in a few, okay?" He went on past, heading for the dance floor, and I just watched him go. That boy was a famous movie star, and I'd never met him in my entire life. So why had he just acted like we were at this club together, like friends?

"There's my girl. Over here, Clo!" Jonas didn't even bother

to get up off the couch, he just waved me over. He had a couple of guys and a girl with him, people I'd met once or twice. I went over to sit with them.

"They didn't card me at the door," I said.

Jonas laughed so hard, he started to cough. "Chloe, you're famous. You don't need ID." He poured me some champagne from the bottle on the table. It was Cristal, and I had no idea who had paid for it.

"But I'm only sixteen."

"Sixteen and famous. Drink up," Jonas said.

I clinked my glass against his. It was the best toast I'd ever heard.

Fame Montage, Scene Eleven

"Free stuff!" I yelled, pushing through the door to the recording studio with three shopping bags. TJ and Sharon poked their heads out of the office, and little Daisy came toddling over with her arms out for a hug.

"What stuff?" TJ asked.

I picked up the baby and swung her around. "Clothes for Sharon—it's like a whole spring wardrobe from Bebe—and an iPhone for you, TJ. With free service."

Sharon actually squealed with excitement as she dug through the shopping bags. "Chloe, are you serious? Where'd you get all this?"

"People send me clothes. But I'm in wardrobe for the show most days, I don't need it all," I said. And Sharon needed it a whole heck of a lot more than me, but I didn't mention that. I don't know how much money a sound engineer makes, but it was definitely nowhere near the money I was pulling in now. "And I'm stuck on my BlackBerry, so who needs the iPhone? But one of these days I'm gonna have to steal Daisy and let the paparazzi see her," I added, nuzzling the little girl's cheek. "Then all the fancy baby-clothes companies will send me things for her!"

"Then now's your chance," Max said from the booth. "Just walk out the door."

"What?" I cried. I put Daisy down and headed for the front window. Sure enough, there were three cars in the little parking lot, guys hanging out the windows with gigantic cameras, shooting away. "What are they doing here?"

"Did you drive yourself?" TJ asked.

"Yeah, I took the Escalade."

"They know your car, Chloe. They followed you," Max said.

"Oh my God, this is bad," I said. "This is real bad. I'm not supposed to be here. What if Snap finds out?"

"You didn't see them when you were in the parking lot?" Sharon asked.

I shook my head.

"Then we'll just have to sneak you out," TJ said. "Maybe Max goes out the front and takes the Escalade, and we'll put you in our car while the paps are distracted."

Virgin Voyage Over?

Trouble on set for Todd Linson's first TV outing. Sources say NBC execs have asked for major changes to the pricey series. Drama behind the scenes threatens to eclipse the show's plotlines, which are "deadly dull" according to one high-placed exec. Todd Linson—reportedly dating starlet Kimber Reeve—reworked the concept to beef up the role of his rumored paramour, and star Anders Lee is said to be suing mad. Meanwhile, NBC brass isn't willing to pay top dollar for a thinly-veiled daytime soap. "Virgin" is still on the net's fall schedule, but sources say it's looking more like a midseason slot is in the cards.

"That might work," I said. "Me and Max are friends. He could say he's borrowing my car."

"Great," Max muttered. But it only took a pleading look from me to get him moving toward the front. "Meet you back at the Oakwood," he said, taking the keys from my hand.

"Guess I won't be finishing my song tonight after all," I said.

Fame Montage, Scene Twelve

"What's with the fancy restaurant?" I asked Amanda.

"I'm celebrating," she said, a huge grin on her face. "Or I will be if they ever seat us."

"I thought you celebrated by eating an entire pizza by yourself," my mama put in. "You don't need no expensive place like this."

"Hush up, Mama," I said. "I didn't have to bring you tonight, you know."

"It's okay, honey, I know Early only came along for some free booze," Amanda said. Between her and my mama, it was always an insult contest.

"'Scuse me," I said. I went up to the maitre'd and gave her a Texas smile. "Hi there, I'm Chloe Gamble, and I'm wondering if you can just check on a reservation for us. My friend called ahead—"

"Ms. Gamble, I'm so sorry," the maitre'd cut me off. "I had no idea you were waiting. We've got a table for you right over here." She looked scared, like I might throw a tantrum or something.

"Well, thanks. That's awfully sweet." I waved Amanda and Mama over, and we sat down at a table set for five. The waiters immediately rushed over to take away the extra plates, but it was clear that this wasn't the table Mandy had reserved.

I made a note of this new aspect to my life: I did not need a reservation, not even at the priciest restaurant in town.

"So what are we celebrating?" I asked Amanda.

"Me, thanks to you," she said. "You're not the only TV star at the table. I just closed on a deal to be a judge on *Design Your Life*!"

"That new reality show?" I cried. "Mandy, that's incredible!"

"What is that, some *Project Runway* rip-off?" My mama sniffed.

"Yes, and who cares?" Amanda said. "I'm a judge! It's thanks to you, Chloe, you're always telling people I'm your stylist."

"You are," I said.

"Honey, we all know you take care of your own style," she said. "But thank you. Really."

"That's what I'm here for," I told her. "I ain't stopping until everyone I know is rich."

From the H METER blog

—**Buzzing up:** THE RUFFIANS. It Girl CHLOE GAMBLE admitted an addiction to the band, but rumor has it her attention is only on lead guitarist Max Tyrell.

—**Buzzing down:** JONAS BECK. Is his girlfriend stepping out?

E-mail from Travis Gamble

Coop! You're never gonna believe this! Remember that pic of me and Tiger on the links? You saw it on People.com or something, right? Well, so did the Callaway people because they sent me ANOTHER set of clubs! They show up at my door with a note that says sorry we forgot to get you your own set so you had to borrow your sister's. And then they call up Marc (our publicist) and tell him he should "encourage Travis to take Chloe golfing with their matching clubs."

HAHAHAHAHA!!

Anyway, when you finally get your ass out here, there's a sweet set of clubs waiting for you.

Sorry I've been lame about staying in touch lately. Always busy with Sasha, the girl's got a full schedule. I don't even have time to work—had to turn down two modeling jobs last week. It's worth it, though, cause she is SMOKING hot.

Nika Mays's Manuscript Notes: Celebrity Feud

"Nika, you just got a nasty call from Jules Berg at Virtuoso," my assistant said, sticking her head in the door.

"What? I barely even know her," I said. Jules and I had been assistants together back in the day, but she'd gotten promoted at Virtuoso two years ago and I hadn't seen her since. Agents at the biggest house in town don't associate with assistants from The Hal Turman Agency.

"She said to stop the crap with Kimber Reeve or she'll put her publicist on it." My assistant shrugged, but I knew exactly what was going on. Chloe.

I picked up the phone and called Marc. "What did Chloe do to Kimber Reeve?"

He laughed. "Oh, she had me send flowers to set saying good luck on the reshoots for *Virgin*. She put in a note that said 'True friends are there for you when times are tough,' and signed it 'Your pal, Chloe.'"

"Marc, that is flat-out bitchy," I said.

"I know!" he cried. "It was hilarious."

"Stop enabling her," I said. "Unless you want a full-out celebrity feud between Chloe and Kimber."

"It's not the worst idea," he said. "But let's just see how the teen-star-with-her-own-TV-show tactic works out before we resort to that."

"So no more bitchy flowers to Kimber?"

"No more," he promised.

Fame Montage, Scene Thirteen

"Max! Look at this place," I said, as soon as the manager let me in the back door of the Troubadour in West Hollywood. Max and his band were just about to go on. Jude and I had been smart enough to sneak in this time so we didn't have to deal with the mob of photographers out front.

"Yeah. It's packed." He sounded annoyed. "Biggest house we've ever played to."

"That's good, right?" I said. "What's with the attitude?"

"Nothing. It's just . . . nothing." He leaned over and kissed me on the cheek. "Thanks for coming."

"I never miss a show," I said.

"Yeah, that's what I hear." Max turned away and leaned over his guitar, tuning it.

"You told the media that you love the band. Now it's in every puff piece they do on you," Jude said, pulling me away from Max. "All these people are here to see you, Clo. Not The Ruffians."

"Oh." I thought about that for a moment. "But it's publicity. Get people here, let them listen, and they fall in love with the band. That's how you get a following, that's how you get a record deal. Isn't it?"

"Yeah." Jude chewed on her lip. "But I'm not sure it's how Max wants to do it."

I looked over at him, his dreads falling over his face so I couldn't read his expression. Max was a terrific producer — "Lucky Bitch" was about a million times better because of him. I could believe he wanted to make it on his own, just like I did. But he didn't need to.

"Everybody gets successful because of me, that's the deal," I said to Jude. "Why should he have to do things the hard way?"

She shrugged, and I went over to Max and slipped my arms around him. His whole body stiffened up, but I didn't let go.

"Sing that song for me, okay?" I said into his ear. "The one about the beach? It's my favorite. It's sexy."

Max took a deep breath. "You actually do like my music, huh? I didn't even know you were paying attention."

"You think I'd let just anybody produce my songs? I want the best, and that's you."

He turned to look at me, and for a brief crazy second I thought he was going to kiss me. But instead he pulled back and got all professional. "'Lucky Bitch' is ready, Clo. TJ and I were talking about it yesterday. It's a surefire hit."

"I know it is." I stepped away from him.

"What are you going to do with it?" he asked.

"I'm gonna release it, what do you think?" I said.

"You can't. Technically it belongs to the Snap Network." Max looked a little flushed, like maybe he was only talking about "Lucky Bitch" to keep me from touching him again.

"Tell you what, you let me worry about the technicalities and you just go out there and play," I said. "Tonight isn't about me. It's about you."

Fame Montage, Scene Fourteen

"Here it is," Jude said, throwing open the door to reveal a huge loft overlooking downtown Los Angeles. "The whole thing."

"It's nice," I said, watching while my mama and Amanda and Nika scattered out to inspect the wood flooring, the views out the big windows, the office, and the darkroom set up along one wall.

"Congratulations," Sean said. "My assistant is working on the papers to incorporate you; it should be done by Monday."

"Thanks." Jude bit her lip and bounced a little. "Look, Clo,

I'm going to set up my wall of headshots right over there next to the door. Then I'll hang some of the fashion stuff on the other side, and I'll put a couch and chairs there as a little waiting room."

"Sounds great," I said.

"It's nice, it's great." Jude made a face. "Is that really all you have to say?"

"Well, you ain't seen my favorite part yet," I told her. "Here it is." I handed Jude a gorgeous gift box and watched her open up the sign I'd ordered just yesterday. It was thick and gold, and on it were the words JUDE MORGAN PHOTOGRAPHY.

Jude gave a little gasp. "For the door?"

"Yup," I said. "For the door of your very own studio!"

She threw her arms around me and held me tight. "Thank you, Chloe. I wouldn't be here without you, you know that."

"That's what we said right from the start," I told her. "You help me make it big, and then you rise with me." I pulled away and grinned at her. "Didn't take us long, did it?"

Jude laughed. "From nothing to superstar in six months, Clo. I think it's a record."

"There's just one question," I said. "What comes next?"

chapter nine

E-mail from Travis Gamble

Big news, Coop—me and Chloe are moving out! Clo finally talked
some sense into my mama (she bribed her) and got her to back down
on the legal emancipation thing. Sean the lawyer says it will all be a
done deal by the end of the month, so after that we are adults! Least
as far as the money goes.

Anyway, Chloe says adults don't live in one-bedroom glorified
hotels with their mamas. She thinks we need a place that's more
glamorous than the Oakwood, because now that she's so famous I
guess she's embarrassed by where we live. She's got a point. Sasha
won't even come over because she doesn't want the paparazzi to
snap her there. I don't know, Coop, who the hell cares where you
live? I mean, the Oakwood was good enough when we first got here,

so why is it so shameful now? Just because we have money? Seems pretty shallow to me.

Who cares, though, because in our new house I will have my own room! Me and Clo got a big-ass place in Los Feliz. It's kind of near Hollywood, but our place is up in the hills so we have great views. And that's right, I said HOUSE! We're renting this place, but that means we're also renting gardeners and a cleaning lady, at least that's the agreement. And it's furnished because some big old English actor owns it and he comes over like once every two years but he keeps the house just in case. Amanda said she'll help Chloe decorate it more in her own style, because they say it's a bachelor pad. Works for me! Anyway, I have my own room and bathroom and so does Clo. Plus, get this, there's a pool table! I can't wait to move in.

Weirdest thing is that my mama's not coming with us. She's gonna keep the place in the Oakwood. She likes it there cause she's got this ass-wipe porn producer friend who treats her nice, and nobody cares if she's drunk all the time, and besides, it's not up to her. Chloe said we're moving and you're not coming and that was that.

Mama can't stand up to my sister but I'm getting better at it—I made Chloe put my name on the lease. We're going to split the rent 50/50. Clo thinks I'm an idiot for wanting to pay anything when she makes so much (you can't even believe how much she got just to do an ad for Abercrombie. Like ten of my underwear shoots. It's unreal.) But whatever, I'm still making good money too. That Chanel ad with Sasha paid crazy dough, and last week I got 20K just for showing up to a party. I shit you not. I walked in the door, I had a couple drinks, I got my picture taken with the DJ, and I left with a check in my pocket. They said they'd triple it if I brought Sasha, but she had a yoga class that night. I did it again the next night, this club flew me over to Vegas and put me up at the Venetian. Plus they gave me ten grand to go to the new nightclub they just opened. It was me and Paris Hilton, dude! I think she got way more than ten grand, though.

But Sasha threw a fit about that one. TMZ put up pictures of me at the first party, and then in Vegas, and they were all "Where's Sasha?" and "Why is Travis Gamble partying alone?" and "Is Trav cheating on Sasha?" WTF? I go to a party, and I'm cheating? The photos were just me looking like a dork, trying to dance. Sasha wasn't mad that I was sleeping around, though; she knows that shit isn't true. But then I told her I was going to the Vegas place again for the big fight and she was all, "Stop taking those jobs!" She doesn't want to deal with all the drama in the gossip columns. I say she should just come with me, then they wouldn't talk trash AND we'd both get paid, but Sasha says she's not that kind of actress and she doesn't want to be one of those couples. Whatever that means. Sounds like an insult, doesn't it?

I'm doing it, though. Sorry, but I don't get offered huge movies every week like she does, and now I've got rent to pay(!). That's the other thing—I haven't gotten any jobs since that commercial I did with Sasha. Nika told me that would open up lots of new opportunities, but lately I just get paid to party. I had an audition for a Gap ad last week, but I had to skip it because Sasha had a premiere we had to go to. And I missed a TV audition a while back cause we were at a dude ranch—Sasha needs to ride horses in her next movie. But so what if I skip a few? There should be lots of auditions now.

It's weird, I get so much press now, I'm always in the magazines as "Sasha's Boy Toy" or "Chloe's Brother." Doesn't that make me famous? If I'm famous, I should get acting jobs, right? Chloe says I spend too much time with Sasha and that's why I don't have any auditions, but I think it's because my agent is screwing up. Nika's got new clients and they all get work. I'm gonna have to light a fire under her ass, as my daddy would say.

Shortcut

"You sure about this?" Travis asked me for about the thousandth time. "You could get in huge trouble."

"You put that song online from here and nobody will be able to trace it, right?" I said, nodding toward the door of the Internet café on Santa Monica Boulevard. We were parked right outside, in Max's car, and I had on a baseball cap with my hair shoved up inside. I couldn't risk getting caught by the paparazzi, not here.

"Maybe they could tell that it came from a computer here, but that's it," my twin said. "Probably not even that."

"So what's the problem?" I said.

"The problem is you don't own the song," Max put in. "If it's a hit, Snap will want the money from it. They'll sue you."

"They can't sue me if I didn't do nothing wrong," I said.

"If they come after me, I'll just say I don't know how it happened."

Max just shook his head. He wasn't used to the way I operated.

"Clo, you were all up in Mama's face because she was a threat to your job on *Cover Band*," he said. "Now *you're* being the threat."

"That was before the show was a huge hit; things are different now," I said.

"It's your funeral." Trav opened up the back door and climbed out of the car. I watched him disappear into the Internet café with a disc in his hand.

"'Lucky Bitch,' here we go," I said.

"Ms. Gamble, I'm so glad you could make it," Dr. Cardillo said when I walked into the St. Paul's Academy fund-raiser two days later. They were holding the party in the Beverly Hills Hotel, and the place was swanky, with ivory linens and fine china on the big round tables. There were enough crystal chandeliers in that place to light up the whole world. Outside, the valets had been parking Porsches and Beemers and more than one Bentley. I'd known our school was the best one in the Valley, but I hadn't realized there was quite this much money involved.

"I wouldn't miss it for anything, not after y'all have been so nice to me and Trav," I told the dean. "I hope you

256   Ed Decter

don't mind that I brought my friend Jude. She's such a great photographer and I thought maybe she could take some pictures of this wonderful event." Jude's camera also shot video, but I didn't bother mentioning that part.

"That's a terrific idea," he said, reading the business card Jude handed him. "We've got a professional photographer, but—"

"Jude's the set photographer for my show. She's very up-and-coming," I said.

"Well. Please send me the proofs and we'll see what we can do," Dr. Cardillo said to Jude.

"Excuse me, I'm going to say hello to Coach," Travis said, taking off toward Coach Ibanez. I was a little surprised to see a teacher here among the wealthy parents, but the school's champion soccer team was a big reason why people sent their kids to St. Paul's, so I guessed that the coach would be good for business.

"Chloe Gamble, is it?" I turned around and found myself staring into the eyes of Richard DiPetrillo, the most famous Mafioso in the world. Well, the most famous *actor* of Mafiosos in the world.

"Yes, I'm Chloe. It's so nice to meet you, Mr. DiPetrillo." I stuck my hand out and hoped it wasn't trembling. This man was a legend.

"Are you a student at St. Paul's?" he said. "My son never mentioned that."

Richard DiPetrillo's son went to St. Paul's and I didn't know it? Maybe I should've gone to classes more often.

"I'm a sophomore. But I'm afraid I've been away for a while, working. . . ."

"My son's a freshman. Beneath your notice," he said, laughing.

"I doubt that." I laughed too.

"Can I get a photo?" Jude asked, snapping without waiting for an answer.

"There's our girl," somebody else said, stepping up and greeting DiPetrillo with a kiss. "Rick, I see you've met Chloe. She's our client."

I stared at the woman. I'd never seen her before in my life, and I knew it because I would've remembered her less-than-terrific nose job. "I'm Andrea Liddy, senior partner at Webster and White," she said. "Sean's boss."

"Of course! I see your name on all my papers," I said. "Do you have a kid at St. Paul's?"

"No, but I'm an alum, so of course I donate every year," she said. "Can I get one of those pictures? I'd love to show it to my niece."

"Definitely. Smile big," Jude said, shooting us.

"Chloe, come meet Ari Friedman," Dr. Cardillo said. "He's been asking if you were going to be here."

Jude and I followed him through the crowd of people in black tie, diamonds and sapphires dripping from every arm, neck, and ear, the delicate smell of flowers drifting from the table centerpieces. Every single head turned as we passed, every single person there was watching me even if they wanted to pretend they weren't. We were going to meet Ari Friedman, one of the biggest movie producers in the world, and somehow it was because he wanted to meet me, and not the other way around. This room was filled to the brim with money and power, and yet I was the biggest star here.

"Jude, keep shooting," I said to her. "You can use this footage in the documentary of my rise to superstardom!"

"You're sure about this?" Trav asked as we listened to Dr. Cardillo give a speech during dessert. The guy sounded a little drunk, but nobody was paying much attention anyway. We all knew what he wanted—a big, fat check at the end of the night.

"I'm sure. The song's gone viral in what, a day and a half? Now I want to push it over the top," I said.

"What about Snap?" he asked.

"Don't worry. I got this one," I said just as Dr. Cardillo finally called my name. It seemed to wake everyone up, and there was a wave of applause through the ballroom.

"Come on up here, Chloe!" he called. "Chloe's been nice enough to agree to sing for us tonight, maybe a song from that show all our students are always talking about!"

All the rich grown-ups laughed like they were hip just

because they'd heard of *Cover Band*. I gave them the Girl Next Door smile and beauty pageant wave as I stepped up to the mike and adjusted my Dolce & Gabbana dress.

"Hi, I'm Chloe Gamble," I said.

Applause.

"Y'know, Dr. Cardillo, I think I might sing something else tonight," I said, smiling over at his table. "I wrote this song a long, long time ago; I'd almost forgotten all about it! But I heard that somebody leaked it onto the Internet today, and I guess people like it. So it's kind of in my head, and I'd like to sing it for y'all, if that's okay."

More applause, and a few raised eyebrows. I met Jude's eye. She was standing in the back of the room, and her camera was on me. And as I started to sing "Lucky Bitch," I watched its little red light glowing, telling me that I was being recorded on video.

Video that Trav would put online at the Internet café on our way home tonight.

Because what's a song without a video?

Sean was waiting for me just inside the studio gates the next morning. He stepped right in front of Jude's car.

"Well, that can't be good," Jude said. "I hope you know what you're doing, Clo."

"I'm making my own destiny, that's all," I said. I rolled down the window and he came over. "If you want to see me so bad, you can just call me, you know," I said.

"You can't go in there," Sean said. "Jude, pull over. Chloe, my car's on the street outside. We'll go to Nika's office."

"What are you talking about? My call time is in ten minutes."

"They might just fire you if you walk in there right now. We've got to do damage control." Sean opened my door and for a brief, crazy second I thought he was going to haul me out of the car by force. Which would've been kind of sexy.

"Okay, calm down, I'm coming." I undid my seat belt and winked at Jude. "Have fun at work! Text me and tell me what people are saying."

Sean didn't say a word until we were back on the freeway, headed up to The Hal Turman Agency in the Valley. Then suddenly he laughed.

"What's so funny?" I said.

"You. You just can't let things lie. You always have to push, don't you?" He shot me a sideways glance. "We all heard about your little stunt at that fund-raiser last night. There's a video on YouTube."

"Already?" I said, as if I didn't know.

"I think you put it there yourself," Sean said.

I opened my mouth, and then I closed it again. Had he seen us at the Internet café last night?

"You're not as clever as you think you are, Chloe," he said. "That song of yours was leaked online first, and suddenly there's a video of you singing it? At a totally inappropriate venue? You're trying for another YouTube hit like you had with 'I Could Care.'"

"So what if I am? That song gave me a whole career. A pretty darn successful career," I said.

"You're not allowed to release your music while you're on the show. You're not allowed to sneeze unless Snap says so." Sean sounded exasperated. "You know that. You know they own your music. We talked about it."

"What if I said it was an old song? They wouldn't own it if I recorded it before I signed their contract, right?" I said.

"*Is* it an old song?" Sean asked.

"I got a don't-ask-don't-tell policy on that," I said. "Does Nika know we're coming?"

"Who do you think sent me to get you?" he said.

"What the hell kind of stunt was this to pull?" Hal Turman bellowed. "Do you know that I had *three* irate people screaming at me before I even finished my Ovaltine this morning? Even goddamn Quinn was handing me my ass."

I wrapped my arms around myself to keep warm in Hal's meat locker of an office. "Why can't we meet in *your* office?" I asked Nika. "Can't you yell at me yourself? I don't need to hear Hal."

"You'd better start hearing me, young lady," Hal said. "Because you are on course to get yourself kicked right out of a cushy job. You think it was easy landing you that show?"

"Yes, Hal, I do," I said. "All it took was me releasing a song and a video on YouTube. The first time I did it, I got a TV show out of it. Who knows what I'll get this time?"

"What are you, crazy? You think this You-Turn thing is going to make you a movie star?" Hal's face had turned practically purple, he was so mad. He looked like my daddy used to look whenever Mama got to pushing his buttons and he got ready to push back. "This could ruin you! This is a breach of contract, and you are up against an entire network! This isn't some shortcut to fame, missy. There are no shortcuts in this business!"

"What Hal means is that there are a million girls who would kill for the lead in a TV show," Nika cut in, probably to stop Hal from having a heart attack, which looked like it might happen any second. "A million girls who would behave themselves and do whatever their contract said. *Your* contract explicitly states that Snap owns whatever songs you write, record, produce, anything. What were you thinking, Chloe?"

"And then to get up there in front of the whole town and act all cutesy about it!" Hal cut in.

"I was thinking that I have a hit song, and I know it. You want me to wait for the rest of my contract before I release it? That's years, Nika," I said. "I didn't want to wait."

"You see? She wants a shortcut!" Hal yelled. "She's twelve years old, and she wants to get everything right away."

"I am sixteen," I said to him.

"The point is, your impatience made you do something very, very stupid," Sean cut in.

I stared at him. "Did you just call me stupid?"

"Yes," Sean said. Nika and Hal were quiet now, and looking at their faces I could tell they were worried. You're not supposed to call your star client stupid, I knew that much. "It was a dumb idea, and you knew it was a dumb idea, and you did it anyway because you think you're untouchable."

"That's right," I said. "I read the papers. I know what the ratings for *Cover Band* are. I know how much fan mail I get, and I know how many magazine shoots I've done in the past month. I'm the biggest thing the Snap network has got going. You think they're gonna *fire* me over one little song?"

"Well, that's our argument," he said, turning to Nika. "Should be a fun meeting."

Nika rolled her eyes, but she picked up the phone like she knew exactly what he was talking about.

"What meeting?" I asked.

"The one we're going to set up with the Snap people," Sean said.

"To clean up your mess," Hal added.

Nika Mays's Manuscript Notes: Shortcuts

There are some meetings in Hollywood that are terrifying enough to keep you up all night. Meetings that could go so badly, on such a deep level, that they could conceivably ruin your career. Maybe that's an exaggeration, but I'm not sure. In this town, when fortune turns against you, all your career momentum screeches to a halt. Your friends desert you, the calls stop coming, and you're all alone.

Chloe Gamble had experienced that after her disastrous break-in at NBC. And as I waited for Sean to pick me up for our big meeting at Snap, I wondered if I was about to experience it too.

"It'll be fine," he said as soon as I climbed into his Audi.

"Thanks for driving. I feel sick," I told him. "I know it's crazy, and I'll be completely on in the meeting, I promise. It's just that this was my first contract negotiation and now I feel as if I fucked it up."

"You didn't. We didn't," Sean said. He paused for a moment. "Chloe maybe did."

I laughed.

"You're right about her, though," Sean went on, his voice serious. "She's a star; she's got something. I don't think they'll let her go."

"Can't we just give them that song?" I said. "It's not as if there was a real release. It's just floating around online."

"Why should we give them something they don't own?" he asked. "Chloe recorded that song years ago."

I turned to look at him, and he looked back with a naughty little gleam in his eye that took my breath away. "*Years* ago? She recorded it when she was, what, ten? A song called 'Lucky Bitch'?"

"I think so," Sean said. "I think she was in sixth grade and she recorded it in her friend's basement in Texas by singing into the microphone on an iMac."

"In that case, we definitely can't give the song to Snap," I said, laughing. "I don't know what made me think that she went out and recorded it last week in a professional studio, completely ignoring her contract."

"Chloe would never do that," Sean said.

I grinned, and relaxed back in my seat, my anxiety fading for a little while. Maybe Sean was right. Maybe we could bluff our way through this latest Hurricane Chloe.

From the valet stand, up the elevator, and into the lobby of the Snap offices, I managed to keep my calm. But when I saw the group of people waiting for us on the couch, I felt like puking.

Hal Turman. Chloe Gamble. And her mother.

Even Sean was horrified. "What is your mother doing here?" he demanded. "Early, what are you doing here?"

"Clo told me this was some big meeting about her future as a recording star. We thought it was important for her to have the support of her family," Early said, innocent as a baby.

I grabbed Chloe's arm and pulled her back out to the elevator bank. "What are you thinking? Dave Quinn is going to be here. He is in that room right now! We can't have your mama anywhere near him."

"Mama knows Quinn is here," Chloe said. "Don't worry. She gets a bigger allowance this week if she does what I want."

"Clo, do you really not get how big a deal this is?" I demanded. "You are in breach of contract! They could fire you. This is not the time to be playing games with your mother. Send her home. Now."

"Too late!" Chloe chirped, looking over my shoulder. Quinn had just stepped out of the elevator behind us, along with Leslie Scott and Bo Haynes.

My eyes went straight to Quinn. He was the big fish here, they'd brought him to the meeting in order to scare us. But Quinn's eyes went straight to Early Gamble. He paled, and frowned, and looked just as horrified to see her as I'd been.

Hal and Sean came over and everyone exchanged hellos, trying to be polite but still act angry, which isn't that easy to do when you're face-to-face. But I hardly noticed the awkwardness, because I was too busy watching Earlene. She hung back during all the handshakes, but she made sure to look everywhere in the world except at Dave Quinn. Finally, Chloe stepped up and said, "I'm sure y'all remember my mama, Early?"

Earlene glanced up, straight at Quinn, and she put on a beauty pageant smile and said, "It's just so nice to see y'all again!" Then, her eyes still on Quinn, she slowly brushed her long blond hair back over her shoulder, letting her hand linger.

Quinn's face went from white to red in the space of one heartbeat, and he literally took a step back.

"I heard my Chloe's little song has caused quite a fuss," Early said, slipping her arm around Chloe. "Why, I'd forgotten all about that thing! Isn't it funny how they prey on famous people, all them bloggers and the media? Imagine, digging up some old song like that! They're just out there lookin' for dirt on my girl 'cause she's so big now, and they ain't gonna find any! I raised her right."

Sean turned his face away from her right then, and I had to bite my lip to keep from laughing, or crying, or rolling my eyes. But Chloe just gazed at her mother with love, and I didn't know whether to be impressed by her acting chops or afraid of them. If she was able to lie so convincingly in front of the people who held her whole career in their hands, well, she was capable of anything. (Which I had to admit to the police, eventually. I'm not as good at lying as Chloe was.)

"Well, as you can imagine, we're all very upset about this situation," Leslie Scott said. She glanced at Quinn and cleared her throat, clearly waiting for him to take the lead. But Quinn was staring at his shoes, then at Early, then at his shoes again, and he was obviously useless. "Why don't we go into the conference room and we'll see what we can figure out," Leslie went on, an edge of annoyance in her voice.

"This is a good thing, Leslie, us meeting this way," Hal said, stepping up to walk with her toward the conference room. "We'll work it all out, we don't need lawyers and contracts people talking our ears off. It's a simple misunderstanding."

"I just wish I could find out who released that song," Chloe said, following them.

Sean and I were left with Bo Haynes and Quinn and Early, who were staring at each other. "You look good, Earlene," Quinn said.

"I certainly do," she replied.

Bo shot Quinn a questioning look, then he took Early's arm. "Let's catch up to Chloe, Mrs. Gamble."

She obediently went along with him, and I watched Quinn watch Early's butt as she walked away.

"I'm sure you understand that Chloe needs to keep control of the music she recorded before her contract with Snap," I said.

Quinn turned to me, and I raised my eyebrows. He was busted, and he knew it. But he didn't lose his cool. "If she's going to have a lucrative singing career, Snap needs to be a part of it. We made her famous," he said.

"She made herself. You're just giving her a bigger platform," Sean said.

"It's unfortunate that this current song got out there before we could work out an arrangement for Chloe's music," I said. "And we're certainly sorry that happened."

"You don't think Chloe leaked it herself?" Quinn asked.

"Chloe isn't stupid," Sean said.

"No. No, the Gamble women are very smart," Quinn replied. "But the network already has a deal about Chloe's music. We own it, and she gets a percentage."

"Chloe is a big star, and she's put your network on the map. But she's got an even bigger following because of this song, 'Lucky Bitch,' and her previous online hit, 'I Could Care,'" I said. "The fact is, she owns those songs. Certainly you wouldn't dispute her rights to 'I Could Care.'"

"No . . ."

"It's never been officially released," Sean said. "If you let us release it now, it's a win-win. We've got a deal in place for Chloe to tour with the band in order to promote the show. It would be a nice bonus if we could promise a little solo concert of Chloe's own music. Let her release her solo album while the show's on hiatus, it will have two guaranteed hit songs from her online success, and Snap will get a good-faith percentage."

"Then she tours for *Cover Band*, and you get a bigger turnout: fans of the show, and fans of

Chloe," I said. "You expose the show to people who've only been into Chloe, you give them a reason to watch it."

Quinn sighed and ran his hand through his dark hair. "You know Leslie is the one making the calls here, right?"

"You're her boss," I said. "And really, Chloe is making the calls. She's a supernova and I think you recognize that now."

He chuckled. "Yeah. That runs in the family."

"If you agree to this, Leslie will agree," Sean said. "And we can keep the meeting short."

"Afraid I'll jump Earlene right in front of everyone?" Quinn asked. "Or maybe she'll jump me."

"Afraid that the tension in the room will suffocate us all," Sean said.

"Fine." Quinn turned and strode down the hall toward the conference room. "Let's go tell them the deal."

"So what the hell happened?" Hal Turman asked me as he drove us back to the agency in his boat of a car.

"I made a back-room deal with Quinn," I said. "You always say that the real meetings happen in private and the big meetings are just for show."

"And I'm right," Hal boomed. Then he winked at me, but his expression was a little sad. "I'm usually the one making the back-room deals," he said.

"I had an in with Dave Quinn."

"I'm usually the one with the in," Hal replied.

There was no way to answer him. Hal hadn't had an in for years now, and we both knew it.

"You did great, sweetheart," he said when we got inside, and he shuffled off toward his office. Hal had been a pain in my butt for my entire career, and maybe that's why I'd never realized before just how old he was. I don't think he realized it, either, not until that moment. That moment when I'd made the deal while he was busy telling war stories in a useless meeting.

My BlackBerry buzzed as I dumped my bag on the guest chair in my office. It was Chloe. "So? Is it official?" she said. "I can release my own album?"

"There's a lot of red tape," I said. "But, yeah, essentially."

Chloe squealed. "I can't wait to tell Max!"

"Max from The Ruffians? Why?" I asked.

"Because he's my producer," Chloe said. "We've got two more songs already in the works."

"Clo, you told me 'Lucky Bitch' was old."

"I lied," she said. "But it doesn't matter now, because Snap caved and gave me everything I wanted! Guess Hal was wrong about there being no shortcuts, huh?"

The last thing Chloe Gamble needed was a lesson like that, but I was too giddy with relief to worry about Chloe's life lessons right that second. And besides, there was a message on my desk. A message from Daniel Shapiro, the head of Virtuoso Artists Agency.

I grabbed the phone and called back. "Nika Mays for Daniel Shapiro," I said to the assistant, and then I waited for the typical answer—"He'll have to get back to you."

Instead, the assistant put me straight through.

"Nika," said the guy who ran the biggest, most famous agency in town. "How are you?"

"Fantastic," I told him. We'd never met. I'd read about him in the trades—and the news—for years, but there was only one reason he knew who I was: Chloe. "How can I help you?"

"You can come work for me," he said. "Interested?"

I sank down into my chair, my whole reality suddenly changed. "Um . . ."

Shapiro chuckled. "Sorry to be blunt, I've got a dinner in about two minutes. Jen will set up lunch for us and we can talk it through."

"Okay," I said.

"You've done some very impressive work with Chloe Gamble," Shapiro said. "Very impressive."

And then he was gone, and Jen the assistant piped up to give me the details of my lunch meeting with the most powerful agent in Hollywood. I wrote down what she said and hung up the phone, but my head felt as if it had been stuffed with cotton. I sat and stared at my desk for a few minutes, trying to force myself to work, to get to my call sheet, to check in with little Josh Andrews on his first day of a guest stint on *House*.

I picked up the phone . . . and dialed Sean's number.

"Nika! You won't believe what happened," he answered.

"Daniel Shapiro at Virtuoso wants to poach me," I said.

"Andrea Liddy just promoted me to junior partner," Sean replied.

We were both silent for a minute.

"I'm too excited to work," I said.

"Me too. Let's go get drunk. We're celebrating," Sean said.

"Okay, but you have to come get me, my car's at home."

"I'll be there in twenty minutes," Sean said.

He made it there in fifteen, and I was waiting outside on the sidewalk. "I've got to go home and change," I told him. "If I go out in work clothes, I can't relax."

"What am I, your limo driver?" he joked, but he headed into the canyon that led through the Hills to my place in West Hollywood. He was still in work clothes, but his tie was off and he'd thrown his jacket in the backseat.

"You're a partner!" I cried.

"And you're getting free of Hal Turman," he said. "Not bad for a day's work."

"Was that really it? We basically threatened Dave Quinn to get a good deal for Chloe, and that's why people want to promote us?" I said. "I feel dirty."

He shot me an appraising glance, and my cheeks got warm. "Hey, we weren't the ones sleeping with Chloe's mother," he said. "If Quinn wants to mess around on his wife, he should do it with someone who's not gonna tell."

"He should do it with someone who doesn't have a kick-ass agent/lawyer team," I said.

"We are a good team." Sean's hand on the gear shift was a half inch away from my leg, and I couldn't stop staring at it.

"You want to come in?" I said when he pulled into my driveway. "I've got some Stoli in the freezer—you can have a drink while I change."

"Definitely," he said.

He stood behind me as I unlocked the door, and I could feel his breath on my neck. I pushed the door open, then turned toward Sean. His lips were on mine before I could say a word.

My arms snaked around his neck, his went around my waist, and we fell against the wall, kissing. Sean kicked the door closed as I pulled him into the living room. By the time we hit the couch, he had my blouse off and I was working on his belt.

"We can't sleep together. It'll ruin everything," I said.

"Who said anything about sleeping?" Sean murmured.

"What about—" I began. But then his hand slid up under my bra and every objection I could think of vanished.

Who cares? I thought. *We're celebrating.*

chapter ten

Moving On

"Nika, we're on the front of *Variety* again!" I shouted into my BlackBerry the next morning. "Apparently you and Sean are the hottest reps in Hollywood, and I'm the town's fastest-rising star!"

"All true," my agent said, yawning. I glanced at my watch. It was almost nine in the morning, and I'd been on-set for an hour already. "Nika, where are you?"

"Home," she said. "I got a late start this morning."

"Well, get your butt to the office and work the phones!" I said. "You know what Hal Turman says—you gotta strike while the iron is hot. I need a record deal, *now*."

But Nika wasn't listening. I heard some muffled sounds

on her end, like she'd dropped the phone, and then I heard laughter. Male laughter.

"Bad girl!" I cried. "You got a guy there? No wonder you're late!"

"I'm on my way in right now, Clo," my agent said. And behind her, I heard her guy calling good-bye. The sound of the door shutting. And Nika, still laughing. "Clo? I'll call you from work."

"Okay," I said, and I hung up, stunned.

Nika didn't know it, but I'd recognized that voice. That guy in her house at nine in the morning. Sean Piper.

I handed my BlackBerry to the PA who followed me everywhere, and I walked up onto the set to rehearse the scene I'd be filming the next day. Episode six of *Cover Band*.

"What's up, Clo? You look stoned," Jonas said. He was lying on the bench of the cafeteria table in our characters' high school, reading the script while we waited for the director.

"I just found out something I'm not supposed to know," I said.

"That's the best!" Jonas grinned. "Spill."

"No, it won't matter to you," I said. "I won't matter to anyone except me."

He shrugged and went back to reading. I sat across the table and took a deep breath, trying to clear my mind the way Alan always says to. But there was no way to clear the image of Nika and Sean.

Sean, who wouldn't sleep with *me*. Sean, who turned me down every single time. And Nika, who'd sworn up and down that they were only friends.

"Sorry, Chloe, your phone is ringing," the PA said, running over with my BlackBerry. I glanced at it. Max.

"Hey there," I said, answering it. "Did you read *Variety*?"

"I can't believe you got away with it," he said.

"More than that," I told him. "I can do new stuff now too, I can cut a whole album. I own it all. Snap just gets a percentage."

"A whole album, huh?" he said.

"Yeah. So what do you think, Max?" I asked him. "Are you ready to go public with me?"

"Let's stop by my new house," I said as Max drove us toward his rehearsal space in Silver Lake that evening. "I got the keys yesterday."

"Sweet. You guys need any help moving this weekend?" he asked. I just smirked at him, and he laughed. "Right, sorry. You're the super-rich twins, you can hire movers."

"It's a damn sight better'n the way I moved into the Oakwood," I told him. "With the clothes on my back and one old pageant dress in the trunk of the car. But all I've got to move are clothes, anyway. The place is furnished. I ain't about to pay for an interior decorator who wants me to buy ten-thousand-dollar chairs."

"Yeah, not until *Cover Band* hits season two, anyway," Max joked.

Max turned and drove up into the hills, where the house was perched overlooking Griffith Park. My heart was beating fast as I unlocked the door, and not because I was excited at finally getting my own place.

"Okay, I think this couch could probably go in a museum. It's a Bidermeyer," Max said, wandering into the living room. Sir Paul Holmes liked antiques, the realtor had said, but all the really valuable ones had been taken out and put in storage. He liked antiques, but he wasn't so sure about young renters.

"Trav is taking the room that looks toward the Valley," I said, leading the way down the hall to the bedrooms, "and I'm taking this one. It looks out over Hollywood."

"Are you keeping this bed? It's insane." Max ran his hand over one of the carved wooden posts that led to the canopy over the humongous bed. "All this furniture is incredible."

"It's not really my style," I said, walking right up to Max. "But you can still bend me over it if you want to." I perched my butt on the back of the fancy bed and reached for his shirt, pulling him toward me for a kiss.

Max was so surprised that he just stood there while I pressed my mouth on his. I pulled back.

"Um . . . what?" he said.

"The giant bed. You and me?" I smiled at him, and I began

unbuttoning my shirt, slowly, letting him see the hot pink push-up bra I'd put on just for him.

Max laughed. "Okay, what's going on?"

"I'm tired of waiting," I said, taking off my shirt. "I've been alone for a long time, and I know you want me." I pressed my breasts against him and kissed him again. This time, he kissed me back, his hands sliding around my bare waist. He opened his mouth against mine, and our tongues entwined. I moved my hands up under his T-shirt, and he gave a little moan.

"Let's turn around," I said, not breaking the kiss. I moved off the bed, pressing my hips into his, and twisted around until he was against the bed with me in front. Then I pulled away and looked him straight in the eye as I sunk down onto my knees.

"Whoa!" Max cried. "Hold up." He grabbed my arms and pulled me back to my feet. "Chloe, what the hell are you doing?"

"I thought you'd like that," I said, confused. Don't all boys like blow jobs?

"Well, yeah, I'd like it," he said. "But we've barely even kissed."

"Oh." I felt stupid suddenly, standing there half-naked. Between Sean ignoring me and now Max refusing to let me do this, I didn't know what to think. A wave of anger washed over me. "Sorry, I thought you might want a piece of the girl the whole world wants to get with."

I grabbed my shirt from the floor and pulled it on.

"Hey, don't do that." Max reached for me. "I'm not saying

we're done here. I just want to enjoy the moment." He pulled me into his arms and brushed his lips against mine. "You're right, I want you. I've always wanted you," he murmured.

"But you just—" I backed away. "You stopped me."

"'Cause you're acting like a freak," Max said. "You don't have to go all hard-core on me, Clo. Just, I don't know, let me hold you for a minute first."

"Okay," I said. He tightened his arms around me and I lay my cheek against his chest.

"See, that's not so bad," Max whispered.

"No."

Max laughed. "Chloe, relax. You're all stiff."

I closed my eyes and tried to relax. "I'm embarrassed," I said, and I was shocked to hear those words coming out of my mouth. You should never admit a weakness, and I never had, not to anybody but Travis.

"You can't be embarrassed in front of me," Max said, still hugging me. "We're cool. I know you're not the stone-cold bitch you pretend to be."

He was joking. Sort of. "You do?" I asked.

"Sure, you don't fool me." He began moving his hands up and down my back, sending little chills through my body. I snuggled closer into his arms, burying my face in his shirt. He smelled good, like soap. Max's hand wandered up and began stroking my hair, and I suddenly realized that we were swaying a little, just sort of moving together while we hugged.

"I can't even remember the last time somebody hugged me," I said. Truth. I actually couldn't remember. Jonas hugged me sometimes, but not for long, and not for real. Only when the cameras were on us. Trav would usually punch me in the arm instead of a hug, and my mama only hugged me when she was drunk, and that meant it was really her supporting herself on me so she wouldn't fall. Far as I could remember, my daddy had never hugged me even once in my entire life.

I'd had sex with a couple guys back in Texas, but there damn sure hadn't been any hugging going on there. This was different. Max was holding me, really holding me, his arms tight, his chin resting on my head, his hands stroking me softly. I heard his heartbeat against my ear, and I felt the warmth of his body, and suddenly I was crying.

I bit my lip, trying to stop, but there was a sob building up in me so strong that I just couldn't stop it.

"Chloe." Max pushed me away, holding onto my arms so he could look down at my face. "Clo, what's wrong?"

"Nothing." I swiped at my cheeks, but more tears kept coming.

"Chloe, God, I'm so sorry," Max said. "I didn't mean to make you cry. I wasn't trying to embarrass you."

"It's not that," I said. "I just . . . I can't remember anybody not wanting me. I mean, not wanting something from me. I figured you'd want sex."

Max stared at me, and I wanted to get the hell out of there.

This was not how I thought the night would go. I wasn't supposed to be crying, I was supposed to be having fantastic sex with Max because he wanted me, and I trusted him, and I needed the attention of a guy. I turned toward the door.

"No," Max said, grabbing my hand.

"Yes. This was a huge mistake and now I'm makin' a fool of myself and I don't do that," I said. "Let's just go to the studio."

"No way. You're upset." Max pulled me down onto the bed and wrapped his arms around me again. "Let's just do this, okay?"

I nodded.

"We don't have to talk, or kiss, or anything. We'll just hang out," Max said.

I didn't want to answer him, I thought I might start crying again and it was humiliating. Crying is for losers who can't control their emotions, and I am always in control. But right then, with Max holding me, I didn't feel in control. I felt stressed and confused and, most of all, exhausted. Holding still without talking or scheming or planning my next move, well, that was a thing that I had never done before.

"I'm tired," I said to Max.

"Well, yeah. You're a twenty-four/seven girl," he said. "You don't know how to slow down."

"You slow down, you stall," I said.

"Who told you that?"

"My daddy, when he taught me how to drive the pickup,"

I said. "He was always talking crap, but he thought he was deep."

"Life lessons from your daddy who you hate?" Max said.

"Just 'cause he's an ass don't mean he's wrong," I said. I didn't want to be thinking about Daddy, not then, not ever. But I could picture him clear as day, his trademark nasty sneer on his face and his shiny rodeo champion belt buckle on his hips. "It's lonely on top of the bull."

"Excuse me?" Max said.

"My daddy was a rodeo rider. He used to say it's lonely on top of the bull. He meant that when you're up there riding, you got nobody but yourself. And you're trying to hold on and control the situation, and there ain't no one to help you. You got to be self-sufficient."

"You sure that's what he meant?" Max said. "It sounds to me like he was saying it's lonely, like maybe it would be better if there *was* someone to help."

I'd never thought of it that way. There wasn't a bull alive that could compare to riding the wave of fame in Hollywood. And there sure as hell wasn't anyone to help me. Even Nika was obviously in it for herself—and for Sean. It *was* lonely.

"I hate when my daddy is right," I murmured.

"He's not right. You can slow down for one night without stalling." Max stroked my hair. "Go to sleep. I'll be right here."

* * *

When I woke up, it was still dark, but there was a tiny hint of dawn in the patch of sky I could see out my bedroom window, which was about a million times more sky than I could see out of the Oakwood window. I pushed myself up onto one elbow and glanced around. I was still dressed, but my shoes were on the hardwood floor so I must've kicked them off. Max lay next to me, his arm flung over my waist, his dreads scattered crazily over the pillow.

I sat up and stretched my arms over my head. The house was quiet, only birdsong filtering in from the outside. I frowned.

"What's that face for?" Max murmured, and I turned to him. "You look confused," he said.

"I'm . . . I think I'm relaxed." I laughed. "God, I can't remember the last time I slept so well. I guess my mama's snoring was worse than I realized."

"Nah, it's all because of me." Max's hand crept over to my leg and began massaging my thigh.

"It is," I said, and I meant it. "I wouldn't have slept so well alone, and I know 'cause my mama spends her nights away whenever she feels like it." I lay back down and turned toward Max, slipping my arm over his broad chest.

"Told you I know what you need," he said, grinning.

"Well, I know what *you* need, too." I let my hand move slowly down his chest and over his stomach, and Max gave a little gasp. "You ain't gonna stop me again, are you?" I whispered.

"No." He turned and kissed me. "I'm not crazy."

I smiled, but then I forced myself to pull away from him. "But only if you have protection. Number twenty-nine on the list, don't get pregnant."

Max squirmed out of his jeans, then reached into the pocket and pulled out a condom. He tossed the jeans to the floor and grabbed me again, kissing me gently. Then harder. I closed my eyes and felt his arms around me and his hands moving over my body, his breath coming faster, his lips on my neck . . . and I didn't think about my show, or Kimber Reeve, or Nika and Sean, or anything at all. Just Max.

"Girl, what did you do last night?" Keesha teased me in makeup a few hours later.

"Nothing," I said, not bothering to wipe the grin off my face. "But ask me what I did this morning and that's a better story."

"Mmm, nothing better'n making love in the morning," she said, dotting foundation on my forehead. "Starts the day off right."

"You know, I never got that before, why people call it that," I said. "Making love. It sounds so cheesy, I always figured it was for stick-up-the-butt good girls who couldn't admit they were doing the nasty."

Keesha raised one eyebrow.

"Yeah, I get it now," I said. "Not saying I'm all gooey in

love, but he's a guy I care about for real. And it was completely different with him. Like, he held me while we slept and he kissed me while we . . . you know . . . because he wanted to feel closer to me." I rolled my eyes. "God, I sound like one of them Texas pageant girls looking for a husband."

Keesha laughed. "I didn't know Jonas had it in him."

"He doesn't. She was with Max Tyrell." I jumped at the sound of Jonas's voice, and so did Keesha.

"Jeez! I didn't even hear the trailer door open," I said. "How'd you know about Max?"

"TMZ. Perez Hilton. Even E! Online had it this morning." Jonas looked pissed. "There were pictures of you guys going into the house, and pictures of you coming out this morning."

"Oh my God, I didn't even see a single photographer!" I said.

"They hide in the bushes. Like rats," Keesha said. She glanced back and forth between me and Jonas. "I think I'll get another cup of coffee. Back in a few."

"You could've given me a heads-up," Jonas said when she was gone.

"Sorry." I didn't know what to say. It had never even occurred to me that Jonas would care, it had never occurred to me to think of him at all. "I kinda figured this wasn't an issue with us."

"It's the publicity, Chloe. You know what they're all saying? You're stepping out on me, you're dumping me for a bad-boy musician, whatever. Like I'm just some loser you're cheating on."

"Okay." I frowned. "Sounds more like I'm a cheating whore."

He shrugged.

"But you don't care about that. You care about how it makes *you* look," I said. "Got it."

"It makes me look like I can't keep my girlfriend happy," he said, and I knew he meant more than he was saying. "I just wish you'd told me it was coming."

"I didn't know. Yesterday I found out that the guy I was after wanted someone else, so I just decided to get with Max," I said. "But then it turned into something more."

"Well, good for you." Jonas headed for the trailer door. "Do me a favor, let me say that we broke up two weeks ago. It's the least you can do." He left without waiting for an answer, the flimsy trailer door banging shut behind him.

Keesha came right back in, since she'd obviously just been listening at the door. "Guess that's that," she said.

"I thought we had each other's backs," I said. "We both knew it wasn't real. He's got no right to be mad at me."

"He's mad that it got out, he likes to control his image," Keesha said. "Can't blame the boy for that."

"I guess not." I chewed on my lip, thinking it through. "I better start controlling my image, too, huh? I can't be a cheating whore and still be America's sweetheart starring in a kids' show."

"Girl, you ain't no whore. You heard him—you broke up

two weeks ago. You're just moving on, that's all."

"Yeah. I have a new boyfriend, nothing wrong with that." I smiled as she continued doing my makeup. A new boyfriend. A *real* boyfriend.

"I feel like we're coming out of the closet," Max said when the limo stopped in front of the mini red carpet outside the Chanel store on Rodeo Drive. "Why couldn't we just drive ourselves?"

"It's a big party, I want to drink," I told him. "I want you to drink. And no drunk driving. Number two on the list."

"You and that list." He shook his head.

"What? I'm happy that I'm famous enough to need it," I said. "Ready to come out?"

Max frowned. "You go first, they only care about you."

"You kidding? Everybody's dying to see if I brought you tonight. It's all just rumors until we actually show up holding hands." I glanced out the window at the line of photographers, already snapping shots of me through the glass. "For all they know, I'm with Jonas and you and I are 'just good friends.'"

Max leaned over and kissed me, not letting go until I was breathless. "Let's get it over with," he said. The driver opened the door for us, and Max climbed out first, holding out his hand to help me out of the car.

"Chloe, over here!" somebody yelled, followed by a chorus of other voices yelling my name and Max's. He held on to my hand as we started toward the door of the store, and it was a good thing because my eyes were practically blinded by all the flashes. Me and Jonas had never gotten attention like this, probably because me maybe cheating on him with Max was a juicier story. "C'mon, give us a pose," another guy called. "Kiss her, Max!"

Max yanked on my hand, tugging me into the safety of the door. Inside, the place was dark and the music was loud, as if it was a nightclub, and the bouncers immediately blocked the paps' view of us.

"I don't know how you can stand that," Max muttered.

"It's what I live for," I told him, laughing. "Wait'll you see the pictures all over the Internet later. You'll be happy."

"Not my thing," Max said. "I'd rather be known for my music. So where's your brother?"

"Not here yet." I pulled out my BlackBerry and texted Trav. "He's in the limo with Javier Bronn and Sasha. He says they're pulling up right now. Sasha's gotta be the last one in; she's the big star." I hated saying that; I hated not being the biggest star at the party. But this was by far the most luxe party I'd been to yet in Hollywood, to celebrate the premiere of the Chanel commercial Trav and Sasha had filmed in Spain. It seemed kind of ridiculous to hold a premiere for an advertisement, but it was an excuse to get all glam in a Marc Jacobs dress and get my picture taken, and from what I could see, a lot of other people had come here for the same reason.

"Is that Natalie Portman?" I asked Max.

He peered through the crowd. "I don't know. Go ask her. All you stars are automatic BFFs, aren't you?"

"Fake BFFs, maybe. I want her career, not her phone number." I spotted someone else near the bar, and Natalie Portman vanished from my mind. "No way! It's Kimber Reeve. She's got balls, coming here. She knows my brother is in this thing."

"Uh, we should stay away from her," Max said. "Let's go sit. Travis will find us."

"I am *not* hiding from Kimber Reeve, thank you very much," I said. "Her dress is the wrong color for her skin tone. I look better than she does." I tugged on Max's hand, but he pulled back.

"I'm serious, we're not talking to Kimber. She's . . . got a thing about us," Max said. "She called me the other day when she saw that stuff online about you and me."

"Kimber?" I said, a smile spreading across my face. I hadn't thought about Kimber's reaction to the news that I was with her ex, but now that I did, it made me pretty damn happy. "I didn't know you two were still such buddies."

"We're not; it's the first time I talked to her since we broke up," he said. "And it's not about me, it's about you."

"Really?" My grin got bigger.

"Yeah, she says you're a psycho and that you're trying to steal her life. You tried to take her role on *Virgin*, and now you're dating her ex," Max said. "She wanted to warn me."

I laughed out loud. "Warn you about what?"

"About the fact that you're using me to make her jealous."

Something in his expression made me stop laughing. Much as I loved pissing off Kimber, I didn't want Max getting caught in the middle. "Hold up, you don't buy that crap, do you?" I said. "Kimber's just jealous."

"That's what she says about you."

"Max, I am not using you. And anyway, if I am, I'm using your skills to make my music sound better," I said. "The sex is just a nice bonus." I slid my arms around his waist and kissed my way up his neck.

"You can stop that now, there are no cameras in here," Kimber's voice rudely interrupted the moment.

I felt Max stiffen up, and I pulled my lips away from him, though I made sure to keep my arm around him just so it was clear who he was with. I turned slowly to look at Kimber, and she was obviously halfway to a full-on Early Gamble bender. "Why, hi there, Kimmy! You're wasted," I said.

"You're a freak," she spat. "You think I don't know what you're doing? You want Max because he was mine first. Just like you want every single other thing I have. But you're not going to get it. You're not good enough!"

"I'm good enough that I wouldn't get fired by my own boyfriend from my big NBC show," I said.

"I didn't get fired, in fact," she said. "I've still got my show."

"Oh, but not your boyfriend?" I said. "Did Todd Linson kick you to the curb when he cut your part back down?"

"You're just jealous that people have actually heard of my network," she snapped. "Max, you're really slumming with this one. She's only with you to get at me."

"Back off, Kimber," Max said. "Chloe and I have nothing to do with you."

"Oh, she didn't come to you with some little plan to piss me off by hanging out together?" Kimber said. Max shot me a look, and he shut up.

Score one for Kimber, I thought. The only reason I'd wanted to work with Max on my music was because I thought it would make Kimber mad. But that was back before I knew how good he was.

"Look, Kimber, this here is my brother's party," I said. "He's in this Chanel ad and I'm just here for him. So how about you and me take a break, just for tonight?"

"Bull. Shit." She was slurring her words now, and the strap of her dress had slipped halfway down her arm. If it was my mama, I'd be taking her home right about now. But nobody stepped forward to claim Kimber. "We're not taking a break, *Clo,*" she said. "You've been a pain in my ass since the first day I met you."

"Likewise," I said, with a Girl Next Door smile on my face. Maybe there weren't paparazzi in here, but there sure as hell were a lot of people watching us right now and I was willing to bet a few of them had their cell phone cameras out. "But this isn't about me, it's about Travis, and he's never done anything to you."

I saw her lift up her glass, filled with something amber-colored. Scotch? Amaretto? Didn't matter. What mattered was that she was about to throw a drink in my face. Max stepped forward to stop her, but I was too surprised to move. The drink hit me, but not in the face, it just splashed onto my Marc Jacobs dress. And Kimber's arm hit Max's shoulder, which threw her off-balance on her five-inch stilettos. She went down like a drunken trucker in a Texas roadhouse.

While I stood there with her drink all over my three-thousand-dollar dress, with Kimber lying at my feet, her dress off her shoulder and a breast just hanging out for all the world to see, the door opened and Sasha Powell made her big entrance.

"Everyone give it up for the star of the show! Here's Sasha Powell with Javier Bronn," the DJ announced.

There was a sort of hush, and a few people turned around to look at Sasha, but most everyone else stayed right where they were, staring at me and Kimber.

"Kimber, get up!" I cried, reaching out my hand to help her. She looked dazed, like she couldn't believe what had just happened. So dazed that she let me pull her back to her feet and she didn't even try to scratch my eyes out. "We've got to get you fixed up," I said, loud enough for anyone to hear, loud enough for their cell cameras to pick up. I yanked Kimber's strap back up, covering her breast.

Trav was at my side now, and over his shoulder I saw Sasha staring at me with flat-out hatred in her eyes. "Trav, I am so sorry, this wasn't on me," I murmured. "Kimber just lost it."

"Maybe you should take your friend home," Sasha said, coming over and slipping her arm around my twin brother.

"I am so sorry about all this," I told her. One look at Max was all it took. He grabbed Kimber on one side and I took the other. "Didn't you come with anyone, Kimber?" I asked.

But now she was just crying, a total mess.

"If she did, they're ditching her," Max muttered. "Let's take her out the back."

I hesitated. Kimber was obviously in a bad place at the moment, but that didn't erase the fact that she'd been a complete bitch to me since my first day in Los Angeles. "No, we're going out the front," I told Max. He frowned, but I steered us toward the bouncers. "They can get her car, or call a cab," I said.

Max saw right through me, but he went along. We got Kimber to the door, the bouncers called for her limo, and when the car showed up Max and me helped her cross the sidewalk and climb in back, a thousand paparazzi flashes going off in our eyes.

"Chloe! What happened?" someone yelled.

"Chloe, did you and Kimber have a catfight?"

"Don't be silly, Kimber and I are friends," I said sweetly, letting them get as many shots of my ruined dress—and Kimber's mascara-streaked face—as they wanted.

"Max . . . I'm sorry," Kimber blubbered as he buckled her in. He ignored her and turned to the driver.

"Straight home," he said, and the guy nodded.

Our limo pulled up next, and Max dragged me into it. "Well, that was a waste," he said as the driver took off. "Ten minutes at a party, no booze, no fun, and a fight."

"Are you kidding me?" I said. "That was the best ten minutes I've ever spent!"

A thought flashed in my mind. Rule #15 on the Don't Do list was: Don't have a fight with your boyfriend, or his ex. Maybe I should have been worried I broke a rule. Or maybe I should have been worried I was now above the rules. But what I really should have been worried about is that I didn't care one way or the other. . . .

"Oh my God, that was the most fantastic thing ever," Marc greeted me the next morning. I hadn't been expecting to see him, but there he was, lounging on the couch in Nika's office.

"New couch?" I asked my agent.

"Yeah. Bigger office, new couch." She smiled, but she didn't exactly meet my eyes. *She's embarrassed because of Sean. She thinks I'm mad at her,* I thought. No wonder Marc was there.

"You ever gonna stop moving offices?" I asked her, putting on a playful tone of voice. "What is this, the third one since I met you?"

"Yup. The only one bigger is Hal's. Well, and Bonnie's. But I try to pretend that one doesn't exist," Nika said, matching my tone.

"Who cares? Tell me about Kimber," Marc cut in. "Did she really slap you?"

"What? No," I said. "Where'd you hear that?"

"There are rumors all over the Internet," Nika said. "And a couple of really grainy videos on YouTube."

"Yeah, and about a thousand pictures of Kimber's nip slip." Marc giggled. "I heard she puked on her shoes, is that true?"

"No," I said, laughing. "At least not while I saw her. I bet her limo driver could tell you about that, though. Girl was seriously drunk."

"I have a friend who works for Todd Linson's production company and he says that Linson was definitely banging Kimber Reeve, and they broke up two days ago," Nika said. "He blamed her for all the trouble *Virgin* is having."

"Oh, please. He's the director," Marc said. "Maybe if he wasn't acting like he has a movie budget for a television show, they wouldn't be in such deep shit."

"Can we focus, please?" I said. "We're talking about how much I hate Kimber, remember?"

"Right. Sorry," Marc said.

"So her boyfriend dumped her and she went out and got drunk," I said. "Then I come in with her ex-boyfriend and we both look so hot it's insane. . . ."

"If you do say so yourself," Marc said.

"I do." I winked at him. "Kimber sees me and Max, and she hates me anyway, and she knows I know that *Virgin* is falling apart . . ."

"She feels like crap so she takes it out on you," Nika said. She seemed a lot more comfortable now that we were talking about Max. She even looked me right in the eye for a second. "So, what? She fell out of her dress 'cause she was drunk?"

"Pretty much," I said. "I wasn't even trying to fight; Trav and Sasha are furious at me for stealing the spotlight. But Kimber tossed her drink at me, what was I supposed to do? She made a complete fool of herself, poor thing. I just got her out of there as fast as I could, but I guess it wasn't fast enough if so many people got pictures."

"Yeah. Too bad the only way out was past the paparazzi," Marc said.

I nodded sadly.

"You were just being a good friend," he went on, trying not to laugh. "Everybody said how sweet you were about it. And you look so concerned about Kimber in all the photos."

"Well, we *are* such good friends," I said. And we both dissolved into giggles.

"Girl, I don't even know why you pay me," Marc said. "You are a genius at publicizing yourself."

"Case in point, guess who called me this morning," Nika said.

"Who?"

"Matthew Greengold."

"What?" I practically screamed. "Why are you letting us trash talk stupid Kimber Reeve when you have news like that? What did he want? Wait, was he calling to blackball me because of the fight with Kimber?" I jumped up from the couch, then sat back down. The most famous director in the world had called my agent. I didn't know what to do with myself. *"What?"*

"He didn't mention Kimber, though obviously what happened last night was on his mind," Nika said. "He was calling to check on your availability. For *Frontier*."

"No!" I jumped back up, and I just kept jumping. "Kimber got that part in *Frontier*! It's her role. Oh my God, did she get fired because of her wardrobe malfunction?"

"Kimber never closed on it, I checked. Greengold said he was rethinking some of the casting, and he's been watching *Cover Band* with his daughter, and he can see from the media that you're a good kid and you're obviously talented—"

"And Kimber is not a good kid 'cause she's obviously a lush," Marc cut in, laughing.

"And he wants to know if you're available," Nika finished.

"Oh my God! I'm gonna be in a Matthew Greengold movie! I'm gonna win an Oscar!" I yelled.

"Chloe, slow down," Nika said. "You're not going to be in *Frontier*. It's shooting next month. This is a really late cast change."

"Kimber must've fucked up more than we know," Marc said. "Or else Linson got her fired. What an ass."

"Who cares about her?" I said. "What do you mean, I'm not going to be in *Frontier*? Why the hell not? Does he want me to audition? I'll audition."

"Chloe, it's too soon. You're still in the middle of the season," Nika said. "You're not available."

"Oh, hell yes, I am," I said. "For a huge movie? I am always available."

"You've got a contract that says otherwise. And I am not about to fight with the Snap Network over your contract, not again," she said.

"Was the fight really so bad last time?" I asked her. "Seems like you and Sean actually thought it was kind of fun."

Nika stared at me then, and I wondered if that had sounded as nasty out loud as it had sounded in my head. I didn't care. My agent and my lawyer got off on contract disputes, and that was a fact.

"The ink isn't even dry on your new agreement," Nika said finally. "It's nonnegotiable, Chloe. You can't shoot a movie and your show at the same time. You took the job on *Cover Band*, it's made you a star, and that's that. You can take movie roles when the show is on hiatus and you're not busy touring with the band."

"Even huge stars have to turn down movies because of their TV contracts," Marc said sympathetically. "It's the price you pay for a steady gig."

"Then why'd you even bother telling me?" I said. "Is that your idea of big news—you had to turn down a kick-ass movie role for me?"

"Yes. It's the Don't Do," Nika said. "If Matthew Greengold wants you in a movie, believe me, other directors will want you in their movies. We'll find the right one, at the right time, and we'll make the jump to features. This is a sign that your star is rising, Chloe. Be patient."

I didn't answer her then, because she didn't want to hear the answer that we both knew. I was *not* patient.

E-mail from Travis Gamble

Coop. Hold off on buying that bus ticket. Some shit's been going down here. Maybe you saw it on TMZ, that fight between my sister and Kimber Reeve? Chanel held this big premiere party for the mini-film with Sasha and me (well, they just think of Sasha and I'm "that guy she's screwing who she met on the shoot"). So it's really swank, they turned their whole store in Beverly Hills into a big club for the party and there's a red carpet and all that. I'm with Javier and Sasha in the limo, and we have to be the last people in because they're the big stars. It's weird, Sasha's always complaining about the paparazzi and all the articles about her personal life, but she still wants to get more attention on the red carpet than anyone else. Javier, too.

Anyway, there's, like, a hundred guys with cameras on the way in, and we stand there like idiots and pose. Most of the time they made me stand off to the side so they could shoot Sasha alone, and then when I was with her they wanted us to act like we're making out or something—as if you would ever do that in the middle of the sidewalk with thousands of people watching—but Sasha said no, just arms around each other, no kissing.

Then we finally go inside, and the DJ announces us like we're the starting lineup of the football team at the big game, and there's like a spotlight on us, and Sasha's smiling and I get the feeling there's supposed to be lots of applause, right? But instead everyone is looking at my sister and her boyfriend and that Kimber chick. Chloe says Kimber threw a drink at her, like she's all innocent, but you know my sister is never innocent. She's sleeping with Kimber's ex-boyfriend, for one thing. Anyhow, it's like a big scandal that they got into a catfight. I don't know why; doesn't that happen a lot in Hollywood?

Chloe got the hell outta there pretty fast, if you ask me. And she took Kimber, too. But Sasha hit the friggin' roof! I think she wanted to throw a drink at Chloe too. She just ran straight over to the VIP area and hid for the rest of the night. When I got there, she was drinking bourbon and she barely even looked at me. Seriously, I've been almost living with this girl for a month and I wondered if I should leave because she was acting like I'm a stranger. Finally Javier tells me I need to go kiss her. I'm like, dude, I'm afraid she's gonna slap me. But he's European and he's always got three chicks hanging on him, so I guess he knows what he's talking about. I go over and I grab Sasha and I just kiss her. She tried to push me off, but I didn't let her. I didn't think you were supposed to do that with girls—Chloe would've kicked a guy in the nuts if he tried that shit. But Sasha finally starts kissing me back, then she takes me off to the bathroom and we totally do it right on the counter. *Hot*, dude, I am not kidding.

So we go home and I figure everything's okay now. But the next morning, all the media had were stories about Chloe and Kimber and their feud, and nothing about Sasha and the mini-film. And Sasha is so pissed off that she called her publicist and threatened to fire her! Then she tells me that we're done with Chloe. I'm all, "Excuse me? She's my twin sister. And this wasn't her fault." Sasha just laughs in my face and tells me I'm naive. Like she knows my sister better than I do?

Point is, she's furious and she says she's done with Los Angeles. She hates all the stupid games, and she hates being close to Chloe, so she's moving to her place in New York because people are normal there, which I doubt but what do I know? And she says that if I stay here, we're done. She doesn't do long-distance relationships. But she's totally willing to take me to New York and she says I can get work there and we'll have a blast. I'm not so sure about the work.

I'm not even getting much work here lately; nobody thinks of me as an actor anymore, I'm just Sasha's boy toy. Know what, though? That's not so bad. All I have to do is hang out and have sex with Sasha Powell? I could do worse! Between Mama and her porn friends and Chloe and her bitch-fights and me not working, what's so great about LA? I'm thinking it sounds pretty good to live in New York for a while, especially when Sasha's paying the bills. School's over for the summer, and I'm not sure I'm ever going back anyhow.

So don't come to LA right now, Coop. I don't know, maybe in a couple of weeks you can come visit me in New York.

Nika Mays's Manuscript Notes: Poaching Section

Poaching. It's a standard thing in Hollywood. Agents poach clients from other agents every day of the week. Managers do it, publicists do it. Hell, even the big-name stylists and hair people do it. There's only so much talent to go around, only so many famous actors and directors and showrunners. Those are the people who make your career. "You're only as good as the people you represent, because those are the people who represent you." One of the first things Hal Turman ever said to me.

What he meant was that your clients have to

be stars if you want to be a star agent. You can have a whole list of successful, working clients who get good money to do guest appearances on TV shows, and you'll do fine. But nobody will ever write articles about you in the trades, nobody will ever invite you to speak at their film school, nobody will ever refer to you as a "legendary" agent. If you want to be that kind of agent, you need superstars. There are two ways to get these superstars: You can make them, or you can steal them.

I made Chloe Gamble. I started her career, launched her from nothing. That, let me say it in no uncertain terms, *that* is the hard way to do it. It's much easier to wait for a Chloe Gamble to become a star and then try to poach her. Steal her from her unimportant children's agency and make her part of your client roster at CAA or Virtuoso. Because, let's face it, what starlet would want to stay with Hal Turman when she could be with the big guns at a world-renowned agency? The Turman Agency couldn't offer Chloe the kinds of A-List contacts that CAA could. We couldn't package her entire TV show, we couldn't get her first looks at scripts by Oscar-winning screenwriters. We couldn't even give her the kind of expensive Christmas present that A-list clients at Endeavor get.

I'd been expecting someone at Virtuoso or ICM to try to poach Chloe since the day after *Cover Band* premiered. I had *not* been expecting them to try to poach me.

"Let's get down to business, Nika," Daniel Shapiro said over lunch at Mr Chow. We'd ordered our food, had our iced teas, and the small talk part of the meeting was over. "We've been watching your work with Chloe Gamble, and we're impressed."

"You seem to have a very close relationship with Chloe, hmm?" Adam Cohen put in. He was one of the partners at Virtuoso, one step down from Daniel Shapiro in terms of power. Frankly, I was still expecting a camera crew to jump out of the bushes any second and announce that I was being punk'd. These two guys were superstars in my field. They shouldn't even be talking to me at all, let alone taking me to lunch.

"Yes, we're a team," I said. "A solid team."

Adam nodded. Daniel was busy scanning the restaurant for famous people to schmooze, since he was really only there as a formality, to make me see how serious they were. (Like Hal always said, "If the big fish is at the table, you know the offer is for real.") We all knew what the subtext was: If I left my agency, would my biggest star come with me? Because that's the only way they wanted me—poach the agent to get the client. I was saying yes. I was hoping yes. But the truth was that things between Chloe and me were strained lately. I hadn't spoken to her about my relationship with Sean. I hadn't even spoken to Sean about it, since every time we saw each other face-to-face these days we pretty much ended up in bed. I had a feeling that it bothered Chloe, but I'd been too afraid to ask her.

"Have you told Chloe that you're meeting with us?" Adam asked.

"Not yet," I said. Which was weird enough. Two months ago, Chloe would've been the first person I told. "I'll tell her when there's a reason to."

"Then let's give you a reason." Adam leaned forward, his arms on the table, his eyes locked on mine. "What's your contract like with Hal?"

"Hal's been very good to me these past few months," I said. "I run the New Media division, and I'm a full agent." It wasn't exactly what he had asked, but it was a good enough answer for the moment.

"That's very impressive, but you're talking

about a small, specialized agency in the Valley," Adam said. "Wouldn't you like to play on a bigger stage? There's only so far you—and your clients—can go with Hal Turman. If you want more power, more money, you're going to have to leave him. Think about how your base of operations will change if you join us at Virtuoso."

"It's actually your base of operations I'd like to change," I said.

Daniel Shapiro's attention snapped back to our table. Adam Cohen cleared his throat and said, "Excuse me?" in the tone of voice I'd use with a delusional guy hitting on me in a bar.

"I believe you're thinking too small," I said. "You're wooing me, and Chloe through me. But I think you should go after the big fish. You should go for Hal Turman."

Daniel and Adam stared at me, and neither one said a word. If I were Chloe, I would've put on one of my pageant personas and bluffed it out. But I wasn't Chloe, and I wasn't used to acting, and I sucked at it. At that moment, I was more terrified than I'd ever been before. But Hal always says, if you don't gamble you don't win.

"Buy out The Hal Turman Agency," I said, my voice shaking a little bit. "Hal is a legend, we all know it. He's easy to make fun of, but if there's one thing I know for a fact, it's that Hal is almost always right. He's launched more careers than both of you put together."

Daniel Shapiro's eyes widened, and I got ready to kiss my Hollywood career good-bye. I'd insulted him, sort of, and you don't insult a man like that. But then an amazing thing happened. Daniel laughed. "Go on," he said.

"Hal's past his prime. I'm the future of his agency," I said. "But the agency has a deep client list—virtually all of the under-twelve working actors are with Hal. Chloe's our big name, and I've signed a few other up-and-comers. If you buy the agency, you get the clients, you get Chloe and Josh Andrews. You get my experience in new media, and you get Hal's experience in the Industry."

"We aren't looking to acquire second-rate agencies," Adam said.

"Hal Turman's not second-rate," Daniel replied, shocking me. "The man's a dinosaur, but he's good in a meeting. He taught a class at my college back in the day, and he was like a rock star then."

"He's a has-been," Adam said.

"He's old school. But every bit of advice he's given me has been golden," I said. "Look, I don't even like him. I just think he's good business for you. Buy his agency, install him at Virtuoso as a sort of advisor, an elder statesman. I'll do the heavy lifting."

"We don't have a juvenile division," Daniel said thoughtfully.

"The Turman Agency *is* your juvenile division. We find the kids, we launch their careers, and then you come in and poach them from us," I said. "That's why you don't need a juvenile division of your own. But every other agency in town operates the same way—they come to us for the teen stars. If you buy us, you automatically wipe out the competition. You get all the kiddies."

"What do *you* get?" Adam asked.

"I get a bigger playing field," I said. "I get to be a full agent at Virtuoso; I get to keep my position in New Media. And I get a bigger percentage than your other agents. So does Hal."

Daniel's eyebrows shot up. "No."

"Yes," I said. "It's hard to start a career, and that's what I do. I put Chloe on the map. I created her from nothing. It's more difficult to do, so it deserves a bigger percentage."

"And what about Hal's other agents?" Adam asked. He hadn't answered my argument, and I knew that meant the percentage was still on the table. "What about Bonnie Uslan, isn't she his number two?"

"We'll buy the agency name and we'll take Hal and you," Daniel said. "That's all. The rest will get layoff packages as part of the merger."

No more Bonnie? "Fine with me," I said.

"Good. Make it fine with Hal Turman," Daniel Shapiro said. "That's when it's a deal."

"Absolutely not!" Hal bellowed. "Not on your fucking life, missy! You get your ungrateful ass out of my building right this second!"

Instead, I sat my ungrateful ass down in Hal's office chair and waited for him to yell it out. I just hoped he didn't have a heart attack before he calmed down.

"How dare you, how *dare* you waltz in there and act as if you have anything to say about the future of this agency?" Bonnie Uslan said from the other chair.

"I am the future of the agency, Bonnie," I said. "They came after me. Not you."

That shut her up. Her face looked even more pinched than usual.

"Hal, I see you checking H Meter every day," I said. "I don't think you even went online once the first two years I worked here. Now you do, because you want to read about yourself. We've got buzz. The agency is hot again, Hal, and it's been a long time since you could say that."

He looked at me, his face still red and angry, but he was listening.

"Don't you want to go out on top, Hal?" I said. "This is your retirement package. Virtuoso will pay you a bucket of money, you'll have an office there and you can work as much or as little as you want. And the last time the words 'The Hal Turman Agency' are in the trades, it will be a story about how hip you are, how good you are at launching young stars, and how much money you're worth. It will be about how legendary agent Hal Turman is bequeathing his legacy to Virtuoso."

"Oh, please, Hal doesn't even want to retire," Bonnie started.

"Shut up, Bonnie," Hal said. His old eyes were sad as he looked at me.

"I could have gone to them and taken Chloe. I could've ditched you, Hal," I said. "And I probably should have. But you taught me everything I know."

"I taught *everyone* everything they know," he said. "I invented this business, young lady."

"Damn right," I said. "So do you want the respect that's due you? Or are you going to limp on as a second-rate agent until the bitter end? What's it going to be, Hal?"

Turman goes Virtuoso

Breaking news from the Valley has monster tenpercentary Virtuoso buying out the kiddie-centered Hal Turman Agency. The surprise move is said to be the brainchild of Nika Mays, who reps TV and music star Chloe Gamble for Turman. Daniel Shapiro's office claims "Hal Turman built the child-star industry and we're thrilled to be in business with his company," but sources say Virtuoso will be bringing only Mays and Turman aboard. The move is expected to be quick, with Mays and Turman becoming the de facto kiddie arm of Virtuoso.

chapter eleven

Frontier

"Oh my God, I *loved* that book," the girl at the Astro Burger said to me.

I glanced down at my copy of *Frontier* and smiled. "Me too."

She kept staring at me for a few seconds too long, and I knew she recognized me. I'd gotten good at spotting the exact moment I went from being just some girl to being Chloe Gamble in people's minds. The question now was whether she was the type to play it cool and pretend she didn't know me, or the type to gush about how she loved me and ask for a photo.

"Y'know, I just love your show," she began.

"Thanks, that's so sweet." I stood up fast, grabbed the book, and turned toward the door. I wasn't in the mood for type number two. Then I turned back around and handed her the book. "You want this? I just finished it."

She beamed as if I'd just handed her a hundred bucks, and I went outside onto Melrose Ave. I'd wanted to stake out the Paramount lot just like I staked out the NBC lot a few months back. Back then, I'd been a complete nobody sitting in a Taco Bell. Now, I couldn't even hang out in a burger place for ten minutes without being recognized.

It didn't really matter. I couldn't see well enough from there anyway. I'd been planning to get into the lot through the side entrance, on a smaller street with fewer cars. I figured the security guards there would be more relaxed, that maybe I could sneak in as part of a group. But I'd been on enough studio lots by now to know I was being stupid. Back when I broke into the NBC lot, I had no idea how seriously they took security. I knew better now.

Back when I broke into the NBC lot, I'd gotten a ride in with a delivery guy. I stood on the corner of Melrose and gazed down the side street to where a truck was pulling in to a back gate. Could I find another driver to smuggle me in? I'd just lucked into it the first time. Now, most drivers would probably recognize me.

A couple of people crossing the street stared at me, whispering to each other.

I can't sneak in anywhere anymore, not unless I pull a Britney and start wearing wigs or something, I thought.

"Screw it," I said, and I started down Melrose toward the main gates of the Paramount lot. This place was right smack in the middle of Hollywood, and it was a famous studio where a million hit movies and TV shows had been filmed. Huge stars and Oscar-winning writers, directors, and producers came in and out of this lot every single day. Megawatt movie stars worked here. Billionaires worked here.

But the people I passed on the sidewalk all still stared at me, that shocked smile of "Hey! It's Chloe Gamble!" on their faces. Even here, in the center of it all, I was somebody.

The main gates were for cars, one driveway going in, one driveway going out, the famous double-arched gateway over both. But on one side was a little walking path, under the gateway and to a separate security booth for pedestrians.

I walked right up to the desk, pulled off my sunglasses, and gave the guard a big pageant smile. "Hi. I'm Chloe Gamble," I said.

"Morning, Ms. Gamble," the guard replied. He typed my name into his computer, then frowned. "I'm sorry, I don't have a walk-on for you."

"It is just such a beautiful day, I decided to leave my car at home and just take in some air," I lied. "But I bet they were expecting me to drive on."

He clicked around on the computer, still frowning, and I made a show of checking my watch. How long could it possibly take to see that I was not in their system, not for a walk-on and not for a drive-on?

"There must be some problem. . . ." The guard glanced up at me. "I'm so sorry. Who are you here to see?"

"Matthew Greengold," I said. "And I'm already incredibly late. Y'all wouldn't believe how much longer it takes to walk! What was I thinking?"

He laughed. "It's not a walking town."

"I know that *now*," I joked.

"Let me call the office." He picked up his phone.

"You mind if I just head in?" I said before he could dial. "I hate to keep Matthew waiting, and it's probably gonna take me twenty minutes just to find the right building, your lot is so darn big!"

"Oh, I can give you a map." He dropped the phone back down and a laser printer spit out a color map of the historic studio. "We're here, and you're going to building twelve, so you'll go straight in, take a left, then a right, and the entrance is here." The computer had already circled the building on the map.

"Thank you so, so much. You're a lifesaver!" I reached for the door, which he had to buzz open. "Next time I am definitely driving," I said, rolling my eyes.

He laughed, and buzzed me in, and I walked as fast as I could straight through the door and into the lot. I needed to put as much distance as I could between myself and that guard before he remembered that he'd never called to check if I was expected.

I made it about a hundred yards.

"Ms. Gamble! Chloe Gamble!" somebody called from behind me.

"Damn it," I whispered. I just hoped Marc would be able to keep this whole thing out of the news. "Chloe Gamble Busted Breaking In" didn't sound too good.

I turned around just as the guard from the gatehouse whizzed up on one of the little golf carts they use to get around studio lots. His face looked a little pinched, less friendly than it had a minute ago. "Did I drop something?" I asked, all innocent.

"No. But I called Matthew Greengold's office," he said, and I knew I was busted. "They said I should drive you over, because Mr. Greengold has to leave in ten minutes," the guard went on.

I just stared at him.

"You want to hop up next to me, Ms. Gamble?" he asked.

"Why, sure. Thanks." I climbed onto the seat next to him, he hit the gas, and in about a minute he was dropping me off in front of a building with Matthew Greengold's logo on the door.

I watched him drive off, my head spinning. Why hadn't he thrown me out? Had the receptionist at Greengold's office screwed up?

"Chloe? Good to see you," a tall, cute guy said, sticking his head out the door. "Come on in."

"Okay." I went in and waited for the questions to start.

"Sorry to rush you," the guy said. "I'm Jake, I'm Matthew's second assistant. We've only got a few minutes so let me get you settled and then I can bring you a water or a Diet Coke if you want."

"Sure. Water, please," I said, following him through the posh office. Outside the lot looked beige and bland like every other studio lot, but in here everything was done in polished dark wood and I could tell that the art on the walls was the real kind. "Sorry to barge in on y'all like this," I said. If he wasn't going to mention it, I had to.

"Not a problem." Jake shot me a smile and shooed me into a giant office with a big flatscreen on one wall, an entire living room set up around it, and a desk at the other end that was twice the size of Hal Turman's. "Be right back with the water."

The door closed behind him, and I was left alone with the most famous director in the world.

"Well, this is a surprise," Matthew Greengold said from behind the desk. "I don't think I've ever had an actor show up without an appointment."

"Thank God *somebody* thinks it's weird," I said, and I meant it. "I've been expecting them to toss me out on my butt since the second I got here!"

He laughed, and he got up and came around the desk. Up close, he looked older than I expected, and tanner. "TV stars don't get tossed out," he said, holding out his hand. "Nice to meet you, Chloe."

"You too." I gave him the handshake my mama had taught me before my first-ever beauty pageant. "Thank you for seeing me."

"It's my pleasure. I've been hoping we could get together." He waved me over to the couch and we sat. "Your agent says you're pretty locked up on the show for a while."

"I am, but I don't care," I said. "You're making a movie of *Frontier*, and that is my favorite book of all time. If I had known you were still casting, I would've been pestering you every single day."

"Well, we're really not, we've had the cast set for a while now. I was just mulling it over, thinking of making some last-minute changes," he said. "I watch your show, and you strike me as a girl who's got spunk, as we used to say."

"That's what my agent says, Hal Turman," I said.

"Hal knows spunk. He might have coined the term." Greengold laughed. "Anyway, there's a quality to this character that I think you have, she's young and she's sweet but there's steel in her bones. She's . . ."

"Fearless," I finished for him.

"Exactly." He narrowed his eyes and studied me for a moment. "I get the feeling you have something of that, too, since you spend a lot of time breaking into heavily fortified studio lots."

I bit my lip. "You heard about me crashing the audition at NBC?"

"I also heard you gave quite a rousing speech to the room," he said.

Todd Linson, I thought. He'd been there when I did my disastrous nonaudition for *Virgin*. He was friends with Matthew Greengold, that's what Kimber said. "It was a mistake. I didn't know it then but I know it now," I said.

"And yet you're here, doing it again."

Busted. "Hal says there are no shortcuts, and that the rules are there for a reason. But every time I break the rules it turns out better for me," I said. "I don't mean to be disrespectful to anyone. I just don't want to wait."

He nodded.

"Your movie, it's about a pioneer family. Those people didn't live by the rules, they were in the wild. They made it up as they went," I said. "Well, I think Hollywood is like that. I think it might as well be the lawless frontier, and I think everybody wants to believe that there are rules because they're just too scared to face the anarchy."

Matthew Greengold laughed out loud, and he kept laughing. "How old are you?" he asked finally.

"Sixteen. But my mama says I'm an old soul," I said.

"You certainly are. So if I offered you this role, you'd leave your show for it?" He wasn't laughing now, he was serious. "That's a big risk, Chloe."

"I'm a movie star," I said. "I'm bigger than that show." *I'm bigger than television. I'm bigger than* Cover Band, *and Jonas, and the Goldens, and Snap. And when I take this role away from her, I'll be bigger than Kimber Reeve,* I thought.

"The show is your safety net. You sure you're ready to work without it?" Matthew Greengold asked. "Because the part is yours if you want it."

"I don't need a net," I said. "And believe me, Mr. Greengold, I want it."

Nika Mays's Manuscript Notes: The Big Time

When Hollywood wants to do something fast, it happens fast. The old office in the Valley still had a sign outside that said, "The Hal Turman Agency," but Hal and I were already sitting in our new suite at Virtuoso, a view of Beverly Hills out the windows. In a week, we'd be moving in to these rooms, and they'd lock up the doors of the old office forever.

"How did Bonnie take the news?" I asked Hal.

"She cried," he said, waving his hand as if it didn't matter. "Said she gave me her best years, blah blah blah. She never had the backbone for this business."

I didn't say anything. Somehow the idea of Bonnie Uslan crying didn't fill me with the joy I'd been expecting. My friend Michael hadn't cried, but he had cursed me out when he found out he was being let go in the transition. He said I should've brought him with us to Virtuoso out of loyalty. I didn't feel loyalty to him, though. Or to anyone except Hal and Chloe.

And Sean.

Hal tugged at his tie, frowning around at the sleek low-slung furniture. "It's warm in here," he muttered.

I laughed. "You're never happy."

"I'm happy. You did good, kid." He smiled at me, and I smiled back. It was the closest thing to a thank-you I was ever going to get from Hal, and I knew it.

"When you get your own furniture here from the old place, it will feel more like home," I said.

"Ready for lunch?" Daniel Shapiro said, appearing in the doorway. He had Adam Cohen and two other partners with him, all of them in expensive suits with expensive sunglasses on and the keys to expensive cars in their hands. We were doing a group lunch at The Ivy, where everyone in town would see us, to celebrate the acquisition of the suddenly-beloved Hal Turman Agency, and it was clear that every single one of us would be driving there in a separate car.

I was the only woman in the group, and I was the only one with a non-German car and shades from Macy's. But I channeled Chloe, lifting my chin and making eye contact with everyone who looked at me. It makes you look confident—beauty pageant 101, Chloe had told me. I'm no beauty queen, but maybe I could learn a thing or two from them.

"These offices are great," I said. "We can't wait to get started."

"In my day we'd have a toast," Hal said, looking around like he expected to find a fully stocked bar. I saw a couple of the guys exchange glances. These Virtuoso guys might drink hard at Hollywood parties, but the office was for working. In the pause that followed, I wondered if Hal's entire way of doing business might be out of place here.

Then Daniel Shapiro smiled. "Good man." He called his assistant, and in half a minute she was there with a bottle of Scotch and a tray of glasses. I hate Scotch, but I'm smart enough not to admit it. Hal handed me my glass last, with a raise of his bushy eyebrow.

"Thanks, Hal," I said, taking the glass. It was a test, and I was going to pass it.

"Here's to Hal Turman, the best in the biz," Daniel said, holding up his drink. "And to Nika Mays, the girl with the plan."

Everybody toasted, everybody drank, and the Scotch didn't even burn that badly going down. This was it, this was my new life. I was drinking with Daniel Shapiro, a man I had never even imagined I would meet, a man who hung out with Brad and Angelina on a regular basis. A man who could create money out of thin air, or so it seemed in the Industry.

I wasn't even thirty yet, but I was swimming with the big fish, as Hal would say. This was my new office, my new place in the world, and I had earned it. For one magical moment, my life was perfect.

My BlackBerry buzzed. The caller ID said Leslie Scott. I didn't even have time to frown before Daniel's BlackBerry buzzed too.

"It's Dave Quinn," he said, glancing up at me. All the friendliness was gone from his eyes. "What's going on?"

"I don't know." I hit talk. "Leslie, what's up?"

"What the hell do you people think you're doing?" the head of the Snap Network screamed in my ear. "This is the last straw! We've been putting up with diva antics since the second Chloe stepped onto the set, but this is too far. You rein her in right this second or so help me God, I will see you in court!"

I was fascinated by Daniel Shapiro's face. He was on his BlackBerry with Quinn, and I had a feeling he was hearing the same words I was hearing. His eyes narrowed, and a frown settled in around his lips.

"We gave in to your demands on the music. We handed that girl an unheard-of deal!" Leslie was yelling. "We are *not* going to overlook another breach of contract, do you hear me?"

Daniel Shapiro wasn't looking at me. He was looking at Hal. And Hal sank down until he was sitting behind that modern, low-slung desk, like a little kid in a grown-up office. His old eyes were confused, and tired, and he had no idea what was going on.

"Why didn't Quinn call Hal?" I said, cutting Leslie off. "Why'd he call Shapiro?"

She gave a bitter laugh. "You sold yourselves to Shapiro, now *he* gets the calls."

"Just tell me," I said. "Tell me. What did Chloe do now?"

"She took a role in *Frontier*. Matthew Greengold just announced it. She starts shooting in a week. Which is interesting since we're shooting episode eight of *Cover Band* in a week."

"Okay." I took a deep breath and tried to shove down the panic in my chest. "Okay, Leslie, we'll handle it."

"Bullshit," Leslie snapped. "You didn't even know it was happening. You've got a day. Then we're firing her and we're going after all of you people. One day."

She hung up on me, and I stood there holding the phone like an idiot. I'd never been hung up on before, not in the office. Adam Cohen and all the other agents were staring at me with expressions of delighted horror.

Daniel Shapiro clicked off his BlackBerry, stuck it in his holster, and said, "Looks like we're not having a celebratory lunch today."

"Chloe—," I started.

"You didn't even know she did this," Shapiro cut me off, his voice as sharp as a switchblade.

"Your client takes movie roles and you don't even know she's had a meeting? I thought you said you were on top of her."

"I am. It's . . . Chloe's impulsive," I stammered.

"I don't give a shit. The entire network is riding on her shoulders and they've taken care of her. Did you teach her she can walk out on a contract and get away with it?"

"No," I said.

"Did you tell her it's okay to burn bridges with people like Dave Quinn?" Shapiro was yelling now.

I opened my mouth, but I had no idea what to say. I had no idea how to spin this, no idea how to turn Hurricane Chloe to my advantage this time.

"That's enough." Hal Turman's booming voice cut through the anger in the room. Hal was on his feet, and he didn't even flinch when Shapiro's nasty gaze turned to him. "Back off, Dan. We'll handle it," Hal said. "We'll take care of Chloe Gamble."

IM

COOPERMAN: Trav, you got a sec?

GAMBLEGOAL: No. Driving. Housewarming party for me & Clo.
    Turning into a nightmare.

COOPERMAN: I have news.

GAMBLEGOAL: Clo fucked up bad. I'm gonna go to NYC
with Sasha. I have to tell Clo at the party.

COOPERMAN: You're moving to NY for good?

GAMBLEGOAL: For now.

GAMBLEGOAL: Shit, cop almost saw me. Can't text & drive. Call
you later.

COOPERMAN: Trav?

COOPERMAN: Travis. We gotta talk, man. Call me.

Welcome Home

"Nika and Sean are supposed to bring the emancipation papers
to the housewarming party—if they can stop screwing each
other for two minutes—and then it's official, I am a legal adult
and I make my own decisions," I said. "And my mama's playing
it like she's happy to have all our shit out of the Oakwood. *Her*
apartment, she calls it now."

"You let your mother pack for you?" Max asked as he
steered his car around the hairpin turns in the narrow road
up the hill.

"No, Amanda went in and oversaw the whole thing. It's
just clothes and jewelry and stuff," I said. "I didn't own any of
the crap at the Oakwood, and I don't own any of the crap at
the new house."

"Is that on the list? 'Don't Own Crap'?" Max teased me.

"That's just good business," I said. "Don't buy stuff until you can afford it. And soon enough, I'll be able to afford just about anything I want."

"Why?" Max pulled up to the gate at the end of our new driveway and punched in the code to open it.

"You'll find out. I hope Nika's here," I said. "I've kinda been ignoring her calls all day."

"Why?" Now Max sounded suspicious.

I just grinned at him and climbed out of the car. We were a full half hour late, so all my friends would be there already.

Nika and Sean were in the living room, sitting together on the couch. I could see Marc off in the kitchen, talking on his cell. Jude was taking pictures of the place while Amanda told her where to shoot—she was going to help me redecorate so the house would feel more like mine. My mama had broken open the bar, of course, and Trav was talking to Sasha Powell out on the balcony.

"Here she is," Mama called when she saw me. "Here to celebrate your new house, Clo? Better do it fast before the paychecks stop coming!"

"Hush up, Mama," I said, looking around at all the serious faces. "What's wrong with y'all? I thought this was a party."

"Chloe, you know damn well what's wrong," Nika snapped. "Leslie Scott interrupted my first lunch with the partners at Virtuoso to tell me about your little meeting with Matthew Greengold. What were you thinking?"

"I was thinking that your business lunches are not my problem," I said. "I was thinking that if my agent gets a call from the biggest director in the whole world because he wants to give me a part in his movie, and she *ignores* it, that I'd just better take matters into my own hands."

"I did not ignore his call," Nika protested.

"She told him you're unavailable. Because you *are* unavailable," Sean put in. "You have an iron-clad contract with Snap. There is no way out of it except a major lawsuit."

"We used up our last bit of goodwill with Snap when you went off and recorded a song on your own," Nika said. "I thought you understood that."

"Y'all can just drop the disapproving-parents act, because it ain't gonna work. I can't even believe what I'm hearing!" I cried. "This is me we're talking about. Did you really think I would stop at some stupid kids' TV show? I don't want to be a star on Snap. I want to be a star, period. A movie star. And now I will be."

"By taking a tiny part in a period film?" Nika cried. "At the expense of your professional reputation?"

"It wasn't a tiny part when they were offering it to Kimber Reeve," I said. "It was a pivotal role in an important film. It was her next step on the ladder to credibility!"

"That was just marketing bullshit," Marc said from the kitchen.

"Then it's the kind of bullshit I want said about me," I told him. "Not Kimber."

"Goddamnit, Chloe, is *everything* about Kimber?" Max suddenly exploded. "You're taking a huge risk just to fuck with her? Maybe she's right about you, maybe you do just want to be her."

"I don't give a crap about Kimber," I said. "Taking something away from her is just the icing."

"Is that what you say about me?" Max asked.

For a second I was too surprised to even think. Max couldn't really think that . . . but he did. I turned my back on him and faced off with Nika and Sean. "I told Matthew I'd do it."

"Well, you can't," Nika said.

"It's a Matthew Greengold movie!" I yelled. "It's a huge, star-studded freakin' *blockbuster* movie and I'm going to be in it."

"I cannot keep saying 'no comment' for too much longer," Marc said, waving his phone around. "And Greengold's publicist is getting pissed off by all these calls. Somebody please make a decision about this."

"The decision is made," I told him.

"No, it is not," Nika said.

"You have a steady gig, Chloe," Jude put in. "Do you have any idea how hard that is to get? Most actors never get to be a series regular."

"She got it too fast," Sean said. "That's the problem. She *doesn't* know how hard it is to get."

"I am standing right here," I said. "Don't you go talking about me like I am a child with no clue—"

"Chloe, every single person at *Cover Band* is going to be screwed by this," Amanda cut me off. "Think about that. Keesha will be out of a job. Jonas. Little *Maddie* will be out of a job."

"Yeah, and you will and Jude will. Think I don't know you're just concerned about your own gravy train?" I snapped.

Amanda and Jude both gasped as if I'd slapped them, but my mama laughed. "I for one am certainly concerned about my gravy train," she said. "I hope you and Trav don't think you can move back in with me. Y'all are big independent *adults* now."

"Which means I give you an allowance out of the goodness of my heart, Mama, so don't you start with me," I said.

"And Travis won't be here, Mrs. Gamble, he's coming to New York with me," Sasha said. "The sooner he gets out of this toxic environment, the better."

Everyone else stared at her, but I looked at my twin. His cheeks were red, and he wouldn't meet my eyes. My heart began to pound, hard. "Trav?" I said.

"I'm not getting work here, and Sasha's got contacts in New York. And school's over for the summer," Travis mumbled.

"You're leaving me?" I could barely get the words out. Everyone else in this room hated me right now, I knew that and I could handle it. I was going to be in a Greengold movie, and if it cost me every single one of my friends, well, it was worth it. But Travis . . . Travis wasn't expendable.

"Chloe, you're off on your own path now," my brother said. "I need to find my path."

"Your *path*?" I said. "You been hanging out with Sasha's life coach or something?"

"When this hits the fan, the farther Travis is from you, the better," Sasha said. "You're bad for him."

"Oh, but being your little pet is good for him?" I said. "The boy hasn't gotten a single acting job since he hooked up with you, although maybe he should blame his agent for that."

Nika sighed and shook her head.

"You're insane," Sasha told me. "You might get this one movie, but what other director is going to take a chance on you when you've proven that you don't respect the people you work for? You're unreliable."

"You don't know shit," I said. "You got lucky, you were here when you were two years old; you had parents who got you into the business before you could even talk. You don't know what it's like to struggle, or to do it on your own."

"You have *not* done this on your own, Chloe," Nika said, getting right in my face. "You had all of us, every step of the way. You had *me*. I got you here as much as you did. You rise, I rise, remember?"

"What I remember is that I got famous and because of

that, you got three new offices and a job at a huge agency and lots of money and a hot piece of legal ass," I said.

"That's enough." Sean jumped up to stand with Nika, and everyone else was too shocked to say a word.

"I am the reason that the two of you are so damn big right now," I said. "So I am going to do this movie and I don't care if I have to burn every bridge I have to the Snap Network. You're my agent and my lawyer. This is your job. Figure it the hell out."

"Or what?" Nika said.

"Or I'll find an agent who will."

My mama hooted with laughter, but Jude and Amanda and Marc were silent, horrified. This wasn't like that time at NBC, when everybody stared at me, so quiet and so appalled that I had dared to crash their audition. This was different. These were my friends, and they were supposed to be on my side. I'd gotten them jobs, I'd made them successful, each and every one of them.

But they weren't on my side.

"I want no part of this," Sasha Powell said, heading for the door. "Let's go, Travis."

I stared at my twin brother, and he stared at me. If I had nothing else in my life, I'd still have Trav. That's how it had been since before we were even born.

"It's okay, Trav," I whispered. "You can go."

He smiled then. "No. I can't."

Sasha didn't even bother to say a word. She turned on her heel and stalked out of our new house, not even bothering to close the door behind her. Travis reached out and took my hand. "We'll get through this. You and me against the world," he said.

"Same as it's always been," I said back.

"Well, well. Looks like I'm interrupting something mighty big," a voice said from the doorway. Travis's hand tightened on mine, and I heard my mama's wine glass crash to the ground.

I couldn't help myself, I turned around to face him.

"Did y'all miss me?" my daddy asked.

Get ready for the final act. . . .

It's all happening for Chloe Gamble. She's starring in a movie for the biggest director in the world, recording an album with a producer so famous that even rock stars are in awe of him, winning awards at Cannes, and living the high life in Europe.

Too bad everything else is crumbling around her.

Her no-good daddy is going after Chloe's money and her independence; her mama is dating a shady producer; her agent is too busy with her own career to worry about Chloe's; and her twin brother is a world away, taking his life in a totally different direction.

For the first time, Chloe is truly on her own, and she falls into a downward spiral of Bad Behavior. Chloe's not worried— the rules don't apply to a superstar like her. But when the cops find someone dead in her swimming pool, Chloe learns the hard way that even stars can fall. . . .

HOT MESS
A Chloe Gamble Novel
Coming Summer 2010

About the Authors

ED DECTER is a producer, director, and writer. Along with his writing partner, John J. Strauss, Ed wrote *There's Something About Mary*, *The Lizzie McGuire Movie*, *The Santa Clause 2*, and *The Santa Clause 3*, as well as many other screenplays. During his years in show business Ed has auditioned, hired, and fired thousands of actors and actresses just like Chloe Gamble. Ed lives in Los Angeles with his family.

LAURA J. BURNS is a television and book writer who once dreamed of being an actress, so she's thrilled to live vicariously through Chloe Gamble. She lives in California with her husband and children.

SiMON TeeN

Simon & Schuster's **Simon Teen**
e-newsletter delivers current updates on
the hottest titles, exciting sweepstakes, and
exclusive content from your favorite authors.

Visit **TEEN.SimonandSchuster.com** to
sign up, post your thoughts, and find out what
every avid reader is talking about!

Margaret K. McElderry Books